C

MW01221833

DJ Wiseman

Copyright © 2019 DJ Wiseman

The moral right of the author has been asserted.

Apart from any fair dealing for the purposes of research or private study,
or criticism or review, as permitted under the Copyright, Designs and Patents
Act 1988, this publication may only be reproduced, stored or transmitted, in
any form or by any means, with the prior permission in writing of the
publishers, or in the case of reprographic reproduction in accordance with
the terms of licences issued by the Copyright Licensing Agency. Enquiries
concerning reproduction outside those terms should be sent to the publishers.

This book is a work of fiction. Names, characters, places and events are either the
product of the author's imagination or are used fictitiously. Any resemblance to
actual persons living or dead, events or locales, is entirely coincidental.

Published 2019
Askance Publishing

ISBN 978-1-909009-32-5

British Library Cataloguing in Publication Data
A catalogue record for this book is available from the British Library

Set in Aldine401BT by Askance Publishing
Printed in the United Kingdom

Cover photo courtesy of Jalitha Hewage

DJ Wiseman was born and educated in Essex, UK. Having lived on the South Coast and in Bristol, he settled in Oxfordshire in 1973. In recent years he's lived in Canada, first in Nova Scotia, more recently in British Columbia.

Lifelong interests include travel, maps, reading and photography. For more than twenty-five years he's had a passionate interest in genealogy, discovering branches of his family scattered round the globe.

His writing, both short and long, has been recognised and enjoyed by readers and critics alike on both sides of the Atlantic. He continues to work on ideas for future projects, including a third story in the Lydia Silverstream series.

Other titles
A Habit of Dying *2010*
The Subtle Thief of Youth *2012*
The Death Of Tommy Quick And Other Lies *2016*

Casa Rosa

1

"¡Papatico! Papatico! La policía está llegando! La policía!"

Harry looked up from his book as the girl tumbled through the back door, breathless and excited.

"Slow down, Gabriela. What about the police? Here?" He looked over her shoulder as if they might be following her up the steps from the garden.

"I saw them! It's your friend Captain Diaz, I saw him turn this way. They're in a hurry, they have their lights on."

Harry looked out to the front of the house across the scrubby patch of grass, past the jicaros to the narrow crescent of beach and the sparkling sea beyond. If Gabriela was right, Victor Diaz's car would appear at any moment, having followed the long loop of the track round the property. The policeman made occasional social visits, Harry sometimes thought more to hear the gossip from the bar than to enjoy his company, but the two men could share a beer for an hour or two easily enough.

"Do you think he's come to take me for a ride? He promised he would! Can I go, Papatico, please!" Gabriela implored.

"Maybe, we'll see."

Victor didn't usually call in the morning, or with warning lights on. That sounded like business. Harry couldn't imagine what business the policeman could possibly have that would involve such urgency. A moment later he felt sick at having let the only possibility slip so easily from his mind. It was more than a year, nearer two, since he'd seen Captain Diaz on important business of his own: reporting the disappearance of Estefanía Flores, Gabriela's mother and Harry's live-in housekeeper. This, and only this, would be what brought a police car sliding to a stop in the dust with its red and blue lights flashing. To Harry's surprise

1

a second car, unmarked, drew up less dramatically behind the captain's cruiser.

"Gabriela," he said, lowering himself to be level with her excited face, "let's see what Captain Diaz wants before we ask him about a ride today, OK?"

Gabriela nodded. Something in Harry's voice took the smile from her eyes. "Is it Mami?"

"We'll see in a minute. But yes, it might be about your Mami."

Beside the police car a striking woman in a black suit, her dark hair swept tightly into a bun, was gesticulating angrily at Victor Diaz. Harry caught a few words, enough to understand she was displeased with the speed and nature of their arrival. A woman who could berate a police captain must have some authority of her own.

Harry opened the door as the pair reached the verandah. Slightly behind and out of sight of the woman, the policeman made a calming motion with his hands and put a finger to his lips in a silent call for what, discretion? It was enough to put Harry on his guard, even more than he might have been.

"You are Harry Rose?" she said abruptly, in perfect American English.

"Yes," he nodded. "And you are?"

"We will go inside, señor Rose. I have papers for you to sign."

"What's going on, what papers are these?"

"Papers from the court, issued today."

Harry looked at Victor Diaz as the woman pushed past him into the house, but the policeman only shrugged.

"You're from the court? Serving papers?"

"I have come from the court with the papers. I am from APN, La Agencia de Protección de los Niños. Protecting children, señor Rose. This is the child Gabriela?"

Harry felt the girl tighten her grip on his arm, pulling herself closer in to him.

"This is Gabriela. Have you been in court about Gabriela? Why?"

2

"Do you want me to speak while she is here? She can wait in the car with the sargento."

Wait? For what? The woman had said nothing, yet her whole demeanour was threatening, sinister. He had a vision of Gabriela being taken from him and driven away once the door had closed. "No, she can stay," he replied, with as much calm as his growing fears would allow. "Is it about her mother, about Estefanía? Is there some news, some development?" Harry looked to Victor Diaz for answers. Why hadn't he warned him, given him a chance to prepare Gabriela?

"No, señor Rose," said the policeman, glad of an opportunity to speak. Harry noticed the formal address, clearly this was not an occasion for first names. "This is not about la señorita Flores directly. There are some questions, some rumours. La señora Mejía will explain."

"The court heard several serious allegations, señor Rose. They are detailed in the papers, but let me summarise. First, you keep the child, Gabriela Flores, here against her will, mistreat her while she works for you cleaning your house and other tasks. A slave in all but name." She spoke slowly, holding Harry with a fixed stare, making no reference to the papers. "Second, you deprive her of education by not allowing her to attend school. Third, that you may be responsible for the death of her mother, la señorita Estefanía Flores. And fourth, señor Rose, fourth although it is the first amongst crimes, you have sexual relations with the child, who cannot by her age give consent. Pederasta, señor Rose, you know this word?"

"No, I haven't needed it. But there's a word very like it in English."

Discussing the finer points of language at such a moment felt perverse, and yet it was all he could answer. The allegations were numbing, so grotesque he could find no words to counter them. Anger welled up inside him ready to burst on this self-righteous agent of child protection. The policeman caught the snarl roll across Harry's lips as his jaw set with teeth bared.

3

"Señor Rose," he said firmly, "I urge you to caution at this time. Do not complicate this with regrettable action."

"Papatico? Is it about Mami?"

Gabriela's face had crumpled and tears had started in her blue eyes. Harry scooped her up and she clung to his neck.

"No, Gabriela, not really, there is no news of your Mami, nothing that we hoped for." The tightness of the girl's hold round his neck and the trust she put in his sheltering arms brought him back from the brink of lashing out, in voice or worse.

"What are the papers you have? A confession to sign?"

"Ha, no. This is nothing to make jokes of, señor Rose. The papers show what the judge has heard and taken note of. They tell you when he will make a decision about how he will proceed. They tell you he has authorised me to take Gabriela to care and safety today if …"

Harry took a step backwards, still holding Gabriela close to him.

"No! She is safe and cared for here, right here."

Fight or flight? Harry's mind raced over ideas for escape, where to run, places to hide, where a fifty-nine-year-old white man clutching a brown-skinned girl of seven might find refuge on this island paradise. Flight was impossible – at least for the moment. It would have to be fight. One word offered a glimmer of hope.

"If, you said if. If what?"

"If I decide that Gabriela is in danger. Moral or physical. Or both."

"Neither. She is in no danger. Moral or physical. Look at her, see for yourself, would she cling to me like this if I threatened her?"

"She is the daughter of la señorita Estefanía Flores, your housekeeper?"

"Yes, so far as I know. No, I'm sure she is."

"It is not usual for a housekeeper's child to be held this way by the employer. She treats you like her father."

4

"I treat her like a daughter, so yes, of course she does."

"Where does she sleep? Show me her room. No, wait. Say nothing, señor Rose. Gabriela, please will you show me where you sleep? ¿Por favor, me mostrarás donde duermes?"

"Papatico?" she whispered in his ear.

"Yes, please show the lady anything she wishes to see."

"Will you come?"

"Yes, of course, but you lead, show la señora Mejía the way."

He lowered her to the ground, but she kept hold of his hand as she led the way to her bedroom. It was the smallest room in the house, but had all that a child should need and more than many on Isla Concepción. She'd stopped sharing with her mother when she'd grown beyond babyhood, so he'd bought her a good mattress to go on an old frame. Her threadbare teddy was on her pillow along with her stripy pyjamas. By her bed was a photo of her mother with the year-old Gabriela in her arms. Beside it was Harry's tattered old copy of Winnie The Pooh, with more books on shelves under the window. A map of the world was taped to the wall, along with a tourist map of the island. A brightly-coloured illustration of the solar system was pinned to the ceiling above the bed.

"Gabriela, do you always sleep here?" asked the woman.

The child pulled an awkward face and looked up at Harry, uncertain as to how she should reply. He sat on the bed and she stood between his knees.

"You may say, say the truth, say what happens."

She cast her eyes down before she spoke. "Sometimes I go to the beach to look at the stars and fall asleep on the sand and Papatico says I mustn't go out in the night while he's asleep."

Arsenia Mejía allowed the hint of a smile to flatter her mouth.

"He is right," she said gently, leaning down close to Gabriela. And having been allowed by the child to become a confidant of her sins, asked in the same gentle tones, "And do you sometimes sleep with Papá in his bed, does he sometimes come to yours?"

"When I have bad dreams, and I cry and he comes to me."

"Thank you Gabriela, thank you for telling me these things," she said as she stood up. "One day soon I may have to ask you more questions, about Papá and your Mami. Will you you tell me the truth then?"

Gabriela nodded slowly.

"She has someone's blue eyes, señor Rose."

"She has her own blue eyes. It means nothing."

Harry and Gabriela followed the woman out of the little bedroom and for a few moments she stood surveying the house, weighing her options. "Ha!" she said abruptly, and moved to the kitchen, where she opened cupboards, then the fridge. Unspeaking, she closed it slowly, gave the sink a cursory glance, then rejoined the motionless trio. La señora was about to address Diaz when instead she turned to Harry and took a step towards him, closer to him than she needed to be, invading his space to demonstrate the power she held.

"This is not what I was expecting," she said, close enough that he could feel her breath as she spoke, "not what I'd been led to believe. Here is what will happen today. Gabriela will stay here for now. Read the papers, señor Rose, read them well. You will sign to say that I gave them to you. And I'll write the conditions on them. The girl must stay on the island until the judge decides the next action. A week from now, Thursday, he'll decide. You will bring her each day to the police to show that she is well. You must give up your passport and your computer. You have a computer here? Yes. El capitán Diaz will give you a receipt for them. All this is very fine," she said, waving vaguely round the room but without taking her eyes off him, "but there is also the question of what has happened to the child's mother to be answered."

A stillness enveloped the house and the silence within seeped out to quiet the rustle of the trees and the lap of the ocean while accused and accuser looked hard into each other.

"Two more things you should know, señor Harry Rose, two things. First, you cannot keep a girl, a child, like a stray dog when her mother disappears, even if you treat her well. It is not allowed and for good reason. There are laws. Second, the time for certain men from the United States to come here as they wished and do as they wished with our country and our children has passed. We are cleaning them out, one by one. If you are one of these, despite all these fine appearances, then be warned we will clean you out too. You will be a warning to others. You will not like prison here. Do you understand?"

"This is Gabriela's home, she knows no other, she's never lived anywhere but here."

"Read the papers."

★

They walked barefoot together at the edge of the water. Forty metres out, the reef took all the energy from the waves, leaving no more than ripples along the blazing beach. The trees and bushes crowded down as close to the sea as soil allowed. All was vibrant colour: tropical green gashed with yellow and red and purple, pink sand so bright it hurt the eye, the glittering turquoise of the shallows, the blue vastness above them.

When they'd come out of the house they'd turned left at the water's edge, headed south along the shore towards the line of rocks where the sand came to an end and the undergrowth was too dense to walk further. Three properties shared this idyll: Harry's, the middle of the three, the grand Fairchild house they were slowly approaching and the less well-appointed home of Ernest Portillo, between Harry's and the point.

Gabriela had wailed as soon as the woman and the policeman left. Harry had cuddled and soothed her until she stopped, but she clung tight to him for an hour. He could have cried too, cried with frustration, or roared with anger at the injustice of it all. But a worm of guilt also found its way in: he knew he should have made some proper arrangement for Gabriela, but each day they'd hoped Estefanía would walk back into Casa Rosa. And besides, on Isla Concepción there was never any rush and they led good lives. To shake the branches of *la burocracia* might only have complicated things.

When they'd both recovered a little from the shock, Harry had read the court papers. As he did so, the seriousness became clear to him. He could read Spanish well enough, but he'd need help to understand the legal niceties. And a lot more help if he was going to fight for Gabriela to stay with him. Although it was Gabriela who filled his thoughts, he was dimly aware that he was also threatened. He needed to think. How better than to walk by the sea?

"Gabriela," he said after they'd been silent for a few minutes, "I must go to the city, to San Felipe, to see Elena and Julio. You might remember them, they were here a few times, they have children, Cristela and Stuart, they're a lot bigger than you. You played with Cristela. They stayed a few nights."

"Was it before Mami went?"

"Yes, a little before."

"Cristela sang with me, we made up songs."

"I'd forgotten that, yes, you did."

"Can I come with you, Papatico? Please."

"No, Gabriela. Another time we'll go together, I promise. You must stay here to see Captain Diaz at his office tomorrow, we talked about that. How will it be if you stay with Pippa for a few days?"

"Can I paint with her?"

"If you're good," he said, deadpan. It was their private ritual. He would make her goodness a condition of a treat and she would wait a few seconds and then ask am I good? And he would make a show of deciding before telling her she was good enough.

On this occasion they were interrupted by a door slamming and a woman's angry voice from beyond the trimmed hedges of the Fairchild house. It was old and rambling, but had a style missing from most modern villas. Harry had been inside a few times, invited by Bill Fairchild for a beer or a barbecue. It felt like a house in which Hemingway or Clark Gable might appear at any moment, or where you might catch a glimpse of a young Elizabeth Taylor lounging by the pool.

"She will come out. Can we go back, Papatico?"

"Who will come out, la señora Fairchild? I didn't realise they were here at the moment."

"Yes, I don't like her, she's mean."

"To you?"

"No. She's mean to Natalia and to Adrián."

"Is that the maid? And the gardener's boy?"

"I hear her. If I'm there she says nothing, but if she can't see me she shouts and calls Adrián idiota and sometimes," Gabriela leaned into Harry and whispered, "pequeño malparido."

"Well, that's unkind. I wouldn't have guessed that, she always seems quite pleasant. Did you know that when your Mami first went away they were very kind and helpful?"

Gabriela pulled her don't-know-don't-care face and tugged Harry round to retrace their steps. By their own house Harry stopped to look at the place he'd owned for ten years and enjoyed in one way or another for twice that. He'd borrowed it frequently from an Englishman, a colleague on the hydro project, then when he'd moved on, Harry bought it from him. It was the Englishman who'd planted the rose garden below the verandah. Harry was no gardener and the roses struggled to survive the extremes of heat and rain, but when the day was right, he'd sometimes catch their delicate scent in the evening air.

With sadness Harry remembered Estefanía Flores enjoying the roses too. He could push all manner of evil from his mind, believe and hope for Gabriela's sake that her mother would return, but the longer she was gone, the more likely she was gone for good. Of her history and circumstances he knew almost nothing, but chance had put them together and when she'd needed a job and a roof for her new baby and he'd needed a housekeeper, Estefanía and Gabriela moved in. A month's trial turned to six and six turned to years.

"Looks like Ernest has visitors," Harry called out, squinting into the glare at a shirt-sleeved figure standing by the car parked near his neighbour's house.

Gabriela was watching her toes sink into the sand under the gentle lap of the crystal water. She looked up towards the point, where the track ended near Ernest Portillo's house. "They were here before," she said, returning her attention to the disappearing toes.

"I'm going to the house to call Pippa. I must get started, don't worry, we'll be all right. Coming back?"

"In a minute."

"OK, stay close today."

★

Pippa Maddingly arrived in a similar fashion to Victor Diaz but without the flashing lights. Her ancient Peugeot and the way she drove it were well known on Isla Concepción. The old 405 was a miracle of make-do-and-mend while Pippa's driving was a miracle of survival. She slammed the door and bounced onto the verandah with the lithe energy of someone half her age. At fifty-five she retained her good looks and youthful agility. When complimented on either she'd attribute them to her blameless life and healthy living, although neither claim would have stood close examination.

Harry had known Pippa as long as he'd known the island. She'd been first introduced to him as one of the more exotic examples of the local fauna, and so she'd proved over the years. At times wildly eccentric and always fiercely independent, Philippa Imogen Maddingly-Hughes was as English as the day she was born, despite spending most of her adult life in Central America. She supported herself through her art, painting and teaching others to paint. Her large canvases were filled with the colours that surrounded her and the surreal beasts of her imagination. It was a powerful cocktail, enough to draw a steady trickle of buyers from the United States and beyond to the little gallery in San Felipe, the sole outlet for her work.

Once, and sometimes even still in Harry's imagination, they might have been more than occasional lovers. After the initial flowering of lust had subsided, their friendship had flourished and grown to a deep affection. When he'd called her for help

10

Pippa's response was instant and unqualified, as he knew it would be.

"Where's Gabriela, where's that darling girl?" she cried as she opened the door.

"Out front, or up in her lookout tree more likely. She won't be far."

"Harry! For God's sake man, today of all days, you should know where she is. I didn't see her on the beach. Do you know there's a stranger parked by the point?" Pippa demanded.

"We saw them earlier, visiting Ernest I thought," he replied, a little lamely.

"Come on, I want to see her."

They went down onto the sand with the intention of locating her but with an eye to checking the visitors. The black car remained, shimmering in the heat haze, although there was no sign of the occupants, nor of Gabriela. A sudden anxiety swept through Harry, all the more disturbing for having no foundation. He turned back to the house and was about to call her name and run when she appeared on the steps.

"Hello, Pippa's here," he called out brightly, disguising his fears.

She ran down to meet them and Pippa swept her up and spun her round as she always did until the child squealed with delighted fear.

"You are growing so fast! I won't be able to do that much longer."

"Pippa, will you help her get some things together for a day or so? I want to get away, get the next ferry."

"Of course we will. You get going. Gabriela and I will have a great time, won't we?"

Wide eyes and a big smile gave the answer. Harry put his arms around them and whispered his love to them both.

"I love you too, Papatico."

A few minutes later he threw a bag onto the passenger seat, then swung the old pickup round Pippa's car, slowing to wave at them both. For all the world might see, he and Pippa could so easily be Gabriela's grandparents. Instead, in the eyes of the state at least, they were nothing to her. And now far worse, he'd been cast as her abductor and abuser. The full weight of his mission to San Felipe bore down upon him. It was nothing less than Gabriela's future, the shape of her life, at stake.

At the turn on the track he wondered if Gabriela might have run from the house to her spot in the big savannah oak, but he saw no one. Fifty metres later he noticed the car previously parked at the point was also leaving. Its presence had been vaguely unsettling, it was not a place where tourists visited unless they were lost. Strictly speaking the track from the road was part of the Casa Rosa property, but he'd never put up signs and so far as he knew there had never been any. He was pleased to see the car leave, one less niggle in the back of his mind.

The drive to Concepción, the one sizeable town on the island, took only a few minutes. Concepción had always been the nearly town: nearly big enough for a proper hospital, nearly popular enough with tourists for more investment, nearly important enough to become a city, nearly close enough to the mainland for a new road and a bridge to replace the ancient and unreliable ferry. At one time or another schemes had been proposed to remedy all these deficiencies: some had nearly come to fruition. But any spare resources had never quite reached beyond Puerto Reunión on the mainland, leaving Isla Concepción permanently stuck in second gear.

Harry would have dearly liked to find Victor Diaz and hear his side of the story, perhaps receive a few insights out of earshot of the intimidating señora Mejía. But catching the ferry was more important, it was the last crossing of the day. Sharing his predicament with Elena and Julio in San Felipe was more urgent than listening to Victor's excuses for not warning him, not least because Julio had become one of the capital's most respected lawyers. Like Pippa Maddingly, Elena and Julio were dearly trusted friends, and Harry was godfather to their son Stuart. Julio's assessment of the court papers would be critical.

As Harry inched down the slope to the loading ramp he wondered whether he'd make it. As usual, *Espíritu de las Islas* was crowded with people anxious to not be trapped on Isla Concepción overnight. The rusting vessel took forty or so vehicles plus as many other passengers as could be crammed on. Drivers could sit in their cars for the half-hour journey or find a space under the awning on the deck above. The boarding-passes on the dashboard were no guarantee he'd get on the boat and he was ready to abandon the pickup and walk on if he had to. One thing he knew was unlikely to get him on board was any complaint or argument. Once, many years previously, he'd remonstrated with a seaman when it seemed he'd been denied boarding while there was space available. Within a very short time a harbour officer had appeared and declared his vehicle 'unsafe for loading.' Then he'd watched impotently as the next two cars in line had been squeezed onto the last few feet of deck space.

He rumbled over the ramp with maybe five cars to spare and thanked the loader with a few coins. On the upper deck he bought a Coke from the boy with the big red cool-box and stood at the rail looking out over Concepción's little harbour. On the quayside close to the ramp he was surprised to see Victor Diaz leaning casually against his car and looking directly at Harry. Yesterday it would have been shouted Holas! and waves and smiles: today they stared for a moment before Harry gave a non-committal flap of his hand, returned neutrally by Victor with no more than a nod of his head. Was Victor checking up on him? It seemed a bizarre idea and yet this had already been a bizarre day. Perhaps la señora Mejía was also heading home and it was she who the captain was waving to. Harry looked about him for the dark suit and the striking profile of the agent from the APN but saw no one among the campesinos to match her city chic.

As the chains being drawn across the gangway an argument between a man in a white shirt and the loader was gaining volume. The latecomer had no ticket, no boarding pass. No, he was saying, of course not, my pass is in my car, a pass for a car and a passenger. To which the loader was rightly saying but your car is on the dock, not on *Espíritu de las Islas*. As the man's shoulders slumped in recognition of defeat he looked heavenwards and then directly at Harry. Despite the sunglasses Harry thought he saw the look of recognition, a look which lasted a millisecond too long. White-shirt walked back to his car, his phone to his ear. Harry couldn't be certain, but it might easily be the same car as he'd seen near the house earlier.

Two people interested in his movements or simply coincidences? Victor Diaz checking Gabriela had not left the island? And white-shirt, what was his interest, another agent of child protection? Surely not, cloak-and-dagger wasn't likely to be their style. He looked around him as the ferry groaned into life, belching black diesel exhaust. No one looked out of place, no one was paying him the slightest attention, apart from the drinks boy, who saw the chance of another sale.

Thirty uneventful minutes later, he drove away from the quay at Puerto Reunión firmly resolved that if he was being watched then he'd make it as difficult as he could for the watchers. He couldn't imagine a motive, apart from some unspecified connection to Gabriela, but surely the child would be the one to watch. Perhaps she was being watched. He'd call later. At Pippa's isolated house anyone spying on Gabriela would find it impossible to stay hidden for long.

Harry drove the few hundred metres to Maximercado and parked the pickup, then casually strolled inside trying to make his holdall look as empty as possible and inspecting an imaginary grocery list on a scrap of paper. It wasn't unusual for some island residents, especially gringos, to take the ferry to go shopping in Puerto Reunión. Once inside he zigzagged through the aisles, bought water and a couple of bananas before slipping out the main entrance.

At the bus station he immediately bought a ticket to San Felipe, *directo*, then sauntered about, checking his watch and the arrival boards as if he were there to meet someone. Only as the driver was climbing aboard the bus bound for the capital did Harry

14

move towards it, waving at an imaginary friend on one arriving alongside it. A mystified woman waved back. The timing was ideal, it allowed Harry to slip onto his bus as the door was closing. He slung his bag onto the seat beside him and drew the curtain across the window, leaving a crack for him to scan the blur of faces as the bus moved out. He saw no one he recognised, he saw no one watching his departure.

2

The two hours between Puerto Reunión and San Felipe gave Harry plenty of time to think about the reasons for his journey – and about similar ones taken years previously. Not *directo* then, there was no *directo*, only the crawling, dawdling, intimately packed *colectivo* stopping at every house and corner on request. Back then he'd sometimes use it on his trips to the city, trips that might end with more alcohol in his system than his system could take, might end with him waking in a room above a bar in the district favoured by working girls, might end with his wallet emptied and only the emergency notes he'd pinned into his waistband to get him home.

Those were not days or nights that he recalled with any affection, inasmuch as he recalled them at all. They were the dog days between the end of his working life and the contentment of today. The liquor might have been expensive, the bar girls might have been a step up from the street girls, but neither the drink nor the fuck ever gave much more than fleeting pleasure. The first whisky of the night was always the sweetest, always the richest, always the one to swirl the subtle flavours round the mouth and thank god for being alive and able to afford it a million miles from its Speyside birth. The second and the third glasses – all the way to the last – they all promised a repeat of that first delight yet never matched it.

When he hadn't had so much of the Scotch as to be incapable, he'd go with a girl, usually the first to take his arm, the first to offer him plump young limbs and dark eyes and smiling white teeth, the first to pout and lick her lips and play coquette and whisper the pleasures he might enjoy once they'd climbed the stairs, with the price of the room he should take for an hour or two or the night slipped in as a casual aside.

16

In the dull light of early morning their mechanical intimacy left as bad a taste as the stale tobacco and whisky. Sometimes he'd wake as she slipped away, then he'd watch from the window as she trotted across the road to where the last of the all-night taxis waited. Mostly, the girl would be long gone to her day job, leaving only the faintest imprint of her presence. He'd shower to remove the stink of cheap scent and stale sex, then stand at the window and watch as the night-street came grudgingly to day-life. On good days he'd have enough left for a coffee, maybe a plate of rice and beans, before the *colectivo* returned him to normal life, to Concepción, to Casa Rosa and a beer or two with Victor Diaz.

The last of these excursions had been nearly eight years ago. Harry remembered neither the whisky nor the hours that followed it, but snatches of the journey home remained with him. Like all memories, it had been coloured by subsequent events, enhanced by wished-for generosities which may or may not have been felt at the time. But there were a few undeniable facts: he first saw the infant Gabriela Flores that day, cradled in her mother's arms; he first spoke to Estefanía Flores as they shared the lurching ride in adjacent seats; it also marked his last visit to the twin pleasures of Bar Pension Pacífico. He'd often wondered about this, whether it was simply coincidence that his life took a small change in direction just as Estefanía and her baby appeared on its fringes. It had been a week before he'd seen them again, several more before they'd come to stay, temporarily, at Casa Rosa. Mostly he convinced himself there was no cause and effect, the nights in San Felipe ceased because his life had reached the point where they would cease, regardless of a random meeting on a crowded bus. But very occasionally he'd privately wonder if it might also be the presence of the baby Gabriela which cast a different light on his world.

Now, Gabriela was at the heart of this new journey to San Felipe, and Harry wondered if anything from that previous life might seep through time into the present. There was no law against getting drunk nor paying for sex, not now, not then, but if the outcome hung in the balance what grubby secrets might la señora Mejía dig out from his past? Had any of those young limbs been under age for the trade they plied? He thought not, but who was to say at this distance? And who was saying anything at all? That protector of children had not arrived at his house, fresh from court, ready to snatch Gabriela to safety, without someone, somewhere, saying something.

How much of that past life, that pre-Gabriela life, should he confide in Julio? How much would he want to know? Lawyers tended to want to know everything unless the client was guilty, in which case the less they knew the better. As close as Harry was to Elena and Julio, they had never shared intimate secrets. Harry's excesses in San Felipe were his alone to know, he'd never called on his friends during those visits to the city, nor seen any reason to mention them. In more than twenty years of friendship they'd taken each other at face value and never been disappointed.

The scrubby green-brown countryside blurred by through his almost-drawn curtains. No one on the half-empty bus paid him any attention as the video screens blinked out a dubbed soap opera. Across the aisle a young woman, maybe teens, maybe twenties, cocooned in her private headphoned world, watched her phone. The wrong hair, the wrong hands, the wrong face, the wrong everything to be Estefanía, who anyway never had a phone to Harry's knowledge: but maybe the right age. Maybe. Who could tell the age of young people any more? *Colectivo* passengers had bags and chickens and children and babies being taken to clinics or grandparents and they spoke to their neighbours. If Estefanía and Harry had shared a *directo* both their lives would have been different. Gabriela's even more so. But then if Harry had been less drunk the previous night, if and if and if, their lives would also have been different. There was no *directo*, they had sat next to each other, they had met and all that had followed had followed. No ifs.

The lost nights, the chance meeting, the delight of a baby grown to a girl, her mother missing and missed, all these things and more had him back on a bus to the city. Worse, he was behaving like a criminal, dodging imagined pursuers, suspicious of every glance in his direction. And for what? For Gabriela of course, but what was she to him, really? Even as the questions formed themselves, he pushed back the doubts they voiced. He didn't understand how it had happened, but he didn't care: she'd become the child he'd never had, the grandchild he never would have. She'd filled a space he hadn't realised was vacant, not in a rush with a bang on arrival, but slowly over the years as they'd come to care about each other, become fixtures in each other's worlds. It was true what la señora had said, Gabriela treated him like her father, he was her Papatico, and he felt privileged that it was so. Estefanía doted on her, but that didn't prevent her being a good mother. If she was the sun in Gabriela's life, then Harry was her moon.

With a jolt he realised that Gabriela's real father, never known, never mentioned, might now become significant. Whoever he was, perhaps he played some part in Estefanía's disappearance, or was somehow the cause of this day of troubles. Harry was again in danger of seeing conspiracy and intrigue where there was none. But the thought of Gabriela's father, whether as the unseen manipulator of events or oblivious to her existence, remained unsettling. He shifted awkwardly in his seat and as he did so, caught the eye of the headphoned girl opposite. She looked away, unsmiling, dismissive.

*

"Harry!" Elena hugged his neck, reaching up to kiss his cheek before the door was closed behind him. He was family, as much as if he'd been her uncle. No sooner had she released him than Julio grasped him, followed only slightly less enthusiastically by Cristela and Stuart, who knew what to do with their arms in such embraces, but not their faces. At sixteen and thirteen they had yet to outgrow that awkwardness, however much they'd been raised to love Harry.

In the cool tiled elegance of their home with the family as groomed and immaculate as always, Harry felt suddenly soiled and scruffy, the beach bum who's gatecrashed the wedding party.

Julio took his arm, guiding him towards the inner courtyard. "Harry, you look exhausted, come and sit down, have a drink, tell us what's happened. Where is Gabriela? Cristela, some drinks, please."

"Gabriela's safe enough, staying with Pippa, you remember her? My artist friend."

"Yes, of course. But what about the court and the APN? They don't usually get involved in domestic matters, certainly not outside San Felipe."

"I've got the papers from the court, that's what I really need some help with. I think I understand most of it, but the language is complicated, and I need to get it right, I need to know exactly what I can do about it."

"Of course, I will look at them, we will see how serious it is. But tell us what happened."

Cristela brought a jug of iced tamarindo which Stuart poured and handed to his parents and Harry. The family settled round him, Stuart and Cristela each side of him, their parents facing him. They were a handsome couple who'd born two handsome children who grew more beautiful every time he saw them. They'd inherited more than their parents' good looks, both were perceptive and better read than most their ages.

For a few moments they sat quietly sipping their bittersweet drinks while a breeze rustled the palm fronds above them.

"Harry," Elena said, sensing something of what was about to unfold, "would you like Stuart and Cristela to leave us?"

Stuart looked at the floor, waiting for the instruction he hoped wouldn't come. Cristela frowned at her mother, a protest forming on her lips, but it remained unspoken.

"No, better they hear it from me what has happened, what is being said, than from anyone else, even from you."

Elena nodded.

"I'll get to the heart of it right away, the rest is who said what and Gabriela crying and me seeing shadows where there are none.

"The APN, La Agencia de Protección de los Niños, in the person of la señora Mejía, came this morning. They were going to take Gabriela, they had an order from the court to remove Gabriela from the house, where, it is said, I keep her as a slave, prevent her going to school, may have murdered her mother and," he hesitated over the final accusation, as if speaking the words might give it credibility, "and that I abuse her, molest her."

He met stunned, uncomprehending gazes from Elena and Julio.

"Sexually," he added, for the avoidance of any doubt. All the anger and frustration of the day, the injustice of it, the prospect of losing Gabriela, all merged into streams running down his cheeks, his strength and resolve dissolving in the tears.

Elena motioned to her daughter who brought him tissues and let her hand rest on his arm for a few seconds in unspoken sympathy. Despite his distress, the gesture did not go unnoticed. It gave him strength to gather himself again, but without apology for shedding tears.

"Thank you," he said, and put a hand out to hers. "So, that's why I'm here, and if it matters at all, I'll tell you how it all happened and the questions that multiply themselves every time I think about it."

More had happened in his day than he'd realised, and it was twenty minutes in the telling. For the most part the family listened without interrupting him, but Julio asked him to state the detail of signing the papers and whether he had a receipt for his passport. When it came to the part where he'd dodged through the supermarket and played spies with imaginary pursuers he said nothing and excused taking the bus because of an imagined problem with his truck.

When he'd finished he sank back into the chair, sighing deeply.

"Harry, we have work to do, much work," Julio said sombrely. "It all makes sense but no sense. I'll read the papers now, why

21

don't you take a shower while I do that and we'll see what can be done. Not much today maybe, but we'll see."

Stuart carried Harry's bag, saying nothing as they climbed the stairs. Harry was too tired to find energy or invention for small talk with his godson. At nearly fourteen, the boy was almost as tall as Harry and could already look his father in the eye. Raven-black hair and an athletic build disguised the gentlest of natures. When Stuart was a child Harry had seen him often at his parent's house, the little flat with the big mortgage that was their first home, and sometimes at his office when Elena came to visit. Every few months or so the family would come to Casa Rosa for a few nights at the beach, but that and all the other visits had lessened over the years as their lives grew busier. Seeing the boy, enquiring of his progress at school and with his sport and music, the usual attentions at Christmas and birthdays, these were the extent of Harry's godfatherly duties.

"I don't know what to say," Stuart said as he turned to leave the room.

"Then, as I've probably said before, best say nothing."

The boy nodded.

"Life can look so easy, Stuart, especially for people like you and me, we have everything we want. But it can bite you without warning. Then we need our friends, friends like your mother and father."

He nodded again and tried a half smile before escaping.

Harry hadn't been in the shower more than two minutes before he felt the urge to be out of it, doing something, anything, to aid the process. He wasn't sure how long Julio needed to review the papers, but he imagined it to be an hour at least. Behaving as if he were on holiday, enjoying a long shower or lounging on his bed seemed perverse, no matter how tired he was. He dried himself off slowly and deliberately, stretching out the time, then put on a clean shirt and sat on the edge of the bed and called Pippa.

El número está fuera de servicio.

22

It wasn't unusual, Pippa's house phone relied on some ancient technology and was frequently out of order, although thankfully it had worked well enough earlier. The mobile signal was equally weak and variable, the house being on the wrong side of the hills, but he called and left a voicemail.

He flirted with the idea of calling Leo at the Kasanee, the bar he had a small interest in, just to see if Victor Diaz was having a beer. Diaz might be tempted into having a conversation he couldn't have from the desk in his office, he might do a friend a favour and suggest he look in this direction or that. It was tempting, had he been in Concepción he might have dropped in and pulled up a chair opposite the captain and put a fresh bottle in front of him. But that was different, to sit and drink beer and chit-chat until a question was suggested and a careful answer was given, an answer which could be taken this way or that according to the looks exchanged as they tilted their heads and let the cool Cervezas trickle down their throats. Calling, even if he was there, even if he spoke, calling was asking a favour, a big favour, before a word was spoken. There could be no other reason for such a call.

Another time perhaps, let Julio do his work first, no point in asking for a favour before he knew what to ask for. And besides, wasn't he making some assumptions about his friendship with Victor Diaz?

"Harry? Mamá has some food ready. If you are hungry." Cristela was at his door.

The family meal was an important point in the day for Elena and Julio. Whatever else happened they would expect to share their supper time with their children. It was a rule Harry understood and applauded. He expected to see five chairs round the table, perfect place settings, candles as they had a visitor and dishes full of Elena's cooking. Instead, the food was there but no settings, no candles, a pile of plates and cutlery.

"Are you disappointed, Harry?" Elena asked when she saw his face. "I thought we wouldn't want to be formal tonight. And Julio is still busy, he's at his desk, he'll come soon."

23

Elena at her best, thoughtful, caring, efficient and calm. Somewhere in there too, was great love.

She'd been Harry's secretary, inherited unwillingly from his predecessor, long before her marriage and motherhood. He'd been self-sufficient most of his working life and couldn't see how there'd be enough to keep her occupied. And besides, she was young and inexperienced and her English was less than perfect. If pressed, he could probably have found other disadvantages, but it hadn't taken long for him to be won over. His first new project had been overseeing the installation of new generators on the same hydro project as he'd worked on when he'd first come south. Coordinating the replacements involved far more than he could have handled without assistance, despite his first-hand knowledge. Once Harry allowed himself to delegate, Elena grew into the job with a quiet efficiency. In less than a year she'd become indispensable, often anticipating events and potential pitfalls quite independently of Harry.

As the months passed he gradually came to learn more of her life outside of work: how her father's sudden death had left her family struggling to maintain their modest middle-class lifestyle; how, as the eldest of five children, Elena had become the family's main wage earner; how she also supported her fiancé in his struggle to complete his law degree at the Colegio de Abogados.

He'd liked Julio the moment he'd met him and had found nothing to change his mind in the years since. That, rather than him being Elena's husband, was the real basis of their friendship. Harry and Elena were strictly work but Harry, Julio and Elena could be friends. And when Harry's company needed a local lawyer who better than the newly qualified Julio?

Then Cristela had come along a little earlier than they might have planned and amidst all the joy came a diagnosis. *Developmental dysplasia of the hips.* Not life threatening, easily understood and treated – if done soon enough. But argued over by the insurance company and classified as a birth defect, in which case they would not pay for treatment. With their credit already stretched to the limit, Elena and Julio had few choices.

They could endure the long wait for an unpredictable outcome with *El Seguro Social* or they could beg, borrow, or steal enough to pay for surgery that became more expensive the longer it was delayed. Harry took it from his retirement savings without a second thought, joking that they'd have to care for him in his old age.

"There's beer here, Harry"

"Thank you, Elena."

"And eat, you must be hungry."

Perhaps he was, he wasn't sure. He took tamales and chicharrones on a small plate and ignored Elena's raised eyebrows. If he'd been alone, at home, he wouldn't have bothered at all. He'd leave the beer in the fridge and reach down the bottle of single malt. It was certainly a single-malt evening.

Julio appeared from his little *oficina* at the back of the house. He too took a small plate with little food on it and sat next to Harry. He was about to take a bite but paused, all too aware of questions hanging like ripe heavy fruit waiting to drop.

He reached over and touched Harry's arm, much as his daughter had done earlier.

"It is serious, very serious. We must talk. Tonight. But first we will eat. Tell us about Gabriela, we haven't seen her for so long."

⋆

Julio's *oficino en casa* was a functional scaled-down version of his office in Colonia San Luis, the smart professional quarter of San Felipe. The obvious shelves of reference books, the mandatory laptop, a modest TV screen, were all there. The single indulgence was his desk. Not for its size or opulence, nor for its cost. The indulgence was purely sentimental – it had been his first desk in his first tiny office after qualifying. Rescued from an abandoned railway station, he'd first hidden its shabbiness under a green baize cloth. Later he'd restored it to something like its original 1920s beauty, polishing over the worst scratches and dents and the innumerable cigarette burns. The centre drawer had become a little sticky again, the security lock only worked if you knew how to squeeze two fingers into the gap, but it was solid and spoke of heritage and tradition.

"Harry, someone has involved the APN, they don't start things themselves, cases are referred to them for investigation. Can you guess who might have done that?"

"No. I've thought about it, but no."

"Who knew about Gabriela, about her mother?"

"Everyone on the island I should think."

"But you reported it, you said you'd reported Gabriela's mother missing?"

"Yes, I saw the police Captain, Victor Diaz. He wrote out a report, I saw him do that while I was there. He wasn't very interested, more shrugged it off as something that happens."

"And Gabriela, what did he say about her?"

"I could hand her over to someone on the mainland if I wanted, but I said I wanted her to stay, the house is her home, and he said OK and made a note."

"Did you get a copy of this report?"

Harry hesitated. Had he? Not then, but maybe in the weeks that followed, maybe he'd been handed an envelope one afternoon when he'd been at the bar with Pippa and Gabriela dawdling over tiradito and chips.

"I'm not sure. I can get a copy from Victor."

Julio grunted his disapproval.

"Get it quickly, when you are back. Now, why doesn't Gabriela go to school? I know she can read and write and she's clever and better off than being at school, but did you register for schooling her at home?"

"No. But she can't go to school, they won't take her without her registration, her birth certificate. She can't get anything without that."

"I thought she was registered, didn't you say that Estefanía went away to register her?"

"She said she was, she was away two or three days, that was the first time she'd left me with Gabriela for that long. But I never saw her papers, I never asked about them. I've looked through

26

Estefanía's things since then, but I didn't see any registration. I didn't see anything useful at all."

"We can search the registers but it will take time. If she was registered outside San Felipe it might take a very long time. But Harry, even if she is not registered, not accepted in the school, you should have permission to teach her at home. It's small, it's nothing." Julio waved the question away, Gabriela wouldn't be taken from Casa Rosa for such a triviality.

"But it's true," Harry said. "It's the one thing that is true."

"No. It is alleged you prevent her from school. It is different. The school prevents her from school."

"That just leaves slavery, abuse and murder."

"Yes. Less easily dismissed because they are already put in people's minds. Even to say these things leaves a trace of the crime on you."

"A smear. Throw enough mud and some will stick."

Julio nodded his understanding.

"So we must defend these things with seriousness, not simply dismiss them as nonsense. We will show that they are not true. We will need Gabriela. Will she speak well without prompting?"

"I think so. I think the APN agent, la señora Mejía, I think she was surprised by what she found, I think she quite liked Gabriela."

"I will find out about la señora, but that's for tomorrow."

Julio sat back, eyes closed, nodding to himself about some thought or action. He ran both hands slowly back through his hair as if smoothing away uncertainty. He liked Harry, had always liked Harry, trusted him in all things, enough that he was godfather to his son, enough that he knew that the suggestions, the allegations, were entirely false. But someone had made those suggestions, someone thought they might be true, and if not, might be accepted as possible. The court had already agreed that they might be possible, might be true. Why would that be?

"Harry, I want to ask you some questions. Some hard questions. About Gabriela and about her mother. Tell me again how she came to live at Casa Rosa."

"Here's the short version. We sat next to each other on a bus from San Felipe. Gabriela was maybe two weeks old, three at most. We spoke of nothing much. Gabriela was asleep mainly. I held her for a few minutes while Estefanía was in the washroom at San Ramón."

He remembered the day clearly, even though he'd seen it all through half-closed eyes with a dull ache throbbing just behind them. It had been dark and heavy, the air thick enough to drink until the downpour came as they reached Puerto Reunión. Estefanía was also heading to Isla Concepción, it seemed a friend of a cousin had a room and a job.

"I saw her again on the ferry, she was up top, I stayed in the truck. After that it was a few weeks before I saw her again. She was at the bar one evening."

"Was she alone?"

"Yes, alone. Well, she had Gabriela."

She did, she'd had her baby wrapped in a shawl, close to her, but not so close that she was hidden from view, for Gabriela's face was key to the success of her mission as she passed from table to table. She was begging. She stood at Harry's side asking in a whisper for help for her baby, eyes cast down. Anything he could spare, anything at all, they were both hungry. Harry reached into his pocket for some change before really looking at them. It was a shock when he recognised them. He remembered Gabriela's name but her mother's eluded him. He spoke but she didn't answer him, standing uncertainly, head down, unable to run, wary of staying. At the promise of food and drink she nodded, looking at him from under hooded eyes. Still silent, she sat. And still silent she ate the rice and beans and eggs put in front of her and drank the water and a little of the milk while Harry held Gabriela, no heavier than when he'd done so weeks previously. When he asked about the friend, the room and the job she shook her head. *Nada*.

He knew there was a room over the bar, not much, but a room and a bed, one he'd been known to occasionally use himself. Harry thought Leo would let her use it if he asked and if she helped clean up the kitchen later. Leo did exactly that, but not before wondering if Harry had gone mad, then pausing and smiling, nodding to himself, asking if maybe Harry would be back later to visit his new friend. And Leo's suggestion and the way she'd said *thank you* when he left her had reminded Harry of another moment a year or so previously on a cool grey morning in San Felipe.

"What happened at the bar?"

"She needed a job, somewhere to stay. Leo had both so she was at the Kasanee for a while."

"Then?"

"Then, Leo wanted the room and he wasn't so happy about Gabriela. He had no need of help in the bar, not every day. He had it all covered without Estefanía. It was handy to have her there for the odd jobs, an extra pair of hands, but not full time. Not even half time."

"So?"

So, for a few weeks she'd had a bed and a roof and food in her stomach with enough energy to feed Gabriela and the baby had started to put on a few ounces. She'd survived. They'd survived. More than that, they'd both discovered their smiles. Harry couldn't see that going to waste with them back on the streets. He owed her nothing, yet was vaguely responsible for her, certainly in Leo's eyes, and Victor's too most likely, along with a few others who'd seen Leo wink as he told how the woman was Harry's *compañera* from the city.

So, he'd suggested he needed a housekeeper. Only a trial, only a few weeks to see how it worked out. He had the space, he could easily afford a small wage and she could still cover emergencies at the bar for Leo. And there was Gabriela. Harry could see, however indistinctly at that time, he'd already affected her life and whatever he did then and in the future would affect it more. Do nothing and they'd slip out of his life, do something and they'd slip in; it was a fork in the child's road and she'd barely started her journey.

29

So, Estefanía had come. Of course she had, she had nowhere else to go and no money to go there. The room over the Kasanee had been basic, but it was a room, it had a door and a bed and her little bag of possessions was still there when she went back to it. Another room in another place? Sure, maybe that also had a door and a bed. But Harry saw the light dim in her eye and dull acceptance return to Estefanía's face as the new arrangements were suggested. It wasn't a matter of choice, she would do what she had to do.

"I needed a housekeeper," Harry replied to Julio, "she needed a job. Leo said she'd been OK, no trouble and worked hard. It was just for a month, to see if we got along."

"And you did."

"Yes."

"How old was Estefanía then?"

"I don't know for sure, but maybe twenty, I can't see how she'd have been more than twenty-five."

"Not younger?"

Harry knew the reason for the question, knew how doubts about Estefanía's age might play into a malignant imagination. He shook his head slowly. He had no real doubt about her, but the nag about those plump-limbed bar-girls threatened to resurface.

"When did the arrangement become permanent?"

"When the month was up, it became a couple of months more and it's just gone on like that."

"Were you aware of people saying anything about this, about you having a young woman living with you?"

"Not really, Leo always made a few comments but it meant nothing."

"You and Leo own the bar, the Kasanee, yes?"

"No, he owns it and I have a little share. He has a brother too, he also has a small stake."

"Would you give him back your share if he wanted it?"

"Yes, of course."

Julio was silent for a few moments, studying his hands as they rested lightly one on top of the other on the edge of his desk.

"Estefanía was at Casa Rosa for what, six years or so?"

"Yes, a little longer."

"Harry, did you sleep with her?"

Did he?

He hadn't when, after a month or so of him being polite and keeping his distance, she'd asked uncertainly, apparently more curious than concerned, *do you want to fuck yet, Harry Rose?* and he'd said *no* too quickly and she knew he'd thought about it. And she'd been pleased and a little surprised that this was not part of the duties of a young housekeeper for the single man with a home on a beautiful beach on Isla Concepción.

He hadn't a year later when in the small hours of morning he'd momentarily relieved her of a wailing Gabriela and wandered to his bedroom and lay down, whispering a half-forgotten nursery rhyme and Estefanía had come and lain beside him as naturally as if they'd been the child's parents.

He hadn't after Victor and he had sat the whole evening on the verandah and spoken of the women in their lives, of past conquests and easy victories and Estefanía had brought them beers just as Victor had cursed all hookers – pleased with himself that he knew the American word – and Harry and she had caught each other's eye and in that moment were aware of past secrets.

But had he when he came home after a few beers and took a couple of Speyside nightcaps and knew nothing until waking in his bed as the day crept into his room? How could he be sure, hadn't he often imagined it in the early days, hadn't he wanted to, for the comfort of it as much as the pleasures it might give?

"No, not at all, not in all the time she's been at Casa Rosa," Harry said firmly in reply.

"But you had an affection for Estefanía, yes?"

"Yes, I did. I still do."

"Harry, you would not be who you are if you did not love her a little."

31

The evening had darkened to night as they'd talked, while all around them the gentle fragrance of white jasmine from the *jardineras* in the courtyard had suffused the house. From a room beyond the jasmine Stuart was practising an exam piece, Chopin's Mazurka, the notes combining perfectly with the air that carried them. There could scarcely be a better moment to savour than to be in the home of a friend on such a night and allow music and scent to fill the senses and friendship to fill the soul: if it were not for the matter that had brought him there.

"What happened the day she disappeared?"

"Nothing happened at all, not that I know of. We'd spoken about her going away for a couple of nights and me being there to look after Gabriela. Estefanía had been away before, always just a night or two, once it might've been three. She never said where, just that she had to go away. She never offered any information and I never pressed her for it. I think she once said something about her mother, but I can't remember now if it was to do with one of those trips or not.

"We, that is Gabriela and I, took her to the ferry and waved her off. I'm sure she was alone, or she seemed to be alone. We'd done that before, said goodbye like that, even if she was just going to Puerta Reunión for supplies. We went home and we haven't seen her since."

"And no word, no mail, nothing since then?"

"Nothing."

"What do you think? Was it planned, did she mean to leave forever? Or has something happened to her?"

"Not planned. She was a good mother, she loved Gabriela. People do things you never expect them to do, but leaving without a word, no, she would never have done that. If Estefanía is alive then she can't come back, either because she is incapable of doing so, or because to do so would in some way endanger Gabriela."

"You believe this?"

"Yes."

"It sounds like a drama."

"It's what I think."

"Do you think she is dead?"

"Dead or in danger or prevented from returning."

"Did you say this to your capitán Diaz?"

"No, not then, not officially. We've spoken since, but, as you say Julio, it sounds like a drama."

"Who would prevent her, why would they?"

"I wonder if Gabriela's father might want to find her, and Estefanía might want him not to."

"Hmm, it is possible. Do you know anything about him?"

"Nothing. Not a single thing. Estefanía has never even mentioned him."

It was true, she hadn't. And the longer she'd stayed at Casa Rosa, the less Harry had wanted her to. Whoever he was, wherever he was, Harry had come to think of him as vaguely threatening to the comfortable arrangement that he enjoyed more each day. If he appeared on the scene it would inevitably be changed, and not for the better. Even acknowledging his existence would alter the way they were. Harry knew there would be a time when Gabriela would ask about him, perhaps search for him, but that time was a few years away, and until then her Papatico could look after her well enough.

"Perhaps the father is involved in all this, perhaps he wants to discredit you," Julio suggested, unconvinced by his own idea.

"Why? If he knows where Gabriela is he could just come and take her."

Julio nodded, his mind more on the daughter than the father.

"Harry, the allegations about Gabriela, the, er…abuse. I do not need to ask you about them, even if someone else will. But let me ask you this: could someone have seen something, heard something which they might have misunderstood? I think Gabriela was naked on the beach once when we were there, perhaps you were playing a game, maybe something as simple as that."

"Sometimes she goes into the sea without clothes, there's never anyone on the beach. The Fairchilds have their pool and Ernest stays inside. No one else comes there. It's private."

Julio was silent, nodding to himself as if summarising their conversation. After a few moments he said, "You saw they had your proper name in the court papers? How many people know you're really Stuart Henry Rose?"

"Not many. You and Elena. But it also says known as, *conocido como*, doesn't it?"

"Yes, but it shows someone has checked on you, maybe from the property record or your residency."

"Or the bar, I had to register for that too."

"Maybe. You said la señora Mejía thought you were from the United States."

"Yes, but I'm often taken as being from the States. I don't usually bother putting people right."

"But they used your real name, but not your country. Who knows you are Canadian?"

"Well, I'm Canadian and British, I'm both. Few people here know that. Pippa, you, and Elena if she remembers, Victor Diaz maybe."

"Because you gave him your passport?"

"No, he knew before today. I had to register when I took that little stake in the bar, had to show some ID. I showed him the Canadian passport. That's the one I gave him today. I still have my other one."

"You have two passports?"

"Yes, that's how it works."

The door opened a little and Elena looked in on them. "Cristela and Stuart said goodnight to you both, they have gone to their rooms."

Harry stretched out a hand to her. "Thank you, Elena," he said softly.

"We can't do more tonight," Julio said, as he put an arm round his wife, "but there is a little still to be said. I think Harry might like a whisky, and I will join him, yes Harry?"

"Yes, Julio." Weary as he was, Harry could think of no better way to end a bad day.

They settled in the comfortable chairs where Harry had first shocked them with his news, each contemplating a measure of Tomintoul: Julio's taste had been shaped by Harry's.

Julio interrupted their reverie. "Harry, you're worried about Gabriela, about her future, what may happen to her, yes? Of course you are, you are her uncle, her grandfather, her Papatico, she looks to you. If you were not concerned for her you would have handed her over when Estefanía disappeared."

Harry nodded, the glass at his lips, the sweet spice on his tongue.

"Now for a moment look away from Gabriela, and think of yourself. Gabriela is accused of nothing, it is you who are accused. You think losing Gabriela would be the worst thing, wait," he held up a hand to prevent any protest, "no, it would not be the worst. Gabriela would be well cared for, if for no other reason than we know her and would make sure of it. Elena and I have not spoken of this, but I know it is so." He looked to his wife who was nodding her agreement. "And there is Pippa too. Gabriela would not be abandoned.

"But you might be in trouble. The accusations are untrue, we know this, but perhaps there is false evidence behind false accusations. So, we must do everything exactly as it should be done, exactly as the court orders. We must not provide any opportunity for them to say we have failed in anything they ask. The order made was for an emergency, to remove Gabriela. It was a surprise to leave her with you. On Tuesday the judge will consider the case, and has ordered you to appear a week from now to hear the next decision. What is not ordered, but which we will do, is to be ready with some answers before that decision. Tomorrow we will plan how we will do this."

It was true, Harry's main concern was for Gabriela, and yes, in part his own misery at the prospect of losing her, he was her guardian, her champion until her mother returned. Trouble for him he understood, la señora Mejía's lurid threats had left him in no doubt, but he was innocent and innocent men don't go to prison, even if they might lose custody of their housekeeper's daughter.

"Why might I be in trouble? You know it's all untrue, there can be no evidence that would make it true."

"Harry, you are here because you love Gabriela, you love this place, the life you have, you love Casa Rosa, the list is long. And you are here because you have permission, you are 'un residente aprobado', an approved resident. Do you remember the process I helped you through to obtain that, the things you may do and the things you may not do?"

"Well, not the detail, but if I'm convicted of a serious crime then I may lose my residency."

"Yes, but more than that, if you associate with criminals, if you are suspected of a crime that cannot be proven, you may become disapproved, 'un residente no aprobado', without any appeal. The law was designed to discourage gangsters, the organised criminals who want a villa in the sun. There is also a section about 'conducente a una buena comunidad', being good for the community. If it is decided you are no conducente you could also be disapproved. You should be aware of this. Look at what the court has been told and it would be easy to think that maybe you are not good for the community."

3

Harry stirred in the grey minutes before sunrise, drifting uneasily between unnatural dreams and uncertain reality. He recognised the bed, the room, the angle of the roof half-discernible beyond the blinds, all solid things that anchored him in the solid world, from them he could deduce his reasons for being there. But whether the worst of those reasons were dream or reality he couldn't be sure. Mixed with distorted visions from his own childhood were those of the toddler Gabriela drowning, face down in a placid ocean lapping no deeper than her knees, and all because he hadn't called her in for tea. Try as he might she would not respond as he cried out and struggled to reach her while the sand sucked at his feet with every step. Even with eyes half open the horrors from sleep leaked into the waking world.

He propped himself up on his elbows, shaking his head as if to dislodge the images that swirled there, only for new evils to rise in their place. Grunting, he hauled himself upright, exhausted and breathing heavily, eyes determinedly open, willing himself to focus only on a single object. His phone lay beside the bed. He clicked it to life: there were no messages, no missed calls. It meant nothing, just as it had meant nothing ten hours ago.

If he could only think of something constructive to do he would do it, but the fatigue of a night of troubled sleep and waking nightmares urged his head back to the pillow. He convinced himself that doing so could become constructive if he took the opportunity to calmly consider how he came to be where he now found himself.

First, he recognised that much of his trouble had stemmed from his own actions – and inaction. Above all he should've somehow formalised his care of Gabriela. Of course he should, how could he not have? Easily enough, as one day became another and he and she had settled into their life without Estefanía. And he should have made some effort of his own to find her or find out what happened to her, instead of which he'd done nothing at all. If he could admit these failings, know why he had failed, then one day he might confess them to Gabriela. She would surely demand some explanation from him, not today or tomorrow perhaps, but one day. La señora's words ran round his head *you cannot keep a child, like a stray dog, when her mother disappears, even if you treat her well.* It was offensively put, he'd been insulted, indignant: but he'd known, even as she spoke, that she was right.

So much for calm consideration: anxiety twisted his thoughts to the point where he didn't deserve to take care of Gabriela for even an hour, and certainly not pretend that he could replace a real father. He hadn't even been able to look after Max, his only childhood pet, a bouncy mongrel rescued from the local dogs' home. He'd lasted no longer than his first walk by the river without parental supervision. At nine years of age, Harry was a sensible child, one who could be trusted to walk alone along the river bank and not fall in. *Put Max on the lead when you come to the old weir,* they'd said. But distracted by the dog fetching sticks and snuffling for rabbits, he'd come to that place before he'd realised he was upon it and the dog had slithered down the wet bank and into the current below the weir and he never saw him again. He was there, lively and wriggling and playing and then he was not, then there was nothing but the sound of the water, endlessly churning brown foam. The dog's lead was still looped in his hand.

Torturing himself in this way he fell back into a troubled sleep, only to wake with a start to the sounds of the household having risen and busying themselves with their days. Beyond the window the promise of sunrise was forgotten in steady rain. By the time he'd quickly showered and dressed only Julio remained, deep in urgent conversation with a colleague.

Harry found fruit and coffee and returned to the office where Julio motioned him to sit and stay before finishing his conversation. "Good morning, Harry. We've a lot to do in a short time. Ay! you look like a man who did not sleep well."

"I did not, too many things in my head."

"Harry, I have to be in court at eleven. I could ask someone else, but I have a duty. You won't lose by it."

"Of course, I don't expect anything, just advice on what to do next, that's the most I can ask for."

"Advice in a minute, but I have started some actions, instructed a student we have."

Harry's expression betrayed his thoughts.

"She is good, she is in her last two months with us, she will qualify when she is finished. Harry, she is smart, she will do well for you and for Gabriela. She has already started. She is la señorita Indira Chavarria Calderón, you will meet her."

"Yes, I'm sorry, thank you, I'm sure she's...I didn't mean...I'm grateful. Calderón?"

"It's all right, I know you. Yes, Calderón. If it makes you feel better she is a cousin of Elena. But it makes no difference, she is still smart."

Harry felt suitably chastised, any help was welcome, especially an intelligent law student on their final placement.

"Started? What's happened?"

"These are the things I think we should be doing. First, we look for Gabriela's registration. If we find that it may lead to other discoveries. Second we look for Estefanía, by any means we can. I need you to think hard about all the little details you might know but have forgotten. And when you are home and see Gabriela you must ask her too. Next we must address the court in Puerto Réunion on Tuesday, when the judge will next examine the case. It might be better to use someone local, sometimes the provincial courts aren't pleased to have big-city lawyers descend on them. I will look at this.

"And I will try to discover how your troubles have happened, how the APN are involved, and something of la señora Mejía, perhaps she is junior and making a name for herself, maybe

39

senior. We will find out some things and decide on what to do when we know."

"What am I going to do? I can't leave it all to you."

"You will go home and take very good care of Gabriela and make sure she is seen by your Victor Diaz every day. And a paper signed, too, to say he has seen her. Also, you will try to remember things and stay in close touch with me and la señorita Chavarria. Oh, and you will be in court on Tuesday. Someone will be there with you, not me, but someone."

Harry nodded, a little disappointed that there was apparently nothing more constructive he could do than go home and wait.

"So, now we have a little time for the details. What is Estefanía's name and her age, do you know?"

"Estefanía Flores Blanca. I'm not sure of her age, as I said, but when we last saw her she would have been twenty-five, that's my guess. Thirty at the most. I'll ask Pippa, she may know or guess better than I do. And Leo might know, it depends how he paid her while she was at the Kasanee."

"Let me know. What else, she mentioned her mother, what about her father, the town she came from, anything from before you met her?"

"No names, never. The friend of a cousin, the one with a room and a job, he may never have existed, it may have been a story she told or a lie she'd been given."

"But think Harry, and ask everyone who knew her. Any photos we could use?" Harry shook his head. "We'll do our best. Now, Gabriela, what about her. The papers say she is eight but she's seven, yes?"

"She'll be eight on July twenty-first, same day as my mother's birthday."

"What names does she have?"

"Gabriela Flores is all I know, but..." he hesitated over the possibility, "if Estefanía did register her then it's possible she may be Gabriela Rosa, even Gabriela Rose. Before Estefanía went that first time, when she first left Gabriela with me, she asked about my name, Rose, and was it the same as Rosa. I told her we used it

40

as a given name as well as a family name. Then she asked would I mind if she gave it to Gabriela."

"Oh?" Julio said and waited for Harry to continue, but he had his eyes closed, reliving the moment vividly. Estefanía had been offering him something, something precious, but he'd been too pleased with himself to realise just how precious. Seeing her again, with Gabriela laughing in her arms, Estefanía seemed so young and yet so old, so hard, as young mothers can sometimes be when they've born their first child before they're adults themselves.

"I said yes, of course, why not."

Then he added, "Estefanía may have been younger than I've said, it's hard to tell, I'll ask Pippa."

*

He fell asleep before he was out of San Felipe, the swish of the wet road lulling his senses. Elena had intended to drive him but he'd protested so much that she'd settled for taking him to the bus station. He didn't really want her company for the journey, especially as there would be only one topic of conversation. Either that or long silences where their normal chatter about the children or the old times would normally be. And besides, he needed to collect his truck from Maximercado. His lie about the pickup was a very small lie, of no consequence whatsoever, yet he didn't want to be discovered in it.

He woke groggily to the sound of his phone and struggled to find it. *G is fine in town to see captain D when are you back?*

All safe and well. Of course they were, they were never going to be anything else.

Soon ferry at 5 with luck 6:30 without.

A little later it buzzed again, *Come to mine stay over.*

On the outskirts of Puerto Reunión a bridge was being repaired, but the swollen stream had washed away half the road and one vehicle at a time was being allowed across. The bus inched its way forward. At one stop Harry was astonished to see a new billboard announcing the *Reconstrucción del Aeropuerto*

Municipal de Isla Concepción. It showed an artist's impression of a shiny new building with a small jet parked conveniently close. So far as he knew, the run-down old airstrip hadn't seen a plane land or take off for years. Calling it the *Municipal Airport* certainly stretched the truth. He'd explored it once, soon after taking up residence at Casa Rosa. Even then the runway and apron had been lined with weeds where the concrete had begun to crumble. One delightful discovery was an ancient DC3 parked there, quietly rotting away. The story went that it had been impounded for unpaid fees a decade previously. He'd heard talk of someone carrying it away in pieces and making a bar out of it. That notion had come to nothing and he guessed the *reconstrucción* would follow the same path. A little further along, a second board proclaimed a new resort with palm-roofed cabins on stilts over a shallow sea. The set was completed by what he thought was a marina, although the bus moved too quickly to be sure through the rain-streaked window.

No doubt when reality dawned – plus a little lobbying from Puerto Reunión interests – two of the three would be dropped and the mainland would benefit from the third. He settled back in his seat and thought the DC3 could rest in peace a little longer. But what a waste, maybe when his current troubles were settled he should be the one to turn it into a bar. With Leo's help, of course. Leo might be more help than that, if he knew something of Estefanía. She'd lived in that room above the bar for a few weeks, she'd cleared tables and washed dishes on and off for years, she might have said something to someone, something she might not have said to Harry. He'd ask, he'd do what he should have done a long time ago, if he'd cared for Estefanía at all.

The anxieties of yesterday returned as the bus swung into the terminal. If he'd needed to be devious then, what about today? He decided not. If anyone was interested in his movements they would either already know or be waiting at the ferry on Isla Concepción, his only possible route home.

His truck coughed and faltered twice before picking up cleanly on the third attempt and the ferry god smiled too as he clanked down the loading ramp with a few minutes and a few spaces to spare. No policemen watching the departure, no men in white shirts. As the ferry docked at Concepción he briefly considered a detour to see Leo, or even Victor, at the Kasanee, but thought better of it, they would wait until tomorrow. He drove home, partly to check on the house, partly to collect some clean clothes, then headed towards Pippa's place on the other side of the island. Despite the rain and the winding road, it would be impossible for another car to follow him without being detected. He saw no one.

La Plantación was set high on soft slopes above the ocean, land once cleared for a fruit-growing project now long abandoned. The house, a bungalow of colonial proportions, had been placed in a natural bowl of the land, giving it shelter on three sides. From the terrace on the fourth side the gentle descent led the eye across the neglected lawn to the last vestiges of an orchard and from there across verdant green where nature had reclaimed its annexed territory. The shoreline was hidden but the huge sweep of the bay was apparent, the constant ocean as restless as a temperamental lover.

In bouts of enthusiasm Pippa would attempt to restore a rock garden here or lily pool there but she rarely completed anything before it was interrupted by adverse weather or her creative urge finding a fresh outlet. Despite the decay and the faded glory of the original vision, La Plantación was still magnificent and always welcoming.

Gabriela ran from the shelter of the verandah before the truck had stopped, jumping on the running board and hauling open the door. Harry reached down and hauled her onto his lap, from where she clung to his neck.

"Hey there, little lady, I'm pleased to see you, too," he said softly, kissing her head.

"I thought you weren't coming. I thought you'd never come back."

"I'm here now." He squeezed her closer to him and thought how fragile she felt, and wondered if she should be stronger, rounder, taller. "Come on, let's get inside and you can tell me what you've been up to with Pippa."

They scampered to the house where Pippa hugged them in turn as if they'd both been gone for weeks. She held Harry longer than usual, saying quietly, "Harry, Harry, you lovely man, what'll become of us all?"

"All go to hell in a handcart, I shouldn't be surprised."

"Don't say things like that, not even in jest."

"No, I know. It's easy to wish it all away. I fell asleep on the bus from San Felipe. I woke somewhere near Puerto Reunión and it seemed as if it had all been a dream and I'd woken the day before yesterday and everything was where it should be, everything was back in its place. I know it's not, but I want it to be. How's Gabriela doing?"

"A bit wobbly. She's desperate to show you some paintings she's been doing, come on."

They went through into Pippa's studio, almost completely glass-roofed, on the north side of the house. Gabriela was waiting for them, fists clenched and jiggling on the spot in her excitement.

"Papatico, come and see what I've made!"

Beside her was an easel with her latest creation still on it. She'd covered the paper in rich blue, her sea, and populated it with three fishes, all exotic reds and yellows. Near the lower edge a few fronds of dark green kelp stood upright.

"That's beautiful," he said, and it was.

"Pippa said I could do anything I wanted. I really wanted to do fishes. Or planets, but I chose fishes. I did this too," she added, picking up a board resting beneath the easel. She held it up across her chest, her chin resting along the top edge. It was a head-and-shoulders impression of a young woman. Unusually for a child's painting, the subject was shown half turned away. Gabriela had carefully depicted a crucifix on a yellow chain and a pink hair-slide in jet-black hair. If Gabriela painted any young woman, it would only be, could only be, her mother. Harry had been ready for that the moment she stooped to pick it up. The surprise was the pink slide. Regardless of the likeness or the skill in painting, the slide was a personal detail that made it come alive, made it Estefanía. She was never without it, and yet Harry might never have remembered. For Gabriela to have included it seemed astonishing.

Harry felt his face crumbling and tears start in his eyes.

"Oh, darling, that's beautiful," he said through fat lips.

"It's Mami," she said, then, seeing his tears, "Papatico do you like it? Pippa helped me and she has a photo. I cried a little when I saw it."

"Come here, darling." She came to him and they each held one side of the painting, holding each other at the same time.

He looked up at Pippa, "A photo?"

"I took a few when Gabriela was about four, they were sitting on your front steps. Estefanía didn't mind."

"Have I seen them?"

"I don't know, I thought you did. I'll get them."

The snap Gabriela had worked from was the only one Pippa had printed. The full version showed Estefanía holding Gabriela on her knee There were four others still on the camera, all taken on the same day, all showing Estefanía sitting with her daughter on the steps at Casa Rosa. None of them were remarkable. In any circumstances other than the present, they would likely have remained forgotten and unused.

"You didn't put yourself in the painting, Gabriela."

"I only wanted Mami. I didn't want me."

"We'll take them both home tomorrow if they're dry."

"Are we staying here tonight?"

"Yes, I think so, if Pippa will have us."

"Oh yes," Pippa nodded and Gabriela twirled around, beaming her gappy smile.

For the next hour they dawdled away the time until Pippa realised that they hadn't eaten and quickly filled a frying pan with help from Gabriela and encouragement from Harry. It was a happy evening, one in which no mention was made of the troubles surrounding them, nor did those troubles cast a shadow over the simple pleasure of being in each other's company. But when Gabriela had fallen asleep on Harry and been eased off to bed they poured drinks and sat looking at each other not quite knowing where to start.

Finally, Harry said, "You first, how did it go with Victor Diaz?"

"Bloody ridiculous! That's how it went. It was about eleven, this morning, Diaz wasn't there and nobody knew why we were there. Poor Gabriela didn't know what was going on. I told that sergeant just what I thought of him and threatened him with all sorts of things if he didn't do what he was told."

"Poor man, I wonder why Victor didn't make any arrangements. Or la señora from the APN. So what happened?"

"I made him write out a statement that Gabriela had been presented and shown to be well and happy. And sign it and put the time and date on it with one of his stamps. Then he copied it and I told him to put his copy on Diaz's desk and I have the original here in my bag."

"Thank you for doing that, Pippa. I thought it would be more straightforward. Nothing ever is though, is it?"

"Apparently not. Otherwise, we had a very good day and you're back sooner than we thought. I'm so glad you are, you should have seen Gabriela's face when I said you'd be here tonight. Does it mean that it went well with Julio?"

"I don't really know. He asked a lot of questions, the kind you'd expect, he made a lot of notes, then swung into action this morning. I thought I only went to see him for some advice, but it's turned into a lot more. He has a student, an intern, who's going to see what she can find about Estefanía and Gabriela."

Pippa gave him the withering look of a schoolmistress displeased with a lazy pupil.

"Yes, I know, Pippa, all the stuff you suggested a very long time ago. I'm sorry."

"Don't be sorry to me, be sorry to Gabriela. You're her responsible adult, you're *in loco parentis,* or you should be. The trouble is you're more like an over-indulgent grandfather."

"Not fair, she's an easy child, doesn't need much putting right. But I know I need to say sorry to her too. It's a mess."

"Well don't say that too soon either, and not the mess bit either. She's got enough on her plate already. She has it in her head that all this trouble, the APN and you dashing off to San Felipe, she thinks that may be her fault. Something to do with her sleeping on the beach. She was in tears and I didn't push her. And she told me she's scared she'll forget her Mami. And she's scared her Mami has already forgotten her. I could have wept for her. I may yet."

"I may not be too strict but I never tell her any lies about anything. If she asks I tell her the truth," Harry said, a little too defensively.

"But you don't have to tell her the whole truth and nothing but."

"I think she needs to know what's happening, it's her life. Are you saying she doesn't?"

"Not everything, and not always. She's seven, for Christ's sake, not seventeen. She has to put things in context, in perspective. She can't put all the fucking ugly grown-up shit in the context of her seven-year-old world."

The house was suddenly silent, all the more so for the crickets sawing their love-songs in the blackness beyond.

"Julio said something…" he began, with a thought to deflect the point of her anger, but she cut him off.

"Harry darling, I'm sorry for being so cross with you. I'm cross with what's happened and it all comes out as being cross with you. Do you forgive me? You know I love you."

"Nothing to forgive. You're right to be cross. I just kept hoping. I should have done more. I will do more, if I get the chance."

Pippa joined him on the sofa, pushing him across so that she could sit close to him with her legs tucked up beside her.

She held his head in her hands and kissed him gently on the lips.

"You do know I love you, don't you?"

He nodded slightly and said "Yes," very softly.

"I'm still glad we never married, we're better off now."

"I'm still glad I never asked you," he said, half-jokingly, half not.

"You did, you've edited that out. You wanted to get me into bed and thought that was the best way. Little did you know."

"Little do I know."

A truce had been declared.

"Go on, what did Julio say? I interrupted you," she said after a while.

"He said that whatever happened to me, Gabriela would be OK, because he and Elena would make sure she was, and there was you, too. So she would be looked after. I thought about that afterwards, if something happened to me, would you look after Gabriela?"

"In emergency, yes, of course. But you mean something longer term, take over from you and be an over-indulgent grandmother, something like that?"

"Yes, something like that."

"Not sure."

"That's what I thought you'd say. But here's what I wondered next: imagine for a minute that Gabriela is allowed to stay with me, but that they need some extra re-assurance for her welfare. I wondered if you and I, together with Elena and Julio, if we all presented a united front as somehow joint guardians, I wondered if that might be something you'd consider."

"More like godparents with clout, do you mean?"

"That kind of thing, yes."

"Could be. But no religious stuff, I'm not going to perjure myself on that, not for you or anybody."

"Agreed. And taking it to the next step, if Gabriela went to live with Elena and Julio, would you stay in touch, stay in her life? I think you would, but I'd like to know."

"Yes, no question. But she – and they – would have to want me, it would be difficult for everyone if they didn't. Oh Harry, do you think you'll lose her?"

"When I look at it coldly, yes, I do. Funnily enough, I think the better the plans we have for that happening, the more chance of her staying."

"What else can you do, aside from the legal stuff?"

"I have to see if anyone has any little scraps of knowledge about Estefanía, or even Gabriela, anything that might be useful in tracking her down. You might know something, something she said in passing, where she was born, her mother's name, maybe she has a brother, that kind of thing."

"You never asked her these things? Didn't you talk to each other?"

"Of course, but not about personal things." Again he was wounded by the criticism, the implied failure. "Did you?"

"I didn't live in the same house all those years."

"She was private, she didn't talk about personal things, we didn't have that kind of relationship."

"What did you have? You didn't sleep with her, did you, Harry? I always thought you didn't, but…"

"La señora Mejía thinks I sleep with the child and my friends think I slept with the mother. I was fond of her. Julio said maybe I loved her a little and he was right."

"I think she loved you a little too."

"Did she say something?"

"Sometimes she asked me little things about you, had you been married, that kind of thing," Pippa said, and then added pointedly, "The things that people are naturally curious about."

"We know about me, did she tell you anything about herself?"

"She was only sixteen when she had Gabriela, she told me that."

Harry made an involuntary noise in his throat as a trapdoor in his stomach opened. His breath wouldn't come and he was overwhelmed by the sickening sensation of falling from a great height with no hint of how far away the ground might be.

49

Sixteen. Estefanía had been sixteen when they'd shared a seat on the crowded *colectivo*, sixteen when she'd begged the price of a meal from him at the Kasanee, sixteen when she'd moved in, unsure of what he expected of her. Sixteen asked as many questions as it answered.

"Right," he mumbled.

"You had no idea, did you? How old did you think she was?"

"Somewhere around there, eighteen maybe, it's hard to tell," he said, recovering his senses a little. "I must tell Julio. What else might you know? Did she mention her mother or her father?"

"I don't think she was in touch with them. When we were talking about Gabriela being born I said something about her mother knowing about Gabriela and she looked at me and shook her head. Maybe it was a regret she had, but I might've imagined that."

"And Gabriela's...father?" He hesitated over using the words, he had after all, pushed all thought of that anonymous man far, far away for many years.

"Yes, I asked about him too, whether he knew about Gabriela. Estefanía said something like *for now she has her Papatico*. I think she was very happy about that."

"When you say it like that, yes, I think she might've been." He drew a deep breath and studied the ice as he swirled it in his glass. "Look at us sitting here talking about her, with her daughter sleeping in the next room, food in our bellies, gin in our glasses, a roof over our heads. I wonder where she is tonight. Sixteen! Jesus."

The night air, full of the sweet wet-earth smells after the rain, wafted through the room as a breeze disturbed the stillness.

"I want to know how all this has happened, what started it," Pippa demanded. "It could be malicious, you've thought of that?"

"But who and why? More likely someone who's heard half a story from someone else who's got some gossip after a drink or two and then added a few lurid details and passed it on to their friend and...well you get the idea, you know how these things get blown up into something they never were."

"Chinese whispers, we used to call it."

"Well, the last one in line's been outraged enough to complain and here we are. I hope they're happy," he added bitterly.

"I asked you once before about children, whether you wished you'd had any. Do you still feel the same?"

"That was a long time ago, Pippa. What did I say? Probably that I was happy without them, yes? No change there. And there's Gabriela now."

"Do you ever think about us, whether we might've had children? I think about it, but I can never quite make the leap from what we are, what we've been, to what we might have been."

"It was too late for babies, whatever else we might have been."

"Actually no, my darling, not too late, not back then."

"Ah. Too late in other ways then. Anyway, they would've been ungrateful, selfish brats who'd have deserted us at the first opportunity, left us to a lonely old age and never brought the grandchildren to see us."

"You're horrible. Can we sleep together tonight? It would be very nice."

Harry turned to face her, the questions clear in his eyes.

"To remind ourselves of the warmth of another's skin. To be there for each other if the nightmares come. For companionship, Harry, for human touch," she said.

★

Victor Diaz's cramped office behind the public counter was at best functional, certainly not a place to entertain visitors. A ceiling fan endlessly stirred the air, the motion of the blades giving a suggestion of cooling, but too slowly to have any noticeable effect. On Isla Concepción, at the furthermost reach of law enforcement, the constabulary received new equipment only when those nearer the centre had enjoyed first use of it. Everything from the desk to the computer, even the blind at the window, was second-hand. The sole exception was his chair, which Diaz had supplied himself.

51

"Ha! Gabriela! Cada día mas guapa!" he exclaimed brightly, rising to greet them as they squeezed into the space. "It is true, is it not, señora Maddingly, every day she is more beautiful."

Gabriela might have been forgiven for hardly recognising this Captain Diaz as being the same man who'd stood so stiffly beside la señora Mejía and not said a word to Gabriela during the whole of *that* visit. This Captain Diaz had no cap, no tie, no tunic with badges and insignia, no shiny black holster with a strap holding a gun in place.

"And señor Rose," the cordiality remained, but with a subtle switch to the formal, "a pleasure to see you again."

"We have brought Gabriela to see you," Harry said cautiously, unsure how long formality would last with a man he'd called a friend until two days previously. "Pippa brought her yesterday, too. Could we have a document, as yesterday, perhaps?"

"Ah, yes, apologies for that confusion, I was not here and it was you, señor Rose, who had been expected. There is a paper already prepared, here, I will complete it now." He signed the sheets in front of him and handed one to Harry. "And now, is there anything else?"

"Yes, I have something. But in private, Pippa and Gabriela are going along to the bar for some food."

"I don't have long today, señor Rose," he said warily.

"It won't take long. I'll be along in a few minutes," he said, turning to Pippa and giving Gabriela a kiss on her forehead. The two said their goodbyes to Victor Diaz a little awkwardly.

After a moment's silence, Harry turned and closed the door to the outer office.

"Victor, or is it capitán Diaz now, what the fuck is going on?"

"Oh, yes, señor Rose, what is going on? I should not be here alone with you now, you are investigated for some big crimes, do you know that? You think I should be your friend – and do what for you? Make it all disappear with magic? You were surprised when la señora Mejía came to Casa Rosa? I too! She is from the APN in San Felipe, come to make Gabriela safe! I know this an hour before you did, not even one hour! What should I do? Give you warning that you could run and hide? Or maybe I should say *no, you are wrong, Harry Rose is my friend, we drink beer at his house, Gabriela sits in my car and flashes the lights?* That would not be good for me or you. No, I took a small risk and came to show la señora the way to Casa Rosa and flashed the lights and drove too quickly so you would know something was different, yes?"

"Yes, we saw," he said feebly.

"Good. I am Diaz," he said, stubbing a finger into his chest, "capitán de policía, not APN, not investigador, not the judge's man. They tell me you maybe killed Gabriela's mother, you make Gabriela a slave. This sounds like madness, but what do I know, I am a capitán de policía, not APN. So yes, señor Harry Rose, what the fuck is going on? Perhaps you tell me, and then I will tell it to your old friend Victor."

The indignation verged on anger, a shock to Harry who could only sit open mouthed while the fan blades continued their hypnotic journey. Eventually he mumbled an apology, "I didn't think, it's been difficult, I'm sorry," and rose to leave, before he remembered his true purpose.

"There's something I have to ask you," he started tentatively, but Diaz cut across him immediately.

"Listen to me, listen carefully. If I know anything about the APN, about the case against you, if I know anything at all, I would not tell you. If they had asked me questions about you I would not tell you what they were or what I said. If they had been through the files, the bar, anything, I would not tell you. If they had asked me about this person or that person here on Isla Concepción, I would not say who or when. You understand me, señor Rose?"

Harry nodded without comprehension, "Yes, yes, of course. But I wasn't asking that, no, I wondered if you still have the report I made about Estefanía Flores when she disappeared, and if I could have a copy of that?"

"It is still here, yes. When you come tomorrow I will make a copy."

"Thank you, Victor," Harry said, deliberately reverting to the familiar, "and the other thing was Estefanía herself, I wondered if you ever heard her say anything about herself, her family, anything that could help us trace her." When Diaz looked doubtful he added, "It was a long time ago, I know. It's a long shot. I'm asking everybody."

"She spent some time in San Felipe," the policeman said suddenly, "she knew a place there, a district, maybe a street, I don't remember where. Perhaps everybody has spent time in San Felipe."

"Perhaps they have."

As Harry stepped out of the police post he intended to walk the short distance to meet up with Gabriela and Pippa. He didn't know many people well enough to stop and chat, but knew plenty well enough to smile and nod good day. He wasn't exactly well-known, but being taller and whiter than most in Concepción, he was easily identified, even when disguised by a hat and sunglasses. After he'd taken a few steps, a man he recognised as an occasional customer at the Kasanee approached from the opposite direction. Harry's "Hola" died in his throat as the man looked away and passed by without speaking.

For the first time in all his years on the island he felt alien, isolated, unwelcome. A mistaken identity? Perhaps the man was preoccupied with his own troubles, the incident was nothing, easily explainable. Two days previously the same insecurities had thrown up spooks in the shadows as he dodged imagined agents and spies in Puerto Reunión. But his chastening experience with Victor Diaz was fresh in his mind, old certainties were no longer. All around him the citizens of Concepción were going about their Saturday morning business in the bustle of the street stalls, unaware of him standing and staring. The scene was indistinguishable from any other Saturday morning, and yet he saw it from the edge, as a man looking in from the outside. He returned to his pickup, parked in a side street next to the police post, telling himself it would be more convenient anyway, he had no need to walk.

"Have you ordered?" he said when he found Pippa on the back deck at the bar.

"Yes, and for you. Gabriela's fetching the drinks. Leo seemed surprised to see us, the more so when I said you'd be along in a minute. How was it with Victor?"

"Difficult. I hadn't really given any thought to his position at all. But he's doing what he can, he just needs to keep his distance. He thinks it's all crazy, but he can't do anything, he can't even tell me anything. He'll think about Estefanía, if he might know something, some little detail."

"Here's Gabriela, behind you," she said by way of warning.

Harry turned to see, her face a study in concentration as she carried their tray of drinks. Leo was right behind her.

"Gabriela! You have a job here any time you want, OK?" Leo said, congratulating her as she slid the tray with its unspilled drinks onto the little table.

"Hello Leo," Harry said in neutral tones, testing the water by stretching out his hand. Leo hesitated slightly before taking it and holding it firmly.

"Hello Harry, it's good to see you, especially as it is said you had crossed the border and would never return. And other things are said," he glanced at Gabriela, apparently busy with her milk shake, but also focused intently on her Papatico and his friend, a friend who had also known her Mami.

Harry had been mistaken to tackle Victor Diaz head-on, it wasn't an error he was about to repeat with Leo, and certainly not with Gabriela all eyes and ears beside them.

"I'm sure many things are said, and nearly as many are completely wrong, eh, Leo? No, not to the border, but San Felipe. But you know already this is a bad business? Yes, I'm sure you do. So, we've got two things to ask of you, I say we because Gabriela and Pippa and I," he hadn't meant to include Pippa in this way but it seemed natural and she nodded her agreement anyway, "we're together in these troubles."

"Ask, my friend, I can say yes or no." Leo was a big man, a little overweight, his hair thinning faster than he'd have wished and

55

with a wife who loved him deeply but who had ambitions for him and the Kasanee that Leo didn't always share. Like others of his build and age and apparent slowness he was easily underestimated, especially by those who knew less of the world than he did.

"All right then, the first is simple. You will hear things, stories people have heard or add to as they re-tell them, some fantastic, some with perhaps a grain of truth buried in them. Stories of me, perhaps Pippa too, and of Estefanía, maybe even of Gabriela, who knows."

"Yes, there are many stories right now. As I said, you are gone, already across the border, it is said that the police missed you by only five minutes. They say it was a good chase, better than Hollywood."

"Well, perhaps you'd keep those stories and pass them on to me, to us, to let us know what is being said. Maybe there will be a tiny clue hidden in a word, a place, a name."

"Yes, Harry, this is easy, but I don't have all day, I will select from the stories. The second favour?"

"More difficult, time has passed and with it memory and detail. We are looking for Estefanía, we should've looked, I mean I should have looked, a long time ago. We have little to go on. Do you recall anything, however small, she might have said about her life, her mother maybe, a brother or sister, a place she was in?"

"I'll think, but nothing comes now. I'll ask Carla, she may know something small. When Estefanía first came here, to Concepción, I always thought you, er…know her from before. No?"

"I'd met her once, on a bus."

"Ah, I did not know that, I thought there was more."

Harry saw the slight discomfort, but Gabriela's close attention held him back from pressing further.

"There's something else. When Estefanía worked here, how did you pay her? I mean was she on the records, maybe with a note of her age, or birthplace, that kind of thing?"

"Harry, have you forgotten how it started? I paid her with the room upstairs, she and Gabriela were there."

"But you gave her a little money too."

"You know how it works, Harry. Up to a certain amount we can give cash, no questions, it's trabajador ocasional. We have only to say we saw the ID, nothing more."

"Did you see her ID?"

"Yes, for sure."

"Why so sure, Leo?" Pippa asked. "Sorry, but there must be times when..."

"Yes, of course there are times, but with Estefanía Flores..." he started, then paused and spoke directly to Gabriela. "Mi cosita, your Mamá was a good Mamá, she worked hard, she cared very much for you, but when she came here with you I didn't know that, I didn't know her and I didn't know you. So I checked her ID to see if she was who she said she was. And she was. Gabriela, you are growing into a fine girl, you are smart already. Remember this: you cannot trust people you don't know. Know them first then you may trust them. It was like that with your Mamá. You understand me?"

Gabriela nodded without removing the straw from her lips.

4

Gabriela's paintings were safely sandwiched between sheets of cardboard, lightly bound together with masking tape and stowed carefully in her bag of clothes between the seats. She and Harry had stayed at Pippa's again, then somehow when they'd headed off to the police post her art had been overlooked. Halfway home, Gabriela had suddenly remembered them and cried at the thought of their being forgotten. It unnerved Harry a little, Gabriela wasn't a child who cried readily, nor so often as she had in recent days. But then, neither was he, and tears had lately come easily to him. They both had good reason. Even so, he resolved to be more alert to feelings, more so than ever, in the next few days and weeks, who knew what fresh troubles lay ahead.

As soon as he'd appreciated the mistake over her paintings, he'd swung the truck round and they'd returned to La Plantación to recover them. As the pickup bounced back round the hill he wished all his troubles, and Gabriela's, could be remedied so simply. He glanced across at her, saw her vulnerability, how small she seemed under the seat belt he'd insisted she wear in a sudden rush of responsibility. *From now on*, he'd said, and then forgotten to do likewise until she'd yelled *Papatico!* before he'd driven a few metres and Pippa was still waving them goodbye. They would likely be the only people on Isla Concepción buckled up that day – or any day.

She stared straight ahead, not sullen or angry, but simply blank, her usual animated state a thing of yesterday. He guessed she might be drained by the turmoil around her, however calm and reassuring the adults who circled her star had tried to be. She'd lost her precious Mami, perhaps for ever, and was frightened she'd soon lose the memory of her too. A double loss, and for the second, she alone would be responsible. Now for reasons beyond her understanding but somehow also her fault, she might be taken from her home and lose that and him, her Papatico, who made everything possible. Little wonder that she would be flat.

As they approached the track to Casa Rosa, Harry said "Almost home," in that pointless way that adults sometimes try to fill unwelcome silence. At the turn he could see a black car parked at the point. He couldn't be sure it was the same car as previously but it seemed a reasonable guess.

"The men are here again," Gabriela said, matter-of-fact.

"Same as before, you think?"

She shrugged and pulled a face.

"Anything you'd like to do when we get in?"

The face and the shrug were repeated.

"Maybe a quiet time for both of us. It'll be a busy week, a bit different from what we're used to. I think I may have to be away in Puerto Reunión for two or three days. Pippa will be here."

"At night?"

"Maybe, but I think I'll be home too. It may be possible for you to come, but not on the first day. I'll ask and see if you can." He hadn't thought it out, had no idea if it would be possible or not, and cursed himself for raising the subject, all it did was set her up for fresh disappointment. But he would ask, push for it, now he'd thought of it.

When they'd been back an hour and he'd settled to nothing and checked on Gabriela at least four times and she had been sitting on her bed each time, he realised they were waiting. Waiting for the next event to come to them, waiting until it was time to report to Diaz again, waiting until Pippa must come or he must go or news from Julio. Waiting until the end of the week and the judge's decision on the next thing they must wait for.

They could go to the Kasanee, have a chat, have some food. Gabriela could wander between the tables, behind the bar, chat to whoever was in the kitchen, be teased by Leo, be kissed by Carla because she was always there on Sundays. But that was last week, that was what they always did. It was what they always used to do. It would be different today, they would be waiting to come home and everyone at the Kasanee would be waiting for them to leave.

Although la señora Mejía's visit had been shocking, traumatic, as the event receded it became less real, less urgent, less relevant. Yet even as it did so, its tendrils reached into every aspect of their lives. Not just their lives, but into their world on Isla Concepción, and beyond to San Felipe. None of it would ever go back to what it had been, not ever, not even if la señora should magically appear and apologise that she had the wrong house, the wrong Harry Rose, the wrong Gabriela, please continue as you were. Harry could wish with all his heart that it were otherwise, but it would make no difference, there was no going back. He could picture it as innocence being lost, his more than Gabriela's. If he were more honest, he knew it was more a fool's paradise where the day of reckoning had arrived.

He took a beer from the fridge and looked in on Gabriela again. She was lying on her back now, eyes open, her hair pulled out of its ribbons and splayed around her head on the pillow.

"I'll be out front, come and sit with me when you're ready. Are you OK, my darling?" He wanted to go to her, sit with her, lie beside her, comfort her with big arms. But a new inhibition, a sliver of doubt, held him back.

"I'm looking at the stars," she said without looking at him.

"Well, when you're ready."

She didn't reply.

He'd intended to sit on the verandah, but instead he went straight to the water's edge. The rain had stopped but more threatened. It was unseasonable – but wasn't everything nowadays? Old securities were reliable no longer. The cloud cast everything in a different light but it made no difference to him. A chance invitation had first brought him to Casa Rosa and it wasn't the sun that he'd fallen in love with: it was the sweep of the bay, coral sand stretching perfectly to the succulent green which completed the curve, it was the soft lap of the water, never more than a whisper whatever might be going on beyond the reef, it was the marriage of sea and sky and all their moods. But he hadn't bought it with a child in mind. However much he loved it, and he was sure Gabriela loved it too, it could never provide all that she needed. In Concepción they might just scrape by, but what was the point in that?

Movement caught his eye off to his right. It was a rare sighting of his neighbour Ernest Portillo. Harry watched as he walked to the point where he and Gabriela had seen the black car earlier. It had gone but Ernest stood there for a minute or so then turned to retrace his steps. Seeing Harry, he waved and Harry waved back. In another moment he was inside his house, a house Harry had never been invited to enter. He wondered what Ernest did with his days, for it might be a week, a month before he'd be seen outside again. Gabriela, from her observation post in the tree, was an expert on Ernest's movements, or lack of them.

Harry, along with Ernest and Bill Fairchild had united to refuse the best offer they were ever likely to get nearly two years previously. They each loved their beach and their bay and their privacy more than money. The idea of it being dominated by a concrete high-rise hotel was as abhorrent as it was unlikely. A month or two later the lawyers' letters had ceased and nothing more was mentioned. No doubt another beach on another bay in another country received the dubious blessing of that development.

He settled himself in one of the old leather and bamboo armchairs he'd inherited with the house. There were four but the one he chose was the one he always chose. He was sitting in it the evening that Victor had spoken about hookers and when he looked up now he fancied that Estefanía might be about to offer him another beer. On his lap were a notebook and pencil, each about to receive and give their first marks. The notebook was going to be his new beginning. Today would be a small start, the first thoughts and ideas of future actions, of caring for Gabriela completely, with her whole life in mind. A different universe to the holding pattern they'd been in since waving to Estefanía as she was taken away by *Espíritu de las Islas*.

He started with something he'd thought about for months and never begun: a journal for Gabriela. His idea was part scrapbook, part photo album and part diary. Something she could contribute to as much as he, something she could look at in later years and know something of her past. Even to begin it was to admit that Estefanía would not be doing such a thing, to admit she was absent and admit the possibility of her never returning. This was the hardest thing, the more so at that moment. Gabriela, brooding unknowingly on her bed, was once again at a fork in her road, no less than she'd been that day when her mother had begged small change from him. In another week, less, a judge could have chosen a new path for her and their shared lives might be shared no more.

He would buy a scrapbook the next time he was in Puerto Reunión. And while he was there he should consider more of her needs. His mind turned naturally to books, for him the gateway to all knowledge. Gabriela had acquired the same liking, for which he was grateful, it had given them common ground since he'd first read to her one night Estefanía had been working at the bar. But her bookshelf was hardly overloaded and she'd had nothing fresh to sink into for many months. There was no library in Concepción and he'd never enquired about one on the mainland. Even as he thought of the library, he was reminded that there was a library on the island, the one in the school, the school from which Gabriela was excluded. She may not be eligible for classes, but surely she might be able to use the library? And if the library then perhaps other resources? It seemed unlikely, but it went into the notebook, not least because it felt like something he could do, if not today then certainly tomorrow. And doing something, instead of waiting, would be good for both of them.

He fell to thinking of what Elena and Julio and their children could have been doing, and what progress Elena's smart cousin, Indira Chavarria, might have made. Very little most likely, since

62

all offices would be closed. How had they spent their weekends? With families or with friends, socialising or relaxing at home, it was what everybody did, wasn't it? In its way it was what he and Gabriela had done, what they regularly did. True, for some there might be some sporting event, for Elena's Stuart it would be that or music.

Sport and music were both absent from Gabriela's life. He hadn't thought of it as starkly as that before, but the previous vague awareness now hit home forcibly. She'd never shown any interest in either, but then he'd never really given her the opportunity. He wrote *Sport* in the notebook without any idea of how he might bring it into her life, not so long as they lived at Casa Rosa and she didn't go to school. School, it came back to school. Reluctantly he wrote *Music* next, knowing it too had a similar solution. He couldn't sing or play a note, or even hum two notes of a song from the radio. With a pang he recalled Gabriela's happy memory of Cristela *she sang with me, we made up songs*. In truth, it had made no impression on him at the time.

Pippa had art covered, probably better than any school could offer, which reminded him that Gabriela's paintings were still in her bag. They must both be put on display and she should say where. But in frames, maybe, not simply pinned to the edge of a shelf. No, she should decide that too. A moment later he wrote *Art Supplies* in the notebook. It was all very well thinking Pippa had it covered, but that wasn't here at home. He'd been thinking of paint and brushes, but her own easel might be a good idea too. If Puerto Reunión had such a thing.

In that moment the future was bright with possibilities.

He fetched another beer and peeped in on Gabriela. She seemed to be asleep, so he crept closer to be sure. She was. Whatever may trouble a child in the waking hours, whatever frowns or pain disfigure their faces, all are smoothed away in sleep. As if she were not beautiful enough when awake, she was perfection asleep. Bronze lashes rested softly on caramel skin glowing on rounded cheeks, one arm across her chest disguising the little rise and fall of her breathing.

Tears and silences, now an afternoon nap. What next, he wondered, and was dimly aware of a host of troubling behaviours that might manifest themselves in the years ahead. Despite his intervention, she hadn't had the best start to life, there was time enough yet for many repercussions.

An hour passed and he was about to rouse her when she came sleepily out of the house, her face screwed up in annoyance at being awake. Harry held out his arms as she stumbled to him.

"I feel funny," she muttered.

"You feel what, darling?"

"I feel funny!" she shouted.

"What kind of funny?"

"Don't know," she shrugged.

"Do you hurt somewhere? Your head maybe, or your tummy?"

She thought about this while she yawned. "Don't know."

"Well, tell me if you know any more. Before you went to sleep you were looking at your star poster." She nodded. "Then later I saw you'd fallen asleep, you were in just the same place, just that your eyes were closed. It gave me an idea."

"What?"

"Look out there," he pointed at the sea. On the horizon a bright band of light promised a clear night.

"What?" she said again, seeing nothing.

"The clouds are going, I think it'll be clear tonight. Lots of stars to see."

Gabriela gave this some thought. "Will I be in bed?" she asked a little suspiciously.

"I was thinking that maybe we could both go to sleep on the sand, looking at the stars. We could tell each other stories about them."

"Really and truly?"

"Yes, if the clouds go."

Having set a time and a place for something they both wanted to do immediately, they spent the remainder of the day waiting, for cloud to go and night to come. To Harry's disappointment the band of clear sky seemed to approach so far and then no further. They had chicken and rice sitting on the verandah in the last of the light as the sun went down around five, still with little prospect of the promised starry vista. At six it was dark enough to see Venus, bright in the western sky before it set, and Mars following it down soon after. The strip of clear sky had allowed them a sunset and that brief view, but Gabriela was unimpressed.

"Tomorrow then, or whenever it's bright and clear, the next night like that, we'll do it then," he told her. He wished he'd never had the idea, and certainly not mentioned it, it had only set her up for disappointment. She sagged onto him like a collapsed marionette. He let her rest there for a few minutes, stroking her head.

"Have a bath, get ready for bed, then we'll see what it's like," he said. More disappointment set up. He couldn't help himself.

She nodded without any enthusiasm and pulled herself away from him.

The bath came and went, he read a few pages of *Charlotte's Web* to her because it was usually a favourite, they tried squinting through half-closed eyes at the stars on the ceiling above her bed, but it was a poor substitute for the real thing on a sand mattress.

"Still feeling a bit funny?"

"A bit."

He kissed her goodnight but left her light on with instructions to come to him if she was restless, but when he checked ten minutes later she was fast asleep and he clicked her room to darkness.

On another evening like this, Victor might arrive unannounced for a beer and a chat for an hour or two if he was bored with his wife and the Kasanee. Or Harry might take himself off to walk the length of the bay and back, twice if the fancy took him, but tonight he felt the need to stay at the house, close to Gabriela, and he was grateful that there would be no Victor to entertain.

He took the notebook, along with a tumbler of scotch, to his place on the verandah where he intended to resume his review of their lives, his and Gabriela's. Instead, he took a few tastes of the whisky and let his head rest on the cushion, recalling the simple pleasure of lying with Pippa, as she had said, for the companionship of it.

He awoke hours later, cold and stiff, two moths buzzing their wings to destruction against the light bulb. Gabriela was at his side, still warm and drowsy from sleep herself.

"Papatico, can we see the stars now?"

"Maybe," he said, snapping himself awake, "let's have a look."

Together they craned their necks to see the sky. The cloud had gone. Between the black outline of the roof and the moonlit shapes of the jicaros a brilliant vault of jewels had appeared.

"Yes," he said, "yes we can. It's cold, get a blanket and a pillow from your bed. I'll get mine."

The walked only a few steps beyond the trees and lay their rugs and pillows on the sand. Around them the monochrome world slept while the heavens above blazed with light. Heads on pillows they lay close together under the thickest rug and stared up at their show. They said nothing for several minutes, floating in the immensity of space and all the jewelled wonders it held.

It was a beautiful thing and he wondered why he'd never suggested it before. Just as he thought Gabriela might've drifted back to sleep, she whispered, "Tell me a star story, Papatico, please."

"There are so many star stories nobody can count them and nobody knows them all. Some star stories aren't about stars at all, they're about planets, because when the stories were first told thousands of years ago, nobody knew about planets and how they were different from stars. Look now and tell me if you can see a planet among all the stars. You might because you know your planets, but it isn't easy, is it?"

"No."

"Let's find Jupiter." So they did, putting hands up to shut out the light of the moon because Jupiter was a little too close to be obvious. Harry told her how, according to the Romans, Jupiter was the King of the Gods and responsible for thunder and lightning, among many other things. A little lower in the sky they found Saturn, *with the rings round it*, she said. Which accounted for it appearing to have a *slightly oval shape if you looked hard enough*, he said.

"Do all the stars have names?"

"No, not all, there are too many of them, and scientists find new ones all the time, so most of the stars have numbers, not names."

"What's your best star?"

"Hmm, the name I like best is probably Alpha Centauri, it sounds very old and mysterious. Although I like Andromeda too, even though it sounds like a plate of pasta."

"My best is Neptune. Is there one called Gabriela?"

"I don't know, but we could find out."

"Or an Estefanía star?"

★

Clothes. Like Harry, Gabriela had the perfect wardrobe for slopping about at home, in her tree, on the beach, but otherwise had few options. Really she had no options beyond the least threadbare shirt and shorts. Yesterday's idea that he might take Gabriela to Puerto Reunión with him had progressed no further than possibly asking the judge to allow her to leave the island. Now, as he sorted through the clean laundry he realised she had nothing to wear that wasn't tired, and most of it was also getting too small for her. If the judge should ask to see her, she'd need something better than faded shorts and a ragged tee. He couldn't remember the last time, or even if there was a time, when he'd bought her new clothes. There were a few hand-me-downs from Elena's children, some she'd yet to grow into, but nearly everything had come from the second-hand market in town. The last truly new thing were her pyjamas, and they'd been a present from Pippa.

It was unusual for him to be up and doing things before Gabriela had woken, but it had been an unusual night, half in bed and half on the beach. They'd alternately dozed and watched stars until the light of the new day had ended their show and they'd stumbled back to their beds. Letting her sleep in would harm nobody, it would be a hard week for them both.

He'd mapped out the day and having done so was keen to get it started, but she still hadn't stirred when he'd finished his jobs. Looking into her room he saw she'd flung back the bedclothes and taken off her top but was still asleep, arms and legs spread wide.

"Gabriela," he said softly, sitting beside her. He could feel the unnatural heat before he put a hand to her forehead.

"Gabriela, wake up darling," he said firmly, fighting down the urge to shout and shake her shoulders. She was not a child who was ever sick. Once, soon after Estefanía had gone, she'd had a snotty cold that Pippa had given her and been miserable for a week; when she was teething as a baby, she ran a slight fever for a few hours. So far as he knew that was it, that was her complete medical history.

How hot was she? He had no way of knowing, there was nothing in the house to help him. But he knew she was hot enough to need cooling. Had he heard a cold bath was the thing? Or had he heard it was definitely not the thing? A drink, for sure, and a cool compress. These both sounded sensible and undramatic. Pulse? Yes, that he could do. Was she unconscious or still sleeping? Or a little of both? Knowing her heart rate wouldn't tell him anything useful, but he put his fingers to her wrist anyway. Eighty-two, unless he'd miscounted. Again. Eighty-one. OK, fast but not racing. His own was probably not much less.

He fetched a cloth and a bowl of water and ice and made a pad which he put on her forehead.

"Gabriela, hey little darling, wake up."

Her eyelids flickered.

"Come on now, wake up and talk to me a little."

She moaned a long pathetic, "No."

"Yes, my darling, that's better. And you need a drink too."

"I'm cold," she complained sleepily, eyes still closed.

He pulled a sheet up and lifted her a little onto her pillow, then put a mug of iced water to her lips.

"Drink please darling, even a little, here, take your mug."

He held the compress to her head while she did so. She took a mouthful and another and opened her eyes.

"Hello," he said, making himself smile, "good morning." He wanted to tell her how she'd scared him, how hopeless and inadequate he felt. He wanted to say how the more he looked at it, the more things there were he hadn't thought about, the more he'd let her down, but that he would do better, much better, if she gave him a chance.

"I feel funny."

"Hmm, any pain, in your head, what about your tummy?"

She shook her head.

"Any teeth hurting?" he asked in a flash of inspiration. Could second teeth have that effect? He had no idea.

Again the shake of her head.

He sat like that for the next half hour, encouraging her to drink, refreshing the compress until Gabriela said she didn't like it any more and he took her pulse again and it was only seventy-five. Her eyes regained something of their shine instead of the dull glazed stare that was as frightening as the heat on her brow. He left her then, to sleep again, and anxiously paced the house. The day took on a different shape with different priorities. *You will bring her each day to show that she is well* was one of la señora Mejía's conditions yet today she was far from well. He wasn't even sure that he would take her, what then?

Around mid-morning Gabriela found Harry sitting on the steps. She'd put her pyjama top on again and was clutching her bear. Relief and joy filled his heart in equal measure.

"Ah, hello, how are you feeling now?"

She slipped into his arms and settled onto his lap, curling herself as small as possible and said nothing. She felt as warm as she should feel.

"I think we'll go to the clinic when we're in town, I'd like to get a few things and we'll drop in to see Victor. We won't stay long. Let's see how you are."

"Can I bring Héctor? Pleeeease." Héctor bear was strictly a bedroom creature, even a visit to the verandah was unusual, but this was already another unusual day. Harry nodded and she hugged his neck tightly.

Gabriela's fever, apparently gone as quickly as it had appeared, had left her washed out, lethargic. The novelty of it was unsettling enough without the present complications. Caution demanded that Gabriela should see a nurse or doctor but neither he nor Gabriela had any experience of either on Isla Concepción. The simplest place to check was the clinic, part emergency first-aid, part health centre and a long way short of being a hospital, but they found it closed.

In the little pharmacy, tucked away at the back of a convenience store, a young woman was on duty. Harry explained his concern and she came from behind her counter and sat next to Gabriela, smiling and telling her gently what she would do. Gabriela nodded but didn't smile back. Pulse and temperature were taken, throat, eyes and ears were inspected. She touched softly under Gabriela's jaw where glands would hurt if swollen and found nothing.

"She is seven years old?"

"Nearly eight."

"This happens sometimes. What did you do?"

He told her.

"No medicine? No Tylenol, ibuprofen, Advil? Nothing?"

He shook his head, hoping not to have to admit that he had none of them in the house.

"She seems OK now, a little warm," she showed him the numbers, "and tired maybe, did she sleep last night?"

He avoided Gabriela's look and said, "Yes, a little." Mainly floating under the stars, but he didn't need to add that.

"Then rest today and early to bed. Are you her...father?" The hesitation gave away the pharmacist's doubt.

"No, not really."

"It should be her mother or father who brings a child," she said abruptly, her manner cooling in an instant. "There is a register, I must write that I have seen her and who brings her."

"I'm her guardian," he said, because it sounded official and because it was true for practical purposes. When she looked unconvinced he tried a different word, "su tutor."

"I will record this."

She fetched the ledger, green backed and broad leaved, and completed Gabriela's name and age neatly in blue ink. "Tu nombre señor, your name?"

"Harry Rose."

She repeated it and began writing, then paused fractionally between the words. In Harry's mind it was the pause of recognition. News of his troubles had spread to the very depths of the convenience store.

"Señor Harry Rose," she said. "Su tutor?"

Harry nodded. She wrote as he'd said and then a few words of Gabriela's symptoms and advice given. He signed where she pointed.

"If it happens again, what's best?" he asked reluctantly.

"Do you have er, un termómetro medico, er, thermometer?" She'd guessed he did not. "You need one. Under the arm, as you saw. Higher than thirty-eight for several hours then you see the doctor. What you did was OK but you should have the simple medicines. And some drinks, not only water. Here, I'll show you."

The seat-belt rule was overlooked for the trip up the street to the police post, where Harry stopped by the main door. If he could avoid taking Gabriela into the office he would, it might be sufficient for her to be seen in the truck from a short distance. If she was in the truck she could surely be assumed to be well and the paper could be signed without awkward questions.

"Must I?" she asked dully, the little energy from earlier utterly expended. "Can I stay here Papatico? Pleeeease."

71

"Yes you may, unless Captain Diaz needs you to come to his office. But if we wave to you from inside wave back please."

The captain did not need her to go to the office, he was busy with a visitor. The sergeant had the paperwork, signed and ready. He peered round Harry to satisfy himself that Gabriela was present. She waved back when he waved at her.

It was a small deception, probably unnecessary, but Harry was pleased with the smoothness of it. Until he wondered if the pharmacist might be the sergeant's sister-in-law or his cousin or girlfriend. She'd known of Harry's situation from somewhere and it was a small town.

He took the offered paper before saying casually, "We almost didn't come, she wasn't well earlier, but they said she's OK now."

"At the clinic?"

"No, the little pharmacy." He waved in the direction of the store.

The sergeant smiled and nodded. "Good."

★

When they were home Gabriela was still droopy and hot to his touch, not raging as earlier, but caution demanded he check with the new thermometer. He gave her one of the capsules, as directed by the pharmacist, washed down with a glass of the restorative sports drink, also as recommended.

"Can I go to my tree, Papatico?" She didn't usually ask, more often she'd just tell him where she was going.

"Maybe not today, I'd really like you to stay around the house until you're feeling better." He had visions of her falling, breaking a leg or worse, visions that he'd never had previously and she'd been climbing her tree since she was five.

"All right," she said without complaint, settling herself a little miserably with Héctor bear on the verandah.

With his visit to Puerto Reunión in mind, he called Pippa and they agreed she would come to Casa Rosa for the day. And no sooner had they done that than he called back and yes, she would come today and stay the night.

He'd left a message for Julio but it wasn't until the evening, Harry with a scotch already in his hand, that Julio called back.

"Indira Chavarria will come to the court," he said. "La señorita would like to meet you and it will be right for her to be there. She will be your friend, your advisor, she will not be your lawyer, she will be good for you. There will be no lawyers, it will be informal, in the judge's office. The judge will hear from the APN, la señora Mejía almost certainly, another perhaps, we have not heard."

"Should I take anything?"

"Yes, take photos of Casa Rosa, Gabriela's bedroom, the kitchen, all the rooms. Do you have any of Gabriela's drawings, paintings, anything like that?"

"Yes, some she did at Pippa's, and a few others."

"Take them. And any photos you have of Gabriela with Estefanía. Nobody may want to see these things, there may be no opportunity, the judge will decide what he wants to see or hear. You have the papers from your visits to Diaz? Take them too. Take anything else that could be useful."

"OK."

"Harry, Elena has made a suggestion, and I agree, we think it would be good if Gabriela were seen by a doctor, perhaps a dentist too. It might be helpful to have a report showing her development is normal and she is well cared for. The APN may want to do this but we can do it for them, at our expense. I made an appointment for Friday in San Luis, not far from the office, you can stay with us if you wish. Pippa too, of course, if she comes. Maybe she would go to the doctor's office too."

"You think Gabriela will still be with me on Friday? The judge will let her stay?"

"His decision on Thursday? Yes, I think so. These are the first days, the real test will be later, a month, maybe more. La señora Mejía almost made the decision for him last week and she will not find a reason to change her mind. I think the judge will follow her. We will give him every reason to do so."

73

There seemed no way of avoiding it, but Harry still hesitated before saying, "Gabriela hasn't been very well since this morning."

"Ah, that poor girl, it must be very upsetting for her. What is wrong? Is it serious?"

"She has a fever, it comes and goes."

"That is unfortunate. Did you visit a doctor?"

Harry told him the events of the day, but although he couldn't see any connection to Gabriela's sudden fever, he didn't mention the night on the beach. It should've been a good thing to talk about, it was certainly a good thing to have done. He was irritated by his own reluctance, yet it nagged at him that it may have been unwise in some vague and unspecified way, the action of an indulgent grandfather rather than a responsible father, although he was neither.

"La señorita Chavarria has started enquiries for Estefanía Flores and begun searches for Gabriela. There was nothing on the central register, nothing for San Felipe for either of them."

"Estefanía was sixteen when she had Gabriela. She told Pippa. She would be around twenty-four now."

"So young?"

"Yes."

"Anything else?" Julio asked after a pause.

"She was registered, she had ID, she showed it to Leo, at the bar, so she could be paid. But he has no details."

"It's something."

"Do you know how the APN became involved?"

"Not yet. La señora Mejía, Arsenia Mejía, is a senior worker at La Agencia de Protección de los Niños. She is well respected. There is more, but it is all we need to know."

Gabriela lay in bed waiting for him to kiss her goodnight. She was warm to his touch but he hesitated to give her another capsule, despite the pharmacist's advice. He was averse to taking pills himself, and wary of dosing Gabriela if it wasn't really necessary. A week ago every action was instinctive, natural, and now it had to be weighed and considered until he couldn't tell

74

right from wrong. The novelty of the thermometer gave him a minute to make his mind up.

Thirty-seven point three. Perhaps his fingers were cold.

"Papatico?" Her trusting eyes questioned his. The prospect of losing her, seeing her wrenched from her home to who knew where was so painful it was almost physical.

"No pills needed. Good night, my Gabriela, sleep tight and sweet dreams."

She hugged his neck as he pressed his face into the sweet sea-scent of her hair.

"I love you, Papatico."

"I love you too."

Pippa had Harry's notebook in her hand as he returned to the verandah. He poured them both refills and settled beside her.

"You've been making lists."

"She needs a lot. More than I can give her, maybe." Harry waited for Pippa to deny it, to protest that he could provide everything Gabriela needed, but she didn't take her cue. "I've just carried on being the baby-sitter, looking after her until her mother came home. We've both been waiting for Estefanía to walk back through the door. While we've been waiting, Gabriela's grown, she's changed. Estefanía might not even recognize her. And I don't think she'd know her mother.

"I need your help, Pippa, not only this week, but longer, years maybe. Julio thinks the judge will leave her here for now, but later, next month, whenever it is, he may not. Anyway, making a list was my start of doing better, stop waiting and get on with it."

"You know it's not just shopping, don't you? Only it does look a little bit like a shopping list."

"I suppose it is, mainly. But it's not just things, there's music, sport. I don't yet know how to give them to her, but at least they're on the list."

"What about friends? She doesn't have any, Harry, and a girl should have some friends."

"Of her own age? There's Adrián, next door at the Fairchild's, the gardener's boy."

"How old is he?"

He shook his head. Harry had no idea how old the boy was, at that moment he could only recall that Dolores Pérez-Fairchild called him a little bastard when she thought nobody could hear her.

"Listen, you lovely man, of course I'll help, you know I love you both. But you're the lead in this, I'm supporting cast."

He smiled at her a little ruefully and nodded his agreement.

"Now, what are you going to wear to see the judge tomorrow? Usual scarecrow outfit?"

5

The court in Puerto Reunión was housed in a collection of prefab buildings, intended as temporary thirty years previously, after the grandiose nineteenth-century palace of justice had been gutted by fire. The blackened skeleton of that building remained at one end of Calle Santa Ana while the mildewed trailer park of El Tribunal Provincial de Reunión occupied a piece of waste ground at the other. On the dingiest building at the back of the site a small sign denoted El Tribunal Central de Familia.

Harry arrived an hour early, anxious to meet Indira Chavarria with enough time to hear of her progress and tell her of Gabriela. The building seemed empty, no sign or sound of humanity beyond the distant hum of an air conditioning unit. He wished they'd arranged it differently, to meet in a café or a park, anywhere where they wouldn't feel the need to whisper, anywhere more private and less depressing than the little waiting area with its six metal-framed chairs squeezed noisily together.

Soon after he arrived, a smartly-dressed middle-aged woman entered. She forced a brief polite smile before disappearing down a corridor. He noticed she wore black shoes and a black skirt, with well-rounded calves between them. A minute later a second woman of similar age and appearance repeated the action. Harry judged her legs to be less attractive. Probably legal secretaries he thought, in the universal black and white uniform of courts. He'd done his best with his own limited choice of wardrobe, but like Gabriela, he was in need of some new clothes.

For a moment he didn't recognize Arsenia Mejía when she came into the room from the second corridor.

"Señor Rose? What do you want here?"

He stood awkwardly, unprepared for the directness of her question. "The papers you left," he patted the folder under his

77

arm, "It says the judge will consider Gabriela's case today. He'll hear from you, maybe another, that's right isn't it?"

"Yes."

"Then if you're talking about Gabriela, I should be here, he may want to talk to me, I can tell him things if he cares to ask. And if he doesn't care for it, I may tell him anyway."

"It is not usual."

"None of this is usual, señora Mejía."

"We should not discuss things here."

"Gabriela has been unwell since you came to our home. Not serious, but she is very upset, as anyone might expect." He didn't link her illness directly with the visit, but made it plain he saw a connection. His anger and resentment were rekindled in la señora's presence, she who was the personification of his troubles. Sensing her discomfort, he pressed on. "I will take her to see a doctor in San Felipe on Friday, I have an appointment, I will make sure you see his assessment. Shall I take her without permission or will you allow her to leave Isla Concepción, will you sign a paper to say so?"

"I will talk with the judge. It is not the same judge as last week, he is unavailable. La juez Raquel Cruz Renegas will take his place."

Did it change anything, was he less likely to get fair treatment from a female than a male? Might a man's sympathy tip the balance in his favour? It may have been Raquel Cruz's legs he'd been appraising. Now it was Harry's turn to be discomforted.

"There was something else," he said, the confidence gone but a residue of bitterness remaining. "Seeing the police every day, it's difficult, it's unnecessary, especially as Gabriela wasn't well. Once a week, we could do that perhaps. It would be enough."

"I have said already, I will talk with the judge, señor Rose."

He was saved from further antagonising her by the entry of Indira Chavarria. Small and dark, she too was dressed in black, a trouser suit over a white blouse. But it wasn't her clothes that struck Harry so much as her looks. With her hair swept back tightly, bright eyes over a small sharp nose and full mouth, she

78

could have been Estefanía's sister. The likeness was so great he stared at her, unable to speak.

"Señor Rose?" she smiled, extending a hand. He nodded dumbly. "I am Indira Chavarria Calderón. I hope you were expecting me?"

Harry was still staring but he managed "Yes, yes I was." Her voice too, echoed Estefanía's, more cultured, better educated, but the same tone.

"Please excuse me interrupting," she continued, turning to Arsenia Mejía and extending her hand to her also.

"Are you representing señor Rose, is he your client?" she asked warily.

"Ah, no, I have no clients yet, I am in final placement before I qualify. I am here as a supporter for Señor Rose, one with a small understanding of the process."

"Again, it is not usual, señorita Chavarria."

"I understand. Excuse me, but you are señora Mejía?"

"Yes, I am," she replied, stiffening.

"I remember you, señora. We met very briefly at el Facultad de Derecho, at the university. You will not remember me among all the students. You spoke about family law enforcement, how you work with the legal system."

"No, forgive me, señorita Chavarria, there are many students." Arsenia Mejía couldn't help but be flattered and smiled appropriately, forgetting for a moment where they were and why they were there. "Did you learn anything from the talk? I hope you found it useful."

"Very helpful, in particular how you work with wide powers of discretion under guidance from the law and how difficult that can be, how it would be easier if the law was more, er, proscrito. I am not sure, specific I think may be the word here, is that correct, señor Rose?"

"Yes, maybe, I'm not sure," he said uncertainly, a little dazzled by such confidence, such certainty, and in one so young. Harry was already charmed and impressed. La señora Mejía, appeared to have been similarly affected.

"That's very good to know, thank you. I enjoy my visits to el Facultad, but never know if they are useful," she smiled.

"Señora, if you would please tell the judge that señor Rose is here and willing to speak. And also ask that I might accompany him should he be wanted?"

"Yes, I will tell her, thank you. We have other cases today, but I will see what order la juez Cruz will look at them."

The spell Indira Chavarria had cast over the room lifted as Arsenia Mejía left, the warmth and colour fading to shabby grey in time to the click of her steps retreating down the corridor. The deceptions of the beautiful witch Serafina came to Harry's mind. He might need all her powers and more.

"So, señor Rose, good morning. My apologies for ignoring you, it was an opportunity not to miss. I think if we see the judge it will be good."

"I agree. Please call me Harry. That was lucky, having that connection to la señora Mejía, and being quick enough to remember her."

Indira Chavarria smiled a white smile. "No, señor Rose, one day perhaps it will be Harry. As for luck, I have an uncle who often tells me that you make all the luck that you have. I had prepared for la señora, but it was chance to find you together when I arrived. Now, I must tell you of what has been done, although there is very little to show so far. It is a few days only, I believe we should expect nothing so soon."

They sat uncomfortably, using a chair between them for papers. She had notes of every activity started, when and by whom. In her neat handwriting were notes too of fees paid for searches and copies of paperwork. She appeared to have engaged a whole army of clerks stretched across the country, each sifting through civil records, most of which had yet to be included in the central database, looking for references to Estefanía Flores and her daughter Gabriela. But as she had told him, there was little to show for it.

"We have also contacted police and hospitals, asking for Estefanía Flores, but also for unknown females who might match what we know of her. There is a central register for the police but not for hospitals. And the police register is not as reliable as it should be. The search of both may take a long time, we cannot do it ourselves, we must rely on the hospitals and the police themselves. They are busy. There may be fees to pay."

Up until this point Harry had given little thought to costs. Julio had waved aside his question of payment, saying he could never charge for his time, but there were clearly a lot of outgoings that Harry should meet himself.

"You seem to be coordinating the whole thing, señorita, thank you. Are you keeping an account of all expenses?"

"Yes, certainly."

"Good. When the time comes will you let me know exactly how much has been spent? My friend Julio, señor Aguilar, may not tell me."

"I understand. Now, please tell me of Gabriela."

"She's upset. And has not been well, but not serious. Before all this, she was lively and happy despite her mother not being here. We speak often about Estefanía, Gabriela looks for her every day, I think. There is a place she goes, a tree she climbs, she watches the road, who comes and goes. She hasn't said so, but I think she watches for her Mami. I don't know why I'm telling you this, I haven't said this to anyone else before. Perhaps I haven't admitted it before. I'm only just beginning to think Estefanía isn't coming back myself. My darling Gabriela, she..."

The words tumbled out before he could stop himself, the sudden, all-enveloping sadness ambushing his defences. Indira Chavarria's likeness to Estefanía made it difficult for him to even look at her while he fumbled for a handkerchief he knew he didn't have. He took the tissue she offered with an unsteady hand and wiped his wet face.

"Well, what else would you like to know?"

"Later, we can talk later," she soothed.

They sat in silence for a few minutes until Harry recovered himself enough to look at her again. She would have to know why he looked at her the way he did.

"Señorita Chavarria," he began a little shakily, "I must tell you that you very much resemble Estefanía Flores, and your voice, you also sound like her. It's unnerving, I was shocked when you arrived. And I imagine you and Estefanía are of a similar age."

"I am twenty-five, señor Rose."

"We think Estefanía is twenty-four."

The click-clack of heels in the corridor announced la señora Mejía's return.

"La juez Cruz will see you, she may ask you questions. It is not formal, but it is still, er, con respeto, er, with respect. You understand what I mean, señor Rose?"

"Yes."

"And you may come also, señorita Chavarria," she said, the warmth of earlier still in her voice.

As they they followed, Indira Chavarria said softly to Harry, "It is not formal, but act as if it is."

Arsenia Mejía led them to a small office where three chairs had been arranged in front of a desk. One of the women Harry had seen earlier sat behind it, hands folded across her lap, an unopened folder in front of her. A screen and keyboard were the only other items on the desk. They each stood behind a chair until motioned to sit by judge Cruz after the APN agent had introduced them.

"What do you want here today, señor Rose?" asked the judge.

"Thank you for seeing me, juez Cruz," he said, mindful of his instructions. "The papers la señora left with me indicated that the court would consider Gabriela's case today, would hear about what la señora had found and what she had done when she visited so suddenly last week," he couldn't resist glancing sideways at Arsenia Mejía. "It is my duty to be here to provide additional information. I know Gabriela better than anyone else, probably even better than her mother now. If you are hearing about Gabriela, you should hear from me too."

"What would you say about Gabriela?"

"She is beautiful, happy, funny, lively, smart, good at her reading, speaks Spanish and English, knows her stars and planets.

She's well fed and well cared for. And she is sad without her Mami, scared she has gone for ever, scared she can't remember her." He felt the little pin-prick of tears starting in his eye again and forced himself not to look at Indira Chavarria, only at the judge. "And she is more upset since last week, scared she will lose her home and lose me."

No one moved or spoke. Harry composed his face and his feelings and found the tissue he'd been given earlier.

"There's more if you want to hear, just ask. I have photographs of the house, her room, paintings she has done, a list of books she has read."

"Señor Rose," said the judge slowly, leaning forward with her arms on the desk. "I am very pleased to hear these good things about Gabriela, I hope they are true. As for her distress, it is unfortunate, it is regrettable but unavoidable at present. There is an argument for ending the uncertainty, for removing her to a new home now and not waiting for weeks or months."

"There is no…" Harry started.

"No, señor Rose, do not interrupt. I will explain, although I think la señora Mejía may have done so already. La Agencia de Protección de los Niños became aware of allegations against you. And these are very serious. Enquiries were made and information was reviewed by la señora Mejía, who is an experienced agent, who does a most difficult job. It appeared that there was good reason to be worried about Gabriela, there is still good reason. La señora discussed everything with the judge, who agreed, but left the final action to her. That is right, she has the knowledge and the judge acts on her knowledge. When she visits your house she finds some things are not as she expects. She makes a very difficult decision, which is to leave the child with you, even though there are doubts. Gabriela's mother is missing for a long time. Gabriela lives alone with you, a single man, unrelated to her. There is no regular female in her life, her world is confined to Isla Concepción. And she does not attend school."

Harry's anger spilled over. "The school will not have her!" he cried.

"No more!" she demanded, a warning finger raised, then waited to see if he would obey. When he sat silently she let her hand rest back on the desk.

"I will continue for now. The questions over Gabriela's mother are being examined by other investigators and we are kept informed. We are concerned for Gabriela's future. It is normal in such cases when the parents are dead or missing that the child would be with family or with an approved family, where she will learn to enjoy family life and her progress would be checked. If we accept that you have given Gabriela care and attended to her needs since her mother disappeared, even then you are not a father or a mother. You have no authority to keep her. In the best case you are a...cuidador de niños...señora, you know the English word?"

As Arsenia Mejía hesitated, Harry said quietly, "Child-minder," and in that moment was sure of his future and of Gabriela's.

"May I speak, juez Cruz?" Indira Chavarria asked.

"If you have information to help us, señorita, please speak."

"Perhaps. Thank you. I cannot speak for señor Rose, but I can speak of him. Please excuse the emotion, he is greatly distressed by these events. Also the court should know of the intense searches under way for any trace of Estefanía Flores and for details of Gabriela's birth, as yet with no solution. Next, we ask for less severe conditions of movement for Gabriela, and will give a bond if needed. La señora Mejía received this request earlier, but we also make it to the court. Señor Rose intends to obtain health reports to show his good care of Gabriela.

"Lastly, there is something which señor Rose does not know, perhaps the court is unaware too. It is true children may not receive education in our schools if they have no registration details, which is to promote registration and to prevent children from across our borders filling our schools. But I understand there is provision within the law to allow unregistered children to attend school if fees are paid and they are shown to be resident for a certain time. It is in an obscure amendment and I am not qualified to interpret the section. I have written a reference here to assist the court." She passed a note across the desk. "If it is correct then the school in Concepción cannot have known this when they refused Gabriela a place. If Gabriela were to stay with señor Rose and be in school that would be more normal and might remove a difficulty. Thank you."

★

The road ran down beside a stream before a sharp turn across the bridge. Beyond that, tucked away on the right, was the track to Ernest's, the Fairchild villa and Casa Rosa. Once Harry turned onto it and travelled another thirty or forty metres, his imminent return would be clear for anyone to see, especially Gabriela if she should happen to be sitting in her tree.

He stopped the pickup short of the bridge where there was just enough room to get off the road to have a view of the ocean. The stream ran down through the rocks to drop the last metre of its course into the water. To his right the rock wall rose to the height of a house, dotted all the way up with greenery clinging to the cracks and crevices. Everything dripped. It had rained since he left Puerto Reunión. Nothing dramatic, but steady, now and again driven by a sudden gust into a squall, but for the most part falling straight to earth. Or ocean. He watched the pattern of the drops darkening the surface of the swell as it rolled lazily into the land, too deep here for curling waves and foam.

Almost home, yet he needed more time, a few minutes at least, to sit alone and look at the sea, at the infinite greyness of water and cloud, merging perfectly at a point too distant to measure. He needed time to consider his appearance at El Tribunal de Familia where his anger may have sabotaged his own case, where the smart law student may have rescued him, where the judge's *child-minder* stuck like a fish bone in his throat.

The truth of his and Gabriela's positions had been brought home to him, not as the words were spoken by juez Cruz, but afterwards, suddenly, while sitting in a cheap restaurant with Indira Chavarria talking of Gabriela's knowledge of the solar system. Mid-sentence he was overwhelmed by profound sadness and shocked by the self-awareness that accompanied it. It came down to one single event: he was wrong to have allowed Gabriela to continue living at Casa Rosa when Estefanía had failed to return. The better thing would have been to accept the vague offer Victor Diaz had made for her to be cared for on the mainland. She would be a different child now of course, most likely she wouldn't know her solar system at all, wouldn't know all the words to Bowie's *Starman* or what hydro-electric power was. But the one huge disruption to her life, losing her mother, her home and being forced into different care, all rolled into one, would be behind her. She would know other things, things that she didn't know now. Doing it his way, the loss of Estefanía had lingered on and now she had the prospect of losing her home and her Papatico with the frightening uncertainties that would follow. Why had he kept her then, when Victor so casually offered to have her taken away? Was it for himself or for her? A week ago he knew the answer, absolutely, certainly.

In a few minutes he would return to Casa Rosa, hug Gabriela and be hugged back with excitement, maybe a little relief, enough for tears perhaps. And of his day, what should he tell her, what should he hide? He was the master of disappointment, dishing out repeat doses to the child at every opportunity, so why not tell her now, tell her that it will all end in more tears? That's what his guts told him to do. *Gabriela can't put all the ugly grown-up shit in her seven-year-old world*, wasn't that Pippa's scolding of him? More false hope, is that the better way? Then find enough sugar to coat the bitter pill when the moment comes in a week, a month, who knew when?

He could find no reference points, his instincts and love had brought him to this moment when they should have been his strength, yet they were considered unreliable. He might as well be far out on the ocean, beyond sight of land, where all became lost in the grey, while at Casa Rosa, Gabriela waited for word of her future.

With sudden decision, he snapped on the ignition. The engine fired instantly. He would tell her nothing. Nothing had been decided, there was no change from yesterday or the day before, there was nothing to tell. Ifs, buts and maybes were nothing at all.

"Papatico!" she cried as he came up the steps. She hurled herself at him, shouting, "Yay! Yay! Papatico!" As he put her down she pulled on his arm, "Come and see what we've made!"

"Hey, smells really good, what've you been up to?"

Every surface of the kitchen was covered in pans and trays and utensils. Reigning supreme over this bombsite was Pippa, her hair tied up but straggling down her face, an apron he didn't recognise tied round her, and beaming widely.

"This child knew almost nothing about cooking!" she announced. "Well, we're putting that right, aren't we, Gabriela?"

"Yes we are!" they chorused in unison.

He could have cried to see them so happy, a joyous moment in their family life. And if they were not a true family they were certainly as good as most and better than many. Times such as these were worth fighting for, even if the cruel logic of what was officially best for Gabriela suggested a different outcome.

"You two look as if you're enjoying yourselves, tell me what you've made. Or have you eaten it already and left none for me?"

"No!" Gabriela shrieked, "Of course not! Look!" She lifted a tray carefully and drew back the cloth covering it. "Flapperjacks!" she announced triumphantly. And only three squares were missing.

"Flapjacks," Pippa corrected quietly, then more assertively, "Try one, man, for god's sake, taste the goodies, this girl's been desperate for you to get back."

"Mmm, that's delicious. Can I have another?"

"If you're good," she said straight-faced.

This was their private thing, this was how he teased her, always he who said *if you're good*, and she who would ask *am I good*. Now she had reversed it.

He waited the required seconds.

"Am I good?" he asked mechanically, transfixed by her expression.

"Hmmm," she wondered theatrically, looking into the distance, "Good enough," she said, passing the tray back to him.

"And we made cookies, look." Another cover was removed with a flourish. "These are peanut butter and these are…what are these, Pippa?"

"Sultana and raisin."

"Sultana and raising."

"Wonderful!" Harry exclaimed, and he meant it.

"And tonight's meal is in the oven. Chicken and my mother's four-fruit curry. A pretty good day, eh Gabriela?"

"Yes! The best!"

His bag of shopping could wait, what were a pair of cheap shoes plus shorts and tees from Maximercado compared to the joy of cooking with Pippa. As the shopping could wait so could any word of his reasons for being in Puerto Reunión. Gabriela had forgotten or put it out of her mind, Pippa was wise enough to leave it unspoken, why would he break the spell? *Tell her nothing* he'd decided, and it was easier than he'd expected.

Only when Gabriela had reluctantly settled in bed and Pippa had collapsed into a chair, exhausted from her day's activities, was the subject raised.

"How was your day, Harry?"

"In a nutshell, Indira Chavarria was impressive, and I was an arse. Or to put it another way, she was cool and intelligent, I was angry and emotional. I honestly don't know if it was a disaster or went well. The worst part was the judge saying I was only a child-minder. If that's how they're thinking then there's only one outcome."

They contemplated their drinks in silence. A part of him wanted to feel positive about the good things, the possibilities of school, of a health report for a healthy girl. A healthy girl? He hadn't even asked.

"Was Gabriela OK today, that fever, has it gone? When I got home she was so…"

"She was a bit floppy when we went into Concepción, but when we got back she was fine, as you could see."

"Good, I hope she's well, we may have a visitor tomorrow. La señora Mejía may come to talk to to Gabriela. I was hoping you might be around."

"Harry, I have a student tomorrow. When is she coming?"

"Not sure, afternoon sometime. Look, it's fine, I'll be all right, we both will. I won't make a big thing of it, just tell Gabriela she may come, might want to look at her room again, something vague."

"Sounds about right. I'd have thought it was a good thing, her coming back to talk to Gabriela here, not making you take her to some office somewhere."

"Maybe it is. I'll just go and check she's asleep."

She was. Quite beautifully. He knew that in an instant, but he lingered by her bed, watching her in the half-light. Surely one would never tire of seeing a child asleep? He pushed away the thought of her bedroom being empty, her few possessions gone with her to some alien family in Puerto Reunión or god knew where else.

But the idea would not be dismissed, it grew to question what kind of family, one with children already? One who regularly took in the abused and deserted? One who would pay for her schooling? One with a father who'd stand by her bed and rejoice in her sleeping form? And he couldn't avoid the idea of a father who might stand by her bed anticipating different pleasures, the same abuses of which he was now accused. That man would imagine Gabriela to be quite familiar with what he expected from her, compliant and uncomplaining of his hands upon her, while she would be petrified, uncomprehending, wretched, as his grip tightened against her struggles.

He lurched backwards into the light as Pippa came to him.

"Harry," she said urgently, "is Gabriela all right? Jesus, you look awful, what's happened?"

"Nothing," he croaked, "nothing at all, she's fine, perfect. Sleeping like a baby."

"Then what?"

"Imagination," he said composing himself, "like a bad dream, getting frightened of shadows in there in the gloom. I'm all right. Thank you."

Harry spread his arms wide and hugged her close, as much for himself as for her, hoping the physical would distract her from questioning further.

"I must talk to Julio, see what he thinks. And get another drink."

As he could have guessed, la señorita Chavarria had sent Julio a comprehensive summary of the events at court, along with a few references she thought could be useful. Julio was at home working through them when Harry called.

"I think I told you she was smart."

"She is. And very quick, perceptive."

"She is diligent. She researches everything to be prepared. She even researched la señora from APN."

"Julio, how is it they won't allow Gabriela in school, but they'll take her away and put her with another family. What then? They won't get her into school either."

"Two things, Harry. First, authorised families, families where children are taken, may obtain temporary registration for a child and as you know, registration is the key to receiving education and medicine, all the benefits of the state. But secondly, la señorita is correct in what she says about fees, the school should accept Gabriela if you pay. Perhaps you could go to the school in Concepción tomorrow? The sooner you can do this the better." He paused before adding, "Be diplomatic, Harry, they may not know the law."

Harry wondered just how detailed Indira Chavarria's report had been, how many of his undiplomatic comments she'd included. Every word, most likely.

"You know we have another visit from APN tomorrow?"

"Yes, I think it's good."

"Julio, you said authorised families, could I be authorised?"

Julio hesitated before replying, unwilling to cause more distress. "Perhaps, it is not usual, but it may be necessary. We will show that it is best for Gabriela to stay in her home with you. There is something else, la señorita Chavarria is studying another idea on the subject of authorisation. We will see what she finds."

"Will you keep her when she qualifies?"

"Ah, no, I think not, she will take her pick, that one."

★

The pickup juddered over the potholes in the approach road to *Aeropuerto de Concepción*. It was as Harry remembered it, a little more overgrown, more of the fencing laying flat on the ground, and no sign of the advertised reconstruction. The gates by the main hangar were open, as they had been for a decade or more, but as he swung round onto the apron he found another truck, unattended, parked on the cracked concrete. Someone else who was curious about the rumours, no doubt. Harry drove on until they were close to the old DC3. Despite the years it appeared to have declined little since he'd last seen it.

"What are we here for?" asked Gabriela, half suspicious, but with her curiosity tweaked.

"We are here to look at this aeroplane, first to see if it was still here, which it obviously is, and second to see what state it is in."

"It looks crumbly."

"That is a very good word for it. Would you like to fly in it?"

"No!"

"You're right there. It'll not fly again. But I do wonder what it might be good for. Let's walk round it."

They did, swishing through the long grass, avoiding rainbow oil spills and ducking under the grey-green wing. At a few points Harry banged a fist against the fuselage, half expecting to punch a hole right through, but it was sounder than it looked.

"These planes, they were very famous back in the day, there were thousands of them made and they flew all over the world. They were called DC3s, because they were made by a company called Douglas and they gave a different number to the different designs and this was the third. They had other names in other countries, in England it was called a Dakota. They were made in

91

Japan and Russia too, maybe China, you can look on the map when we get home.

"The people who flew them and used them liked them a lot because they were reliable and easy to mend when something went wrong. There are still a few flying today, and a few more which have been put in museums. And there are some which have become bars and restaurants. What else would you like to know?"

"What's back in the day?"

"A long time ago, eighty years or so. So when would that have been?"

Gabriela answered almost immediately, "Nineteen thirty-nine."

"Good. That's history, geography and maths covered in one class."

"Must I go to school?"

"One day, yes. But I don't know when. It may be soon."

"At the school we were in today?"

"If they agree. I think they will, there are rules about who can go and we don't have the right papers. But there may be another way, they'll find out."

She was silent as they completed their tour, then stood by the truck looking up at the nose of the aircraft, a silhouette against the bright sky.

"I wish I could fly," she said.

"Like a bird or in a plane?"

"A bird."

"We could be a plane."

They climbed back into the cab and drove slowly across to the overgrown runway. Harry ran through a make-believe controller-to-pilot exchange and revved the engine ready for takeoff. When he thought his old truck had done enough of that, he eased it forward slowly then gathered speed till they were doing sixty and Gabriela squealed, "Papatico!" and put her seat belt across her shoulder. One-handed he did likewise and slowed into a landing routine to ease her fears, then taxied under controller's orders back to the hangar. Two men in overalls were hauling scrap metal from a rusting pile and loading it onto the back of their pickup. They barely glanced up as Harry and Gabriela left *Aeropuerto Municipal de Isla Concepción* after their brief but exhilarating flight.

Lunch was beans and left-over chicken, although neither of them were interested in food. They waited for la señora from APN until it seemed she might not appear and Harry was relieved and concerned in equal measure. Gabriela fretted and asked to go to her tree, but he was stupidly concerned that she was wearing new shorts and shirt and might scuff or tear them. She made no complaint, but her face told him her feelings. He changed his mind immediately, the clothes were hardly Sunday best.

"But come back in when you see her arrive," he called after her.

Ten minutes was all it took, but Arsenia Mejía was already on the front steps before Gabriela slid quietly in the back door.

Harry extended a hand and she shook it uncertainly. "Señor Rose," she said politely as if it were their first meeting, "may we go inside?"

She had no need to ask permission, she could go wherever she wanted, but Harry appreciated the gesture and stepped aside to let her through. Gabriela was standing in the doorway, blank-faced with Héctor dangling from one hand.

"Hola, Gabriela," she beamed, "Who do you have with you?"

"Héctor," she replied flatly.

"Hola, Héctor."

Gabriela said nothing.

"Perhaps we could sit together for a few minutes, I would like to hear of your day, Gabriela. Will you tell me what you've have been doing?"

Gabriela nodded.

Arsenia Mejía looked at Harry, questioning the sullen nature of her reception. He was tempted to let her flounder, let her see if she could work it out for herself, but he remembered the need for good behaviour, for diplomacy.

"Gabriela and I have spoken about your visit today. She knows you may wish to ask her questions. Gabriela may be nervous, no, more than that, frightened, that if she doesn't give you the right answers you may take her away. I have said there are no right or wrong answers, only truthful answers. Gabriela had an idea that telling you about going out at night and falling asleep on the beach was why you might take her away from here."

"Ah, thank you, señor Rose. Gabriela, what your Papá says is true, there are no wrong answers. When you told me last week about sleeping on the beach, it was a good story, a true story, the kind of true story that made it possible for you to stay here. We will see if we can find more stories like that, yes?"

Gabriela nodded and ran forward to stand by Harry, almost hiding behind him.

He guided la señora into the house and they sat awkwardly while Gabriela squeezed herself into the same chair as Harry. The conversation faltered, Harry unwilling to indulge in small-talk yet conscious of his diplomatic obligations. Perhaps best to start with a relevant topic.

"We went to the school today, to see about enrolling Gabriela. I had been told la señorita Chavarria's suggestion was correct, but the school administrator knew nothing of it. She will check with the ministry."

"Ah, yes, a good idea from la señorita. I myself knew nothing of that but la juez Cruz confirmed the fact. Gabriela will be able to go to school but it may take a week. It is not usual and there is a process. Gabriela, did you go into the school today?"

She nodded.

"Gabriela," Harry said gently, "it is difficult, but please be polite. Remember last week you showed la señora Mejía your room? Perhaps you would like to take her there again and show her the paintings you made with Pippa. And please tell her nicely about our day today. You could tell her what you learnt in your flying class."

"Will you come with me? Pleeeease." she whispered hotly in his ear.

He urgently wanted to go with her, stay with her, be the shield against her fears, not the Papatico who said no to her pleading. Arsenia Mejía found a middle way for them all. "Ah, disculpe, señor Rose, but I wonder if, for now, Gabriela could bring the paintings from her room and show them to me here?" The child seized the chance, detaching herself from Harry and scuttling to her bedroom, emerging with the paintings behind her back before cautiously approaching their visitor. She responded in monosyllables until, forgetting herself, she explained choosing fish instead of stars, while Arsenia Mejía skilfully nudged the conversation to more searching enquiries of her knowledge of other topics. Harry watched carefully as the tension in Gabriela's body ebbed away, even if she checked frequently to see if he was still watching over her.

After a while la señora suggested that she would like to walk on the beach and would Gabriela show her the best places. Gabriela stiffened slightly but looked round expectantly at Harry, seeing if he approved or not. He guessed it was intended to be a walk without him, a walk to delve a little deeper into Gabriela's thoughts about her Mami and her Papatico.

"Yes, our beach is beautiful, and you know it well, Gabriela," he said casually. To reassure her he added, "I'll take a book to the verandah, you can call if you need me."

"Good, thank you, señor Rose."

"There's just one thing before you go," he said, hoping he'd remember the few words he'd rehearsed for this moment. "Señora Mejía, as I said, Gabriela and I have spoken about your visit today, but I have something to add, and I will say it now so that you know what has been said to this beautiful child.

"Gabriela, when you are with la señora on the beach and she asks a question you may answer anything you wish, but be truthful. And if you do not wish to answer then you may say, excuse me señora, but I do not wish to answer. And if you don't know an answer or do not understand then you should say so, because some questions have no answers. You may come back at any time you wish, but politely. Please don't go anywhere you don't want to go and only go where you know you are allowed to go if you were on your own." Seeing their unsmiling faces and fearing he may have been too serious, may have restored the carefully dispelled anxiety, he added, "And do not push la señora Mejía into the water, she cannot swim."

Gabriela looked up, amazed. How could a grown-up be unable to swim?

Harry watched as they sauntered beyond the jicaros and could guess the question of which direction to turn. He guessed the answer too, which was away from the Fairchild house and the possibility of encountering Dolores Pérez-Fairchild. He saw how Gabriela suddenly ran to the water's edge and jumped in the shallows and stood looking down, no doubt studying the flow of sand as it covered her feet. Arsenia Mejía followed leisurely and stood beside her, watching her own feet.

An aunt and her niece enjoying an excursion? The casual observer might think so.

Gabriel appeared to be at ease and he had a sneaking regard for la señora's skills in gaining her trust. He could safely leave them to their walk and settle in his chair with a book. Yet after a page he was up and seeing how far they had gone, checking Gabriela's runs and darts to the water and back. After another page he gave up, resigned to being pre-occupied by the two walkers on the sand. He looked again and couldn't see them. At the top of the steps he scanned the length of the beach and still missed them. As he anxiously started down he caught sight of Gabriela's new red top a little way beyond the trees. She and Arsenia Mejía were lying on the sand almost exactly where he and Gabriela had spent their night under the stars. A moment later Gabriela stretched her hand to the sky, palm upwards and the protector of children copied her action. He knew Gabriela was showing her how they'd hidden the moon so as to see Jupiter, chief among the gods.

6

The rain, drumming on the roof through the night, ceased at daybreak, leaving a countryside wreathed in mist. It drifted along the beach and through the trees in front of Casa Rosa, washing the life and colour from the bougainvillea, reducing the waves to disembodied splashing on the hidden reef.

Harry crept about the house, unable to sleep and unable to settle once he was up. On another day he might have walked on the sand, happy that if Gabriela should wake to find him gone, she'd be unconcerned. But on this day he was reluctant to risk causing her the slightest distress.

Her time with Arsenia Mejía seemed to have gone well enough, they were both smiling when they'd returned. He hadn't pressed Gabriela for details and she'd offered little insight, which Harry had taken as a good thing. There was nothing to hide, nothing that Gabriela could have said that would worsen matters, but there might have been questions which could easily have upset her in a dozen different ways. So today was not a day for Gabriela to be given extra anxiety.

His appointment at El Tribunal de Familia was early enough that he should be on the first ferry of the day. Logic told him that Gabriela would still be living with him by evening, that they would go to San Felipe tomorrow and stay with Elena and Julio as planned, that they were far better placed now than they were a week ago. The threat of Gabriela being urgently removed had receded as sense had begun to prevail, but he was far from confident of the longer prospects. Refuting baseless accusations was one thing, but proving their unique life at Casa Rosa was in her best interest was quite another. Especially in the face of a norm which did not allow for such things.

97

His nagging fear that she might have a recurrence of the mysterious fever as a result of la señora's visit proved unfounded. She woke untroubled and looking forward to a day at Pippa's, where she would paint and read and maybe cook again.

At the last minute Harry decided to take Gabriela via the police post in Concepción to save Pippa the tedious duty and an unpleasant drive, for which she was particularly pleased.

"Wonderful! Now we can have the day all to ourselves," she announced. "We'll walk down to the sea later and look for treasure on the shore."

As he made to leave Pippa handed him a note, "Shopping list. A few things needed," she added pointedly.

Harry kissed and hugged them each in turn, then watched in the rear-view mirror as they vanished in the mist. *Espíritu de las Islas* didn't usually stop for anything, so poor visibility shouldn't be a problem.

Timing, the weather and the importance of his day made for a difficult journey back to Concepción, an unhappy compromise between survival and the need for speed. Survival prevailed, despite a near miss with a fruit truck, but at the harbour he found the number waiting to board the ferry looked greater than its capacity. He'd been wrong before and could be again but it looked doubtful. He recounted the vehicles. No big trucks, but even so it would be a close call. Dumping the pickup would get him on the ferry, but cost him fifteen minutes in Puerto Reunión. Missing this crossing would cost him ninety. No choice.

He swung round out of the line and found a space where the foot-passengers parked. Within a few minutes he was walking onto the boat. He had the thirty-minute crossing in which to compose himself, then a brisk walk to the court. So long as *Espíritu* made reasonable progress he'd be five minutes late at worst. He was vindicated by the sight of the last half-dozen hopefuls being left on the quay, denied boarding to the jam-packed car deck. That was one good decision for the day.

A shout from below him was almost drowned out by a blast on the ship's horn. The crew never needed much excuse to use it, the thick veil of mist would make for a noisy crossing.

"¡Harry! ¡Aquí!"

He looked down at the rows of cars, scanning the drivers until he spotted Leo Morales.

"Harry! Here!"

He descended and slid into Leo's old station wagon.

"You are a saviour, Leo. Can you take me up to Calle Santa Ana?"

"Yes, yes, anywhere. El Tribunal?"

"Yes, it's a big day and I don't want to be late."

"It goes well?" Leo asked with the genuine concern of a friend.

"Maybe, I don't know, OK today I think. I hope."

"Y mi cosita, Gabriela, how is she?"

"Hmm, OK, up and down," Harry said, making the shape of a wave with his hand.

"Mi pobre niña."

Two more blasts of the horn indicated their departure.

"Leo, did you find anything about Estefanía? You said maybe Carla might have something?"

"She has looked. She has all the paperwork, Estefanía's hours and days, and her money, even her signature. All from when she was living at Casa Rosa, but there is nothing with information. Carla remembers nothing of family or friends or places. Yes, she mentioned San Felipe of course, but that is nothing. Carla remembered that Estefanía made phone calls from the Kasanee, did you know? I had forgotten. She always asked if she could use the phone."

"No idea who to, I suppose?" He shook his head. "Thanks, Leo. Something may turn up. Estefanía had a family somewhere, had a baby somewhere. Have you heard any rumours, or has everyone lost interest?"

"There are the beer stories, they are, er, fantastic, I will write a book of them."

"Such as?"

"You have moved your money already, before it is seized, it has gone to Panama, out of reach."

"It's a thought, maybe I should do that."

"You are selling Casa Rosa, you will take any price because you will lose it anyway, then you will go back to the United States."

"I suppose that was predictable. To be honest, Leo, I was expecting worse."

"There is worse, there are stupid, bad things. But I say nothing when I hear them, I let them speak. I tell Carla, Harry is a great criminal, he will be famous, and we will make money because we knew him. Ha! You really want to know, Harry, my friend?"

He didn't really want to hear anything, but some snippet, some word or name might start a thought running, might lead to another and a name or a face. "Yes, tell me."

"Carla heard that the school cannot accept dear Gabriela because she is, er, unable. She is kept drugged to keep her quiet."

Harry hung his head in despair.

Leo said, "Maybe it is enough, eh? There is no sense in it."

"Let me hear it," he groaned.

"If you wish. Yes? This is nasty, about Estefanía Flores. She was una prostituta, huh? She worked for you until she had the baby, had Gabriela. Then you sent her back to San Felipe to get money to repay the debt. When she came back with no money you killed her. She is under the sand at Casa Rosa."

Harry winced with the pain of it. But a part of him, a part deeply buried until a week ago and now exhumed by questions and fears, that part of him was a cold still point in the midst of the pain. *Una prostituta, huh?* Maybe. A heavy stone settled in the pit of his stomach: perhaps they should simply go to a certain district of San Felipe, a district favoured by certain people, and look in the bars of an evening or, later, look in the rooms above the bars where they might yet find Estefanía Flores alive and well.

He took the water bottle from his bag and took a long swallow.

"Leo, a few days ago when we were at the Kasanee talking of Estefanía, asking if you remembered something about her, you

100

said you thought I'd known Estefanía before she came to the island. Why did you think that? Tell me honestly, as a friend. Please."

"Oh, Harry, it is a long time ago, it was an impression. She was begging at the tables one minute then she is sitting with you and you are feeding her, asking me for a room for her. Carla was there, you remember, she looked at me to say who is this and I said a friend of Harry because it looked that way and then the feeling is made and that is all. You said nothing about a bus."

"It looked like she was a friend?"

"Truly Harry? No, it looked like you owed her something."

"Maybe I owed somebody something," he sighed. "Thanks for the honesty, Leo."

★

A slow drip of water from around the skylight revealed the curse of all flat roofs, the pooling rain that always finds a way through, even if it takes years. Some thoughtful employee had placed an old ice-cream tub on a chair to catch the water. A dark patch on the floor beneath the chair indicated it was not always so.

Harry had seen Arsenia Mejía's car, along with two or three others, as he'd arrived at the scruffy court buildings, so he guessed they were preparing the final details of the decision while he waited. It was, he thought, a good thing that neither Mejía nor judge Cruz listened to beer stories in the Kasanee. Yet they had listened to someone's stories, this nightmare had been inflicted on him, and Gabriela, by somebody's imagination.

A few minutes before the appointed time, Harry was surprised to see Indira Chavarria join him in the waiting room, not through the main entrance, but from a corridor.

"Ah, señor Rose, good morning. I have been talking with la señora Mejía, a technical matter, I hope you don't mind."

"No, I don't think so. Should I mind?"

101

"No, no. I will tell you, but first, if you must find some money for a bond in a few days, how much do you think you could have?"

"Hmm, not sure. Immediately, a few thousand dollars. In a week maybe twenty thousand. Will there be a bond?"

"I was hoping to find out, but la señora could not say. So we spoke about if there were a bond how big it might be in such cases. If there is I think it will be ten thousand."

"Today?"

"Yes, but a guarantee will be enough, there would be no cash to hand over. Yesterday I spoke with, er," for once she hesitated, uncertain of herself, "your good friend and my er, mentor, el señor Julio Aguilar, in case such a guarantee would be necessary. He has said he would guarantee an amount greater than that."

"Thank you, Julio," he breathed, while thinking how Indira Chavarria seemed to anticipate every eventuality.

"Tell me, señor Rose, did the visit from la señora go well? Was Gabriela troubled?"

"I think it was OK. Gabriela seemed happy enough afterwards. I was well behaved. Diplomatic. You would've been proud of me."

The almost-lawyer smiled uncomfortably and cast her eyes down, momentarily embarrassed by the slightest hint of something personal. In doing so her likeness to Estefanía Flores was doubled.

Footsteps in the corridor announced Arsenia Mejía, who appeared, smiling. Harry thought how much more it suited her face than the severe look she normally wore. Which, he wondered, was more natural to her?

"Good morning, señor Rose, señorita. La juez Cruz is ready."

They sat in the same office, the seats arranged in the same order as previously. Harry, flanked by the two women, faced the judge. He searched her face for some sign of what was to come but found no clue. His calm optimism of earlier had evaporated, replaced by dread. He was suddenly very tired and old.

"Señor Rose," the judge began, leaning forward in her chair to emphasise her sincerity, "it has been said already that this is an unusual case, and it continues to be so now. I will ask you two questions before giving the decision today.

"First, we will, for the moment, put aside the question of what has happened to Gabriela's mother. You have asked us to believe that you want the best for Gabriela, that you have always acted for her benefit. More, you ask us to believe that you will do so in the future and that to stay with you as she is now is the best that can happen. If we are to accept that you are honest in your feelings, then you should accept that the law, as expressed by the court and the actions of La Agencia de Protección de los Niños, also seeks the best interest of the child. We all in this room wish the best for Gabriela even though we don't agree on what that may be.

"So my first question to you señor Rose is whether or not you accept that?"

Harry knew what came next: accept it then he must accept the verdict, accept that Gabriela will be removed and put in a home or sent to live with people paid to care for her, people who would not know her or understand her. Some extra sense made him hesitate and try to guess the second question. He looked to Indira Chavarria for some expression, a nod of the head, a down turned mouth, but she gave him no clue, not even glancing at him, instead she remained looking calmly ahead. An answer in itself? Arsenia Mejía offered even less, studying the ends of her fingers while she waited for his answer. He wondered if she still had a few grains of sand under her nails from her time on the beach with Gabriela.

"Yes, I accept we all want the best for Gabriela."

"Thank you. Now, when the decision is given today, if you find that some things are not as you would wish, either for today or tomorrow or next week or next year, will you accept the decisions, and will you allow them to be carried through without obstructing la señora Mejía or any other person?"

103

So, it would go against him, they just wanted him to make it easy for them. It was almost a relief to know it. But why the question? Surely he had some recourse to appeal, some way to continue the fight?

"Juez Cruz, if I do not agree with the decision, is there an appeal, some process to have the decision changed?"

"You must consult a lawyer for this answer, señor Rose, someone qualified," she glanced at Indira Chavarria, "but I will say this. If you think we have not complied with the law, then yes you can appeal, of course. If you think we have not taken all aspects into account in coming to the decision, you may bring other things to our attention, today or at any other time. Otherwise, I think no, you cannot appeal. But you must talk to a lawyer. Perhaps you have one already?"

"Yes, I do."

"Good. I ask the question again, señor Rose. Will you accept the decision and not stand in the way?"

"I will fight anything I don't agree with through any legal route I can find. But no, I won't hold Gabriela or take her away and hide her."

"I am very pleased to hear that assurance, señor Rose." She turned to Arsenia Mejía, "Señora, is there anything you wish to say or change before I announce the decision for today?"

She shook her head. "No, nada, gracias."

The judge opened the folder in front of her and took several pages and put them to the back.

"Here is a copy of the order and you will sign to say you have received it and you will do what is required," she said, passing the papers across to him. "I will summarise for us all here today. There are two sections, what will happen now and what will happen in a few weeks. For now Gabriela will remain with you, señor Rose, subject to some conditions. She must start school as soon as possible in Concepción, and we are aware that may take a little time to arrange. As this is an order, any fees will be paid by La Agencia de Protección de los Niños. Next, she may not stay overnight away from Isla Concepción without agreement from the office of la señora Mejía. You must also supply a guarantee of ten thousand dollars today, which will be seized if you fail to do what is asked. You will continue to care for Gabriela which means feeding, housing and clothing her. We have noted that Gabriela will have her health and development assessed in San Felipe. It must be understood that any negative findings may cause a change to these conditions.

"You are aware from previous discussion that there is an investigation by, er, DIC, el Departamento de Investigaciones Criminales into the disappearance of Estefanía Flores? Yes, I'm sure you are. You will cooperate with that investigation. If it is found that you are involved in her disappearance, the order made today will be revised and Gabriela will be removed from your care immediately. I will tell you now, señor Rose, we have discussed the case with the investigator and he will be here today when we are finished. He will ask you some questions."

Harry's cautious joy at those first few words, *remain with you*, was short-lived. As the terms had unfolded he'd become more agitated, now there was this new dimension, even if it was not new at all, simply one he'd ignored. He looked at his supporter, Indira Chavarria, and she saw the set of his jaw and the anger in his eyes.

"It is to be expected," she soothed softly.

"There are other small details, you will read them. But there is the second section which we have decided after very careful consideration of this unusual case. La Agencia will find a suitable home for Gabriela as soon as possible. This will not happen quickly, it will take time, within eight weeks, perhaps longer. It is hoped such a home may be on Isla Concepción to allow her to continue schooling in familiar surroundings. It is also expected that you will make this change as simple as possible for Gabriela."

She closed the folder and let her hands rest on it. Harry would have spoken or stood or raged if he'd been able, but every muscle had wasted away, his head, his arms too heavy to move, his heart too numb to beat.

"Señor Rose, we recognise that you will be disappointed with the decisions. It has not been easy to find the best path for Gabriela."

He supposed he should say something, supposed that in a different world he might thank her for her time and consideration, that they would all shake hands on jobs well done with difficult issues sensitively negotiated. He could do none of these things, neither could he stand when juez Cruz indicated that the process was complete and rose to leave.

Indira Chavarria touched his shoulder and he mechanically followed her from the room.

"Señor Rose," she spoke quietly, but leaning in to him so as to be sure he heard, "you must sign the papers, do you need a little time to read them? We can use an office."

He shook his head. "I'll sign."

He did. She took them to Arsenia Mejía while he sat sipping water from his bottle in the waiting room, slowly recovering his senses. The worst possible outcome, worse than he'd feared, a delayed agony that stretched the torture across every day from now until she was taken from him. And the prospect of that vile day he could not begin to contemplate. And afterwards! Imagine seeing Gabriela in Concepción! He cried out in pain.

Indira Chavarria let her hand rest on his arm. "Señor Rose, Harry," she allowed herself out of compassion, "you can see only the worst of this day. Perhaps when we look again in an hour or two, you may see the best of it."

He couldn't answer, couldn't be grateful for her coolness and logic.

Tipping back another mouthful of water he found a man standing in front of him. He was around Indira Chavarria's age, in a fresh white shirt and with a shock of dark hair falling across his face. He was consulting a sheaf of papers.

"Señor Stuart Henry Rose, also Harry Rose?" he asked.

"Yes. What now?" he snapped, suddenly combative.

"I am Investigador Daniel Scott Ramirez from DIC. I am assigned the case of Estefanía Flores. I think la señora Mejía spoke of me. I have a room, it would be better to go there I think. I have some questions."

"All right, let's get it over with. Do I need a lawyer?"

"Ah, I do not know. You are accused of nothing yet, do you want a lawyer?"

With only a little more provocation Harry thought he might put an end to the day's miseries and punch the man hard in the mouth and settle everything once and for all.

"I thought I'd been accused of a lot of things, isn't that why you're here?" he said too aggressively.

The investigator looked from Harry to Indira Chavarria and back again and saw that Harry was spoiling for a fight, which was not how he wished the interview to proceed.

"Rumour and speculation, señor Rose," he said mildly, "I am looking for Estefanía Flores, to know where she is and what has happened to her. You may be able to help. If you wish a lawyer to be here I can arrange for one, but perhaps we could start before you decide."

Seeing the corner he was pushing himself into, Harry grasped the olive branch offered and took a long breath.

"Yes, forgive me. Let me introduce señorita Indira Chavarria, she's my lawyer today."

"No, señor Rose…" she protested.

"You'll do. In fact you'll more than do." Which was a saying of Harry's mother and the thought of her came to him as he spoke. "La señorita is not qualified yet, but she is very close."

"If you wish," he shrugged, "Please come with me."

They followed him to another small room, similar to the judge's, and with the same utility office furniture. It smelled strongly of rotting wood and stale cigarettes. The investigator inspected the surface of the desk before spreading his papers on it. After he'd run through some simple questions of identification he passed across a copy of the report Harry had made to Victor Diaz when Estefanía had failed to return home.

"Do you recognise this as the report you made?"

107

"Yes, that's it. I have a copy of it also, here in my papers." He tapped the folder on his lap.

"Would you read it all please, tell me if there is anything that you would like to change."

Harry read through the details, the date, the time, the last sighting on the ferry, her age and appearance, what she was wearing. He could see nothing that he'd got wrong. Apart from the age.

"I've since been told that Estefanía was a year or so younger than I thought, otherwise no."

The detective nodded. "You put her address as your address, Casa Rosa. Was that the only address you knew her to have?"

"Yes."

"Investigador Scott," Indira Chavarria interrupted, "There is no recording of this interview, I see you are making some notes. I will also, yes?"

"Please go ahead, señorita." He turned back to Harry, collecting his thoughts again. "Er, señor Rose, did you sleep with Estefanía Flores, were you lovers?"

"No."

"You're sure?"

"Of course I'm bloody sure!" Harry's composure was tested and found wanting again.

"Yes, I understand, but these are questions that I must ask. The next is also difficult. Did you and she have arguments, big arguments about anything, money, the baby, anything at all?"

"No, never. She was easy to live with. She might not think I was easy, but that is different."

"Why might you not be easy, señor Rose?"

"I don't know, she would have to say."

"Yes. I wonder, did you shout at her or strike her for any reason, with your hand or a weapon?"

Was there nothing he was incapable of? Child abuse, slavery, murder, beating a woman after pimping her out? Did this detective sit in the Kasanee and listen to gossip, too? He felt a very long way from home, a lost foreigner, empty and alone in his adopted land.

"No, never. It is not something I would do."

"No, of course. Did Estefanía Flores ever steal anything from you? Money, jewellery, credit card, anything?"

"No. Or if she did I never missed it. She had the run of the house, she could've taken anything, nothing is locked up."

"And did you pay her while she lived with you?"

"Yes, a little. She looked after the house, so she had a home and food. I gave her a little money too, not a lot." And she earned money at the Kasanee, but el investigador Scott could discover that for himself.

"It seems you had a perfect, er, arrangement with la señorita Flores."

"Yes, I suppose we did." Looking back it certainly felt that way, he knew that. But would he have known if she'd been unhappy in it, had he assumed more than he should?

"Could you please tell me how you came to, er, live together and with Gabriela. I wish to understand more of her life at Casa Rosa and before."

Where should he start, with who she might have been, or with who she was from the moment he met her on the bus and nursed her beautiful baby? He chose the latter, it was factual and true, uncomplicated by ifs and maybes. And having recently told the tale he could retell it quite easily, knowing where a question might arise, or feelings might be doubted without the right emphasis and shared insight.

When he'd finished, the investigator considered for a few moments and then asked, "Do you think it is possible that la señorita Flores could have met you not by chance on that bus, but had arranged it that way?"

"No," he said quickly, then, "no wait, let me think." The night was lost to him, the waking only snapshots and blurred impressions, the bus was crowded, they were always crowded. Eyes closed he could see her clearly, the day heavy, the window behind her streaked with mud. She sat by the window, he sat next to her, her bag on his lap along with his own. She was there before him. "No, she could not have known. I did not know, so she could not. It was crowded, she was seated before me. It was pure chance."

"Tell me, señor Rose, do you know anything about la señorita Estefanía Flores that could help me to find her, anything you haven't spoken of?"

"No," he said. There was no value in speculation or imaginings, or fanciful ideas of her being held somewhere against her will. That was for cheap talk washed down with a few beers.

The investigator considered his papers for a few moments, when he finally spoke he seemed genuinely uncertain of what direction his enquiries should take. "Señor Rose, if you were me I wonder what question you would be asking, what do you know that I should know?"

"You should want to know if I'd killed her or not."

"Did you?"

"No. And now you know that, you can save yourself a great deal of time and trouble and look for other answers."

"Ah, that is true señor Rose," he nodded. "Tell me, do you still have any of la señorita's belongings at Casa Rosa?"

"Yes, she didn't have much. Her room is still waiting for her."

"I would like to see it. Perhaps today?"

"Yes, later."

"Thank you, señor Rose. That is all for the moment."

"Investigador Scott," Indira Chavarria said, "do you know we are also looking for la señorita Flores? Can you tell us if you have found any trace of her, anything that might help our search?"

The detective considered this for a moment while his hands continued to slide his papers into a tidy pile. "No, señorita, I can tell you nothing of the case. But if you discover anything we should know then I hope you will inform me."

"Yes, of course."

Harry and la señorita left the decaying building together, happy to leave the detective in the damp little room, happy to breath the open air again. As they reached her car Harry said, "It's almost too much to take in, too much to bear. I have no idea what I should think about first. But here's what I can't get out of my head, I used to work with an engineer, an Englishman whose name was Andrew Scott. He married a local woman. Last I knew, they had a son called Daniel. We lost touch."

"You said nothing."

"It didn't come to me until you asked about what he'd found. Then I remembered while he was shuffling his papers. I didn't seem like the right moment to mention it."

She drove him to a restaurant near the harbour where he looked at the menu without seeing it, so ordered the same chicken and rice as she had. When Indira Chavarria thought he'd had enough time to recover a little perspective, she returned to the subject of Gabriela.

"Señor Rose, the decision today was excellent for you, even though you felt it was not. The judge did everything she could to be correct and to help you. Perhaps in the emotion of the words you did not see the good in this?"

"You're right there, señorita Chavarria. Tell me the good."

"First, Gabriela is still with you, which is most important. It will not be often that the judge hears such a case and the accused keeps the child. La señora Mejía will have persuaded her. Second, eight weeks, maybe more, is a long time to find a place for her. It means they have no immediate fears for Gabriela. The bond, the other restrictions, they are nothing, they simply tell you that you must continue to do as you are doing and it protects them. But the real point of eight weeks is that we can bring new information to them at any time and they will reconsider. And it is not eight weeks, but it is some time which may be eight weeks and may be longer, much longer. They tread a difficult path between what they wish and what the law states for such a child as Gabriela.

"I understand you are distressed, but I believe it is a good result. You will talk with el señor Julio tonight maybe? Ask him his view, he knows better than I."

111

"What was all that fuss about both wanting the best for Gabriela and accepting what they decided?"

"I believe they had a second set of orders if you had disagreed or they thought you would run away with Gabriela. I believe they would have taken her away today if you had answered differently."

"But you said nothing."

"I believed you would give the assurances they were seeking. And if you did not, that too would be for the best."

"You're very cool, señorita Indira Chavarria, very cool indeed. And the detective? I'll see him again this afternoon. What do you think of him?"

"He has a job to do, he must ask questions, he must do his best. I wonder if he has the case because he has an English father so will have some knowledge of differences in er, culture. It is possible."

"Anything else?"

"Perhaps. I think he has already discovered something about la señorita Flores, something which he was uncertain about sharing. And I think it is something which has shaped his questions about stealing and whether you hit her. She may have become known to the police, somewhere. San Felipe would be most likely. We will see if we can find this information too. But if we can't it may help us with questions of our own."

They sat in silence for a few minutes, Harry a little encouraged by her view of the day while she seemed deep in thought, contemplating the pattern of condensation on her glass of iced fresco.

"Señor Rose," she ventured after a while, "may I ask a question?"

He'd already learned enough about her to know a question prefaced in such a way would certainly be perceptive, probably personal and not answering would be as revealing as total honesty.

"Are you still my lawyer?"

"If you wish."

"Then yes, you may ask."

"You knew nothing of la señorita Estefanía Flores before you met her on a bus. But you have an idea of her life before that, yes?"

It was almost exactly the question he thought she'd been wrestling with. Perhaps she'd guessed his thoughts, sensed his fears, after all, she was at least as smart as Julio had suggested. And she already knew the answer.

"A guess, nothing more. A few unguarded words one evening, a look exchanged on another day. So, yes I have an idea."

"Yet you say nothing?"

"It may not be true. I may not want to know."

"You may have to know, señor Rose."

★

No need to pull off the road and consider what he might say of his day. Even in the depths of his despair as judge Cruz had announced their fate, he knew he'd tell her nothing of finding her a new home. The day would come when that needed to be said, but it was not today. It was tempting to think he would leave that loathsome task to la señora Mejía since she was so practised in delivering bad news, but it was spite that told him that. When it came to it, there should be only one person who'd deliver that blow, one person who'd find a way to lessen that bruise.

There was no one to greet him at La Plantación, although Pippa's Peugeot was parked by the garage. He guessed they'd be down by the shore, a good twenty minute walk down the hill, more coming back. He made himself at home and looked for some good scotch he thought Pippa had somewhere. When he couldn't find it he poured a stiff gin and settled himself on the terrace. If he'd seen the house before Casa Rosa he might have fallen in love with La Plantación instead. It was a fine property, even if it did lack a beach.

Just at the point when the light began to fade and the first twinge of anxiety tightened his shoulder he caught movement through the remains of the old orchard. He stood up and waved. As soon as Gabriela caught sight of him she ran ahead, calling out, "Papatico! Papatico!" and then arrived in a rush with her beach treasure, which appeared to be a small beachball.

"Looook!" she exclaimed.

"What have you got there?"

"Pippa says it's a float for fishing."

"I think she's right. It's beautiful." He held the blue glass ball aloft to catch the light. "That's real treasure."

"Pippa says it might be very old."

"Maybe. We'll have to find out."

"Can we stay tonight? Pippa says we can if you say so." She saw him pause ready to place the familiar condition on what she wanted, but she had her answer ready. "And I *am* good enough!" she told him triumphantly.

"Then it's lucky I've brought all we need for our trip tomorrow," he answered as Pippa arrived.

"Which means the day went well?" she asked tentatively.

"I thought not, but I've been persuaded it was a good as we could've hoped for."

She put her arms round him, kissing him and holding him close. "That's very good, Harry. One step at a time. Tell me the details later."

By the time they'd eaten and Gabriela was in bed and ready for a story, she'd still not asked anything of the events in Puerto Reunión. Harry guessed she'd shut the questions away, no news was good news. He and Pippa were behaving as usual, so why should she worry? Even so, he thought she should be told something, if only to unlock more questions. One way in was through the visit of Daniel Scott.

When he'd finished the story, he said, "I saw a policeman today, he came to our home."

"Was it Captain Diaz?" she asked cautiously.

"No, it was a different kind of policeman, an investigator, a detective. He's trying to find out where your Mami could be. He wanted to see where she lives, see Casa Rosa, see her room. He looked at your room too. He liked your maps."

She nodded thoughtfully, then said, "Does he know where Mami is?"

"No, my darling, he doesn't."

"I wish she was here now."

The words released a stream of tears and she wept long and hard into his shirt. Better, he thought, if she were to cry a little more often than bury her miseries. A week ago la señora Mejía's visit had brought a flood, but since then nothing while she'd been around him. He let her sob, stroking her hair until her pain subsided.

"I saw la señora Mejía again today. She asked if you were all right. I said you were. I think she enjoyed her time on the beach with you yesterday. We have agreed that you will stay with me at home. One day that may change, you may live somewhere else but we can't see into the future, so we live each day and hope tomorrow will be even better. If it will change I will tell you, I will help you make a different home. Whatever happens, you will be you and I will be your Papatico. Oh and yes, there was something else, there will be school, next week I think, maybe longer, but soon."

Harry heard himself say all these words calmly, all true but with their stings drawn. He was half-convinced of his own propaganda, perhaps Indira Chavarria had been right after all. But was he right to hide his own true feelings from her, was that how she learned to hide her own? Pippa would have him say nothing of the events so critical to her future, indeed, only a few hours ago he'd convinced himself to say nothing, yet the moment had arrived quite naturally and he'd grasped it. He could only be who he was, he couldn't be anyone else.

"Tonight you can dream of our adventure tomorrow, we're going on the bus. Directo."

115

7

"Please have a seat, señor Rose, el señor Aguilar asked if you would please wait a few minutes, he is with a client."

The smart young woman behind the reception desk was a reminder of just how much had changed for Julio over the years. Harry knew he'd done well, more than well, he'd gained an excellent reputation with the foreign companies of San Felipe as well as respect in the city's legal community. He'd resisted financial pressures and kept his only-what-you-can-afford personal service going and helped establish it as a model for other lawyers in the city. When, as had occasionally happened, a conflict arose between the personal and the corporate, Julio had acted as arbitrator, usually to the individual's benefit and at a fraction of the cost to both sides.

It had been years since Harry had visited the office, which now occupied a whole floor of the building, a long way from the poky room he'd started in. Being told things had gone well was quite different from seeing the evidence.

He didn't wait long for the smart young woman to invite him through to Julio's room. He'd seen no one leave and presumed there was another way out, yet when he entered he saw none.

"I thought you had a client, Julio?"

"Yes," Julio said, mutual affection keeping their hands grasped a little longer than with a normal client. "A conference by video."

"Ah, it's so easy to get out of touch."

"How is Gabriela? The visit to la doctora Arroyo went well?"

"Until she wanted to take some blood. Gabriela wasn't too keen on that."

It had gone well, the doctor was understanding and gentle, not at all the business-like encounter that Harry had feared. Old preconceptions die hard and it hadn't occurred to him that it might be a female doctor, but he was glad of it. With Pippa there too, Gabriela had not minded her ears and nose and mouth being peered into, her weight and height being measured. She breezed through her sight test, read Spanish and English and spoke as well as he knew she could, and was generally a star performer, until he was asked about her immunisations, where his lack of knowledge gave her a zero rating. How could he be so neglectful, how could he not know anything of something so critical? Neither was Pippa exempt from implied criticism: if she presented herself as the caring protector then she should have at least some knowledge of Gabriela's dental visits. It wasn't the time or the place to protest their innocence, to recount their histories. The doctor would learn what she needed from testing the child's blood, even if their ignorance demanded she drew enough for several samples.

There were no immediate concerns, a report would be sent, although a visit to a dentist was recommended, Gabriela's mouth may be a little overcrowded. Harry wondered when the perfect smile had become as important as preventing cavities. He shuddered at the prospect of braces disfiguring her face.

"La doctora, she took a mouth sample, a swab for DNA?"

Harry nodded.

"Good, I asked she should do that. It may be helpful," Julio said, then seeing Harry's doubtful look, added, "For her mother, for Estefanía."

There was only one set of circumstances under which such a sample might be useful and neither of them named it. Instead, Julio struck a lighter note.

"And what have you done with Gabriela and la señora Maddingly now?"

"They've gone to Pippa's gallery, she had business there today and Gabriela will enjoy it. Then they are shopping for Gabriela, you'll see them this evening."

"We're all looking forward to it." He smiled, pausing again, a signal that business was about to resume. "Harry, la señorita Chavarria has told me everything that happened in Puerto

117

Reunión, I have the papers here. She said, too, you were very unhappy with events. Are you still? You know, really, it was a very good day. You and Gabriela have gained the trust of la señora Mejía and she has persuaded the judge."

"But in the end I'll lose her, they'll take her away."

"It is possible, yes, but now there is time for another result. If Gabriela had gone last week or yesterday, then it would be a different matter, then I think it would be difficult to bring her back. Now we can make a different solution, we have many avenues. La señora Mejía could not say so, but I believe she too will want us to find a different solution."

Harry wouldn't let himself embrace Julio's optimism, a grudging acceptance of the possibility was as close as he could get. And there was still the small matter of murder.

"Is there any trace of Estefanía yet?"

"La señorita Chavarria says not, but she has started something new with the city police here in San Felipe to see if they have anything. It is a puzzle that we cannot yet find her registration, la señorita has said there are few places left to look. And the search for Gabriela is the same, she and her mother are not in the city lists, they can only be in a rural town, somewhere small where the records have not yet been centralised. There is less to search but it is slow work. I'm sure we will find them soon. It will answer some questions when we do."

"But not what has happened to her. Did la señorita tell you about the detective, Daniel Scott Ramirez? I'm sure he's Andrew Scott's son. You might remember him, I think you met him once or twice."

"I will find out, if la señorita has not done so already," he said, smiling at the thought she would have overlooked anything. "She works hard for you, Harry, she is good for you and for Gabriela."

"Yes, I think she is. Do you see a likeness in her to Estefanía Flores? I do. It's unsettling."

"No, but I do not remember la señorita Flores well."

They sat in silence for a moment, Harry all too aware that there were a dozen unanswered questions buzzing round his head, but unsure of which topic to settle on. Julio saved him the decision.

"Harry, we have discovered one thing today. It is no more than we had guessed," he said slowly. "It may make you, er, angry again. The source of all these events, it was a call to La Agencia, to APN, a message left a month ago, on a Sunday, the office was closed. La señora Mejía informed la señorita Chavarria, here, I have the text of the call."

He handed Harry a printed sheet with a transcript of the call in Spanish, an English translation beneath it.

A woman's voice, speaking in Spanish, call origin unknown:

Attention! There is an American who keeps a small girl as a slave in his house. He beats her and uses her for sex, she is eight years. He keeps her alone, with no contact, no schooling. He killed the mother and buried her there. He lives at Playa de Rosas on Isla Concepción. He is named Rose. He is evil and cunning. Be careful.

Harry read it twice, then read the original. The translation was close enough, although stilted as if done from a dictionary. After all that had been said, after all that had transpired since the poisonous accusations had been made, the text was sterile. The words had no fresh sting, contained no foul inventions of abuse that might rekindle his anger.

"I don't know what I was expecting," Harry said. "Something worse, something more disgusting, more specific. This is something else, a dead thing. And Playa de Rosas? Where does that come from?"

"I was not sure, but I looked on your Casa Rosa file, it is there, it is the whole property from years ago before the pieces were sold, where your neighbours are now. Maybe it was the name even before that, when there were no houses."

"So who would know that, who would say Playa de Rosas? Someone local?"

"It is possible."

"Have you heard the message, Julio?"

119

"No, only this, why?"

"I wonder if it was an angry voice, a tearful voice. Reading the words typed out like this they don't seem angry or tearful. They seem cold, precise, deliberate, nothing else."

"Being read from a paper, perhaps."

"Something like that, but we'd have to hear them. And do you see there's no concern for Gabriela? She's not even named, she's just a girl."

"There is a reason for that, it is not Gabriela who is the motive for this, it is you. We know it is false, and if it is false Gabriela does not need saving, it is Harry who needs saving. The work for Gabriela, all that la señorita Chavarria has done, will continue, we will find her, and her mother, somewhere, but we should also start looking for why, even if it is no more than malicious gossip."

"Are people really that nasty? They would say such things for the sake of some petty grudge?"

"Someone said such things, someone wishes you harm, Harry. It was not said for Gabriela's good health. We must keep that in mind. Also remember they made accusations to fit what a stranger would see in the way that you and Gabriela live, and how her mother is missing. The accusations become plausible," Julio referred to the papers in front of him, "here, la juez Cruz said so, *it appeared there is good reason to be concerned*. Someone made the accusations knowing they would fit, knowing they would be investigated."

"But where to start looking?"

"They may show themselves if it seems their accusations have come to nothing, so for now I suggest we do nothing, we save our energy but stay alert."

Harry nodded in agreement, even though he was unconvinced. When there was so much at stake, doing nothing did not come easily to him.

After a few moments' thought, he said, "The same might be said if their accusations had been successful."

"Perhaps, we have a little time now to consider our actions. La señorita Chavarria has asked for two things from you. First she would like to see some of the papers from the Kasanee, she said you'd seen papers from la señorita Estefanía Flores' employment there, papers with the address on them?"

"Leo mentioned them, yes I can get copies."

"Good. And also la señorita asked if you would write down as much as you can remember of the conversation you had with la señorita Estefanía when she left Gabriela with you. She emphasised that any actual words used might be helpful. It is an idea which she has, a legal question, she has asked to not tell me anything until she has researched it." He lifted a hand to forestall any criticism. "I said yes. La señorita is not foolish, she will not waste her time, she does not like to waste mine."

★

Gabriela hung back behind Pippa as they came into Elena and Julio's home. She knew the family were not strangers, but neither were they everyday friends. Pippa's flowing skirt offered a safe haven from their exuberant greetings until she spied Harry coming into the house from the courtyard.

"Papatico!" she cried, darting forward to be swept up and cling to his neck. He carried her close to Elena and Cristela so she could be kissed and purred over from the safety of his arms.

"You remember Cristela? We were talking about her the other day, about making songs together when she came to see us at home."

So this was who she'd been thinking of. Her eyes widened in appreciation. "Can we make another song. Pleeeease?" she begged.

Cristela beamed, being remembered by a child with such enthusiasm is rewarding for anyone at any age. "Yes, come on, we'll make a start."

She looked for approval from Harry and slid to the floor as he nodded, all fears dispelled.

"For a few minutes, Cristela," her mother called after her. "We'll eat soon." She turned to Harry. "Stuart is away tonight, he has a soccer camp in Lorenzo. I'm sorry he's not here to see you, Harry. You will have his room and Pippa, you and Gabriela will share the guest room, if you don't mind."

Despite being thoroughly modern in almost every aspect of her life, Elena had a conservative streak when it came to sleeping arrangements. The announcement forestalled any awkward discussion. Harry even wondered if perhaps the soccer camp was a white lie and Stuart had been farmed out to allow unmarried adults to have separate rooms.

"Thank you, Elena," he said, drawing her to him and kissing her forehead, "that will be perfect for us all."

At the evening meal, as they all sat round the table passing plates and raising glasses, reminding each other of the happier events of the day, Harry couldn't help but wonder at the family he might've had. It was not a great sadness to him, he had chosen the single way or, as with Pippa, it had chosen him, and his wondering was curiosity rather than regret. But if he had taken a different route he couldn't see how his table could be happier than the one he sat at. He'd been adopted by Elena and Julio at least as much as he'd adopted them. Their loving gift of being godfather to Stuart had meant far more to them than a mere token of temporary friendship. They had even turned a blind eye to his patent lack of religious conviction and he had responded by making vows in the sight of a god who didn't exist. He and they had understood both compromises but had made no reference to them.

And Pippa, sitting easily between Cristela and Gabriela might be grandmother to both, a confidant to either. With no greater stretch of imagination she might be Harry's wife, although there was good reason that she wasn't. Commitment to one person was impossible, as she'd made plain very early in their relationship. So far as Harry knew, there'd never been a string of boyfriends, or girlfriends, but Pippa prized the possibility of such things. To tie herself to only one, even to the most eligible man on the

122

island as she had once described him, was to give up that freedom and all others. Looking at her now, so easy in her own skin, fascinating to both the child and the teenager, a reliable friend and still the occasional lover, Harry saw his own good fortune quite clearly.

Cristela was growing into the delightful young person her formative years had promised. Harry could guess there were moments when she exasperated her mother, less so her father, as teenager girls so easily can, yet she was a wonderful endorsement of their parenting. In considering Cristela he couldn't help but let his eye come to rest on his smiley, smart and loving Gabriela. He could only hope someone would feel the same about his parenting in eight or nine years' time.

The idea ambushed him, causing him to choke on his wine, spilling it down his front and prompting those who loved him to fuss round him as he gasped for breath at the same time as he tried to brush away their attentions. He struggled to the bathroom, to cough and retch in private and bitterly recall that his parenting was all but done, he might have no say in Gabriela's life beyond the next few weeks. Eight or nine years was a fantasy. When he raised his face from the sink, his reflection reminded him how ill-equipped he'd be, had already been. Despite the joys of stargazing, of sharing *Winnie The Pooh*, of playing the indulgent grandfather, he'd done little in the way of real parenting. He didn't even possess a thermometer or a packet of aspirins until the last few days. How easily wine and amiable company lulled his senses to forget the reason they were all gathered in San Felipe on a Friday evening.

One small point of light shone through the gloom threatening to envelope him: Gabriela was still with him, he could still be grateful for that. She was still as much a part of the family downstairs as anyone else at the table, yet he couldn't let himself hope for a future together. Preparing for the worst would soften the blow, this was the mantra he'd been raised to, this was how he'd lived his life, even if he'd frequently advised others differently. He was uncomfortably aware that such preparations had done nothing to ease the pain when la juez Cruz had declared la Agencia would find a suitable home for Gabriela. He'd prepared for that outcome, yet still it had come as a hammer blow. And all Julio's optimism and Indira Chavarria's cool legalities felt like straws to be clutched at, rather than reasons to be hopeful.

"Harry, are you all right?" Pippa's voice, low and urgent outside the bathroom door.

"Yes," he croaked, "Down in a minute."

His tired reflection stared back at him, revealing all the signs of ageing that the sun and sea cannot conceal forever. The streaming eyes and coughing fit had not helped his dishevelled appearance. For tonight, for tomorrow, for the next eight weeks, he would hide his fears as best he could. He took off his shirt and splashed cold water on his face then used the shirt to dab it dry. In the room he pulled a clean one from his bag, took some deep unhurried breaths and tried to recall the pleasures of family mealtime. As he opened the bedroom door he heard Gabriela delightedly squealing "Cristela!" The spell had not been broken by his hurried exit.

At the table Elena and Julio had each left a little food on their plates so that Harry should not have to finish his alone. Gabriela hardly noticed him, she was fully engaged in a story Cristela was telling her about school, that new world waiting for her in a few days' time. It would be a distraction for him, but for Gabriela, what? More anxiety or the joy of learning? Something of both, most likely.

When the two girls left the table, the conversation faltered. Each of the adults had a wealth of interests and knowledge and news from which they could fill an evening with laughter or reminiscences, yet the single subject of Harry and Gabriela blotted out all others. Elena and Julio became a little agitated, exchanging frequent glances and just as frequently finding something interesting to study on their plates.

Harry thought the unspoken should be released and saw a way to do so. "Well," he said after the longest silence had been punctuated by girls' laughter and music from another room, "there's one thing we haven't talked about tonight, our children. I assume we all agree how lucky we are?"

"I certainly do," said Pippa, "luckier than all of you, I'm further from having my own than any of you, yet I have all the benefits. Gabriela and I had a brilliant afternoon, she is such a loving child, even through all this nonsense with the police and courts and doctors. Then your Cristela treats me like her long lost aunt. Lucky? Yes. Thank you."

"We are blessed, Harry." Elena reached out a hand to him as she spoke, letting it rest on his, looking him steadily in the eye. "Julio and I have something to ask you, something we hope you'll approve of, but you must be the judge."

Harry looked from Elena to Julio and back again. Neither spoke immediately. "Ask away."

"Elena and I have talked much about this since you were here a week ago," Julio started. "We touched on the subject then, you may remember. It is simple yet not easy to say. We have agreed to make an application to become a family for Gabriela, una familia adoptiva, but we will only do this if you agree. There is more to be said, there are some difficulties for sure, but that is what we are asking. Harry, if you do not agree, this changes nothing, changes nothing between us."

So, while he'd been poorly preparing his head for the worst, Elena and Julio had thought practically, lovingly, of making the best of the worst, such was their care and affection. But a thread of betrayal and abandonment mixed a bitter taste to honourable intentions.

"You think they'll take her, then?" he snapped, more defensive and abrupt than intended.

"Ah, dear Harry, that is one of the difficulties. If we make the application, and let us assume we were accepted, it is possible they will see it as a wonderful solution where everyone is happy, and so they will order it to be so. If we do not make an application they may still decide Gabriela is better elsewhere and we miss the opportunity. We do not want to make it easy or encourage them to move Gabriela, but we want to be ready if they do. As your lawyer I believe there is still a very good chance your beautiful Gabriela may stay with you; as your friends, your family, we will do anything we can."

"I don't know what to say. Thank you, yes, thank you should come first, but…" he trailed off into confused silence, his head spinning. The idea raised as many questions as it answered, and it appeared to undermine his position completely. Once the process was set in motion he'd have no chance, la juez Cruz and la señora Mejía would seize the offer immediately, they could scarcely do less. Their duty would be done, their actions vindicated at the same time as avoiding most if not all the tears and disruption to Gabriela. And she could keep her part-time Papatico. Perfect. Perhaps it was, perhaps for Gabriela there could be no better outcome. So how could he stand in the way of that?

"I need time to think," he said after a few moments. "Elena, you've said nothing yet, speak to me please."

She smiled and tightened her hand on his. "It is difficult, Harry, it is all difficult. I don't know what is right, but I know that if you want this, we will do it. We've spoken," she glanced at Julio with the slow look of a lover. "For us it is easy to say yes. You know what we think of you both. Gabriela should have you in her life. This would be a way. We would love her and care for her too."

"Have you said anything to Cristela or Stuart yet?"

She nodded. "They are very happy. They think it would bring you here more often. And they would spend more time on the beach at Casa Rosa. We would not make our decision without them. But also we knew what they would answer."

"And if Estefanía comes back?"

It was so easy to speak as if she would not, they had all been thinking she would not. Estefanía Flores did not feature in their plans or the conversation. But Gabriela had not yet given up on her mother and Harry gave her a voice in their cosy best-of-both-worlds mapping out of her life.

"It changes everything." Pippa had been silent, an observer not a contributor, until that point.

"Yes, it does. I must think what is right, what is best when it feels as if nothing is better than what we have now. But one thing everyone always overlooks, sometimes I forget it myself. All those months ago, nearly a quarter of Gabriela's life, when Estefanía left, she asked me to take care of Gabriela until she returned."

★

Early evening, the lights beginning to twinkle around Concepción, a warm breeze rippling the water by the Kasanee: together they made one of his favourite settings. Add in good food and a beer on the table between him and Pippa, Gabriela busy being entertained by Carla, Leo at his engaging best behind the bar, and there could hardly be anything wrong in the whole world.

"I think I'm getting numb to the awful," he said dully, "I'm sitting here, sharing a meal with you, Gabriela's off with Carla, the bar's gently humming. It's as if nothing's changed. Anyone watching would think the same."

"Yes, I know," Pippa said. "I remember being in a restaurant, a bit like we are now, a few days after my father died and catching myself laughing at some trivial thing. I remember thinking exactly that, anyone watching would think nothing had changed. And of course for the watcher, nothing has."

"What do you think I should do?"

"That depends on what you want. If you really want to keep Gabriela, something like it is now, at Casa Rosa, the two of you, then you should fight for that until you win or the cause is lost. But I know you aren't sure, you poor darling, I know you want the best for Gabriela, and you're not sure what that is. We none of us are. It can't go on as it was, that's already gone, she'll be at school in a week and in its way that's a huge change. And for the good I think, although not the way it's happened."

"And Elena and Julio? I think they have the most loving of motives, but it felt strange to hear their plan like that. I still don't know what to think."

"Harry, my advice is to do nothing for now, just as you told them. Wait and see a week or two more, there are things we don't know, things may look different in a week. Someone once said a week is a long time in politics. It's a long time for anything these days. I know you want answers, but have patience, this will come out right, I know it will. So yes, do nothing about that wonderful offer, there's time. They can get everything ready, get their paperwork and references and police reports, they can do all that and then wait. Let's see. Let's see about Estefanía, who she really is, or was, it'll come out somehow. This señorita Chavarria of yours seems to be pretty smart, let's see what she can discover."

Harry was mindful of the last conversation he'd had with that señorita of his, so he chose his words carefully. "About Estefanía, it may not be good, did you think of that?"

Pippa looked at him in astonishment. "Might not be good? Dear God, Harry, it was never going to be good! Did you think it might be? She was honest enough, she was a good mother in her way, she has a lovely child and I know you were fond of her, but the Blessed Madonna she most certainly was not."

"Do you know something?"

"No, Harry, I don't. Do you?"

They looked at each other, each wondering if their friend had unshared knowledge of Gabriela's mother and why it would be withheld.

"No," he said, "I could guess at this or that, but it wasn't good things that brought a sixteen year-old girl with a new baby on a one-way ride to nowhere."

"Do you think the friend with a room and a job ever existed?"

"Estefanía must've thought so," he said after considering for a moment. "I can't see why else she'd have come here, she didn't know anyone else on the island."

"Maybe she was running."

"To or from? Either way we've no way of knowing now. I never felt she was looking over her shoulder, did you?"

Gabriela interrupted further discussion by appearing clutching two beers and with an envelope tucked under her arm. "Papatico! Beer from Carla!" she announced, carefully settling the cold bottles on the table.

"Thank you. What else have you got there?"

"Carla said to give this to you, some papers you wanted."

He took the envelope and peered inside. A dozen or so sheets, copies of a selection of Estefanía's time sheets from her days at the Kasanee. He drew them out. Nothing remarkable, but exactly what Indira Chavarria had asked him to collect. There was Estefanía's name and address at the top of each, the working week in a grid below with a few hours completed, at the bottom her pay and her signature. Her address was given as Casa Rosa, Isla Concepción. Her signature was almost child-like on the earliest pages, more fluent as the years progressed. On the first, unaccustomed to signing, she'd written most carefully a fuller version of her name, *Estefanía G Flores Blanca*.

It made no difference, but it was something.

He was about to show the signature to Gabriela, surely a keepsake and an item of keen interest, or so he thought, but he caught Pippa's look at the crucial moment. She'd guessed the contents of the envelope and was glaring at him with narrowed eyes and pursed lips that said *don't you dare show that to her.*

"Thank you, my darling," he said casually, "some details about the bar, I'll look at them later. Will you say thank you to Carla please."

She took the empty bottles and danced away.

It was a small deception in a universe of lies, but made greater by being unnecessary. Either way, he hated deceiving her, even over such a small matter. One day she would know her mother's real names, just not today.

"What was that?" Pippa hissed through gritted teeth.

"The time sheets. Estefanía signed one of them with her full name, here see for yourself." He passed the envelope to her.

129

After she'd studied the papers for a few moments she said, "And you were going to show this to Gabriela?" shaking her head in disappointment.

"She should know, she will know," he said defiantly, all too aware of his thoughtlessness. "I wasn't thinking."

"No, Harry Rose, you were not."

They sat in a huffy silence, not bothering to find words to break it. The buzz of the Kasanee slowly subsided around them as the patrons drifted away into the darkness of Concepción's ill-lit streets. Leo came to them as they were on the point of finding Gabriela to leave. Harry told him something of how the court had gone after Leo had dropped him off, plus a little of their trip to San Felipe. He was a good friend, but not one who needed to know every detail. In return Leo recounted another fanciful theory he'd heard across the bar: a drugs syndicate, the 'bigger picture' behind Estefanía's disappearance. It brought a wry smile to Harry's lips, but no humour.

"Leo, have you heard anything about the airstrip being revived, or a marina? There are signs on the road from San Felipe, there was a hotel too, but that was face down in the mud."

"The marina? Ah, someone else mentioned that. They saw a picture on the poster and decided it would be right along there." He waved further along the street where, after a few more businesses and a hundred metres, the road and the quay crumbled away to nothing by the disused slipway. "Where else would you put it, huh? It might be good for business, maybe we should offer to run their bar for them?"

"Ha! Maybe we should. What about the airstrip?"

"Every year someone thinks they can do something."

"There's the old plane too, the DC3? I still fancy doing something with that, just for the hell of it."

"You have the money, Harry? You know I'll be happy to spend it for you." He laughed loudly and clapped Harry on the shoulder.

It was as if nothing had changed.

Gabriela was asleep on Pippa's shoulder the moment Harry eased the pickup out from behind the Kasanee. They'd stay at La Plantación before heading home next morning.

"You know," Pippa began softly as they left the town, "you might not need to look further than the Kasanee to find someone with a grudge against you."

"Have you anyone in mind? Surely not Leo? There's nothing he could hold against me, I trust him completely."

"No, what I mean is, you are better known there than anywhere else. Who knows you in San Felipe or Puerto Réunion? Maybe once, while you were working, a lot of people knew you all over the country, but not now."

"Grudges can last a long time. They can fester for years."

They could: he knew well enough the bitterness that could still rise like bile from incidents more than half a century ago. When the demons are loose in the sleepless hours before dawn, he'd conjure violent revenge for the ill-use he'd suffered from those appointed to power over his young life. But it was never long before the same demons, or their mothers, turned on him for his mistreatment of younger souls when he in his turn had reached the apex of that unholy institution.

The pickup bounced through the potholes close to the turn for La Plantación and snapped him back to the present. Surely enough demons already without summoning the old familiars.

"I have some scores I'd love to settle. Right back to school days. I shouldn't be surprised if others feel the same about me. But that's where it stays, they won't come looking for me after fifty years. Not in this corner of paradise."

"Then who, and why? If you knew one you'd know the other."

"Well, we know it's personal to me, nothing to do with Gabriela. So it's revenge for some injury or perceived injury. They've waited a long time for it, Estefanía's been gone nearly two years. Maybe they've only just tracked me down. I can't imagine anything I've done recently to upset someone enough for this."

They followed the twisting track up and over the saddle before slowing at the final curve to the house. In the moonless night, clear and sharp, a billion suns flickering above them. It should be a night to tell star stories and sleep on the sand. Perhaps they could fetch cushions and lie on the terrace.

"Tonight? It's late," Pippa said doubtfully when he suggested it.

He stopped by the house and looked across at her in the half light, so much the protective mother with an arm round her child just stirring from sleep. Conformity to the norm was not usually her way, the child must have tapped into that instinct.

"Yes. Tonight. Because, if not tonight, then when? How many more nights do we have like these? And there'll be none better even if we live for ever."

"For once Harry, you're right."

Gabriela roused herself, first confused as to where she was, then happy to prepare herself for bed. While she did so, Harry and Pippa arranged cushions and pillows and blankets at the edge of the terrace where it began to slope away from the house. Only at the last moment did he tell Gabriela of the plan.

"Can we?" she squealed with joy.

"Yes, bring Héctor, we can stay all night if we like, or go to bed later if we're cold."

"And Pippa?"

"Is that all right?" he asked, after all this was something they had only done together, never with anyone else.

"Yesss!"

Together they settled themselves into their bed, Gabriela snuggled between Pippa and Harry. Their breathing settled to a slower rhythm as they floated into the wonders above them, absorbed into the night. When they'd become part of the heavens themselves, Harry began to speak of the stars. He named her favourites, guiding her eyes to the south or west, to look right or left until she was journeying effortlessly along the starways between the galaxies.

"This is so beautiful," Pippa said.

"Do you like it?" Gabriela whispered to her without taking her eyes from the sky.

"Very much."

After a few minutes Harry brought Gabriela's attention to Arcturus and Spica, although she wasn't sure she could really tell which stars he was talking about.

"Never mind," he said, "you're looking at the right part of the sky. Concentrate on the two brightest ones. There are many stories about those stars and the stars around them, this is one of those stories.

"A very long time ago, before anyone knew how to make fire, there was a very old man who lived with his daughter. The people who first told this story thought that Arcturus and the stars around it were all that were left of the old man, while Spica and those stars were all that remained of his daughter. The daughter was very beautiful, but you already know that all daughters are beautiful, and the old man was very old. And again, you already know that old men are always very old. This particular beautiful daughter had two great talents. First, she could sleep anywhere and often did. She wasn't lazy, but she loved to sleep, especially under the stars. Her second talent was her skill with a bow and arrow, she was the finest archer of all her people."

"What was her name?"

"She had many names but for tonight we will call her Spica. And her father, we'll call him Arcturus."

"Can we call her Gabriela?"

"Yes, Gabriela was her first name, so she is Gabriela Spica. So, where were we? Oh, yes, the bow and arrows. It became colder and colder as winter covered the land with frost and snow. Their land was a long way from here, in the north where it gets very cold and very dark in the winter. One night, when the old man was so cold he couldn't stand it any more and his daughter Gabriela Spica was sleeping again, he woke her and said, take your bow and launch an arrow into the very centre of the spinning universe and bring down fire so that we can be warm.

She wasn't keen to get out of her bed, but she did as her father asked because she was a very good daughter."

"Did they have a Mami?"

"They must have had a Mami once, but she doesn't come into this story. So Gabriela Spica went outside into the cold night air, raised her bow and shot an arrow straight at the heart of the universe. Her aim was perfect and the arrow brought down fire. Her father quickly gathered it up and took it inside their house and began to make himself warm. His beautiful daughter went inside too and made herself warm and fell asleep by the fire."

"Did the house catch on fire?"

"No, because they had made a special place for the fire. But they were the only ones who were warm and the old man kept the door shut to stay warm. Out in the cold, cold forest, a deer smelled the fire and made a plan. He put twigs and moss in his antlers then went near the house and danced and sang in a most attractive way. The beautiful Gabriela Spica woke up and heard the singing and liked it so much she opened the door. The deer came inside and continued to sing and dance which amazed the old man and his daughter. While they weren't looking, the deer bent his head to the flames and set light to the twigs in his antlers and ran out of the house and gave the fire to all the people in that land."

"Is it a true story?"

"It is so old that nobody knows if it's true, but like all very old stories, it gets better and better the more it's told."

8

"Let's have a day of not doing very much. We both have some new books, we could make a start with those."

They were almost home, the last few turns before the dip down to the bridge, clear blue above and late breakfasts inside them. If there was a day to not do much, Harry reckoned this was it. There was nothing pressing to be done and after the ten days they'd had it would do them both good to slop about. Their night under the stars had set them up well, despite having woken stiff and cool a little before dawn and stumbled to proper beds.

"Papatico, can I go out?" Gabriela said, without great enthusiasm.

"If you like. We'll put your new things away first, help me with that."

By the time they'd unpacked their bags and she'd paraded in some of her new clothes as they unwrapped them, the best of the day seemed to have gone. A steady breeze had sprung up and high cloud streamed in from the south, the usual forerunner of rain later in the day, although such signs were no longer to be trusted. The coffee on the verandah he'd been looking forward to suddenly seemed less appealing as the brightness of the day faded. Nearby a door banged shut in the wind. Gabriela slipped back into her usual beach clothes despite his suggestion she wear something new, something which might actually fit her.

"Not far today, please. Usual rules." he called after her as she headed out the back door. She turned and smiled, nodding her agreement. Seeing her there in that moment, framed by the doorway, he thought how lucky he was that she was such an easy child to live with. Not that he had experience of any other.

He tried settling, first to read then with his notebook, but found no concentration for either. A vague anxiety came over

135

him, as if waiting for a visitor who was late in arriving, yet he expected no one. The door banged again, Ernest's he guessed. The rising wind made him think of Gabriela in her tree, she was bound to be in her tree. He should call her down, but as he stood to leave the house the wind died to nothing. From the verandah he surveyed the beach and found it as deserted as ever. A gust ruffled the jicaros and the door or window, now certainly Ernest's, slammed against its frame once more.

Three times was too many. From the bottom of his steps his neighbour's house was half-hidden, so he walked further out along the beach. It was the side door, open by the look of it, with the screen swinging loose on its hinges. Of Ernest himself there was no sign. When the wind dropped there was no sound but the soft lap of water on the sand. Uncertain of himself, Harry waited to be sure he had the source correctly identified. As he turned away to look towards the Fairchild villa, the wind rose again, catching the swinging door and hammering it against the side of the house.

"Ernest!" he shouted as he headed towards his neighbour's, but there was no answer and the only movement was from the errant door. At the bottom of the steps he called again, then once more as he reached the verandah. This was as far as he'd ever been invited previously. The place was not unlike his own, but smaller, older perhaps, and shabbier. One of the two chairs was broken, the other had stuffing leaking from its seat cushion. Another smash of the door reminded him why he was there. He called again and peered through the window but could see nothing through the slats of the blinds. At least he could go and close the door and wedge it shut if need be.

At the side of the house he found the inner door open, held firm with a wedge. The screen door had a broken catch and he was about to close it with a rock to keep it so, but second thoughts made him place the rock so as to keep it open. He stood in the threshold and called again, loud enough that anyone in the house could not mistake his presence. He listened carefully but there was no answering call. Still Harry resisted the logic of entering, still he expected Ernest to come round the corner and ask him what he was up to.

Stepping back onto the verandah, Harry surveyed the beach. Everything as it always was, with the subtle difference of a changed angle of view. He bellowed "Ernest!" as loud as he could but only the wind answered him. At the door he hesitated briefly again before cautiously entering the kitchen. All appeared to be in order, no huge pile of dirty dishes nor a half-eaten meal on the table. In the living room he paused, letting his eyes become accustomed to the gloom. A sofa and two armchairs round a low table at one end, a dining table and chairs at the other. On a desk behind the sofa a screensaver whirled its ghostly pattern on a monitor.

A sound, or a hint of a sound, from another room took Harry's attention. He spoke Ernest's name again, softly as one would to a companion so as not to startle them. In the bedroom, also dark behind closed blinds, he found nothing but the unmade bed. A second bedroom held piles of books and boxes stacked against a wall, again with no suggestion of what could have drawn him there. The bathroom was equally uninformative. Turning back to the living room Harry saw what he'd missed before, a lamp overturned on the floor by the dining table. He moved forward with the idea of righting it and in doing so suddenly became aware of a human form lying beside it, white shirted, dark legged, limbs arranged as if in readiness for the chalk outline to be drawn.

A low groan escaped his lips as he stood motionless, staring at the body, wanting it to be a deception of the darkness, no more than a rug dropped on the floor, taking human shape to frighten an intruder. He would have to go to it, to Ernest, for surely it was Ernest, he would have to check for life although he was already convinced he would find none.

He could do nothing without light. Slowly he moved to the window and raised a blind enough to let him see the whole room. From his position by the window the body was again invisible, concealed behind an armchair. It might not be there, it might have been no more than a trick of the light. But it wasn't.

Harry stepped over him, over Ernest, for there was no mistaking him once there was light on his face. He was lying on his front, eyes closed, his head turned with the left cheek on the floor. As Harry touched his face he noticed a dark smudge of blood, no more than a graze, near Ernest's right temple. He cupped his neighbour's wrist in his hand, his fingers gently probing to find a pulse he knew would not be there. Some disengaged part of Harry's brain noted how Ernest's arm and wrist were still pliable and that death may have been very recent. Or days ago. The analysis went only so far before his knowledge was inadequate.

He should do something, he should do something urgently.

Gabriela. She should not see this.

"Papatico?"

He looked up, shocked that he could conjure her voice so easily. But it was no super-power, she was in the kitchen doorway, her arms hanging limp at her sides, eyes staring, her face expressionless.

"Gabriela, darling," he croaked, then placed Ernest's wrist gently back on the floor. Ernest was gone, Harry's duty lay with the living. He stood up and gingerly stepped across to her, then knelt beside her and wrapped his arms around her. She moved stiffly to keep sight of Ernest's body as Harry tried to block her view.

"Is Ernest dead?" she asked tentatively, more curious than distressed.

"Yes, I think he is. I'm sure he is."

"Why?"

"I don't know, he may have been very ill." He could have added *or he may have hit his head*, but he didn't.

They stayed like that, locked together, Gabriela looking past him at Ernest's corpse, for minutes or seconds, it was hard to measure the movement of time. Then Harry remembered that he needed to do something urgently and he eased her away from his embrace.

"Gabriela," he said quietly and evenly, looking her straight in the eye even though she was transfixed by the sight of a dead person. "We must call our friend Captain Diaz so he can decide what should happen now. We will go together and then come back."

She turned reluctantly, looking back at Ernest until she couldn't see him. He held her hand as they walked back to Casa Rosa, he feeling the need to speak but finding no words, she walking mechanically beside him, unable to quite comprehend how death meant someone could be there one minute and gone the next.

The number for the police post in Concepción gave an out-of-hours answering service. This was no emergency, but it wasn't something to be dealt with at leisure tomorrow. He could call Puerto Reunión, but it would mean delay and explanations he could do without. It occurred to him that Victor Diaz might be at the Kasanee, settling to a beer before his lunch. Carla answered when he called. Yes, Victor was there. Harry breathed again.

As he asked for him to be brought to the phone there was an urgency in his voice that Carla didn't recognise. "Harry, what is wrong? Are you all right? Gabriela! Mi cosita! ¿Ella esta bien?"

"Yes, Gabriela's all right, she's fine."

Then the policeman was there. "Señor Rose, what is so urgent?"

Harry told him.

"Ah, yes, that is urgent. Do nothing señor Rose, I will come. The sargento too, I will telephone, do nothing." The line clicked dead.

Harry wanted Gabriela close to him, but was wary of her wanting to go back into Ernest's house. She still clutched his hand as they retraced their steps along the sand, pausing momentarily to look up at the blank windows, now with one blind raised. There was no need to stand guard, to preserve a

139

scene, for there was nothing and no one to disturb it. They walked out to the point where they sat looking across the ocean, whipped into whitecaps by the stiffening breeze. From their position Harry could keep an eye on both the track and the house.

"Is Ernest dead for ever?" Gabriela said after they'd sat for a few minutes.

"Yes, my darling, for ever. Some people think otherwise. But as far as anyone really knows, it is for ever."

Gabriela considered this in silence, before asking, "What will happen?"

"We'll see when our friend arrives, he'll decide what happens. But I expect he'll call a doctor, not to make Ernest better, but to tell us why Ernest died and perhaps when he died. Captain Diaz will need to know those things."

"Will they bury him?"

"No, not here, not today. Maybe tomorrow, it depends what the doctor says about him. But I expect they'll take him away."

"Where to?"

"I'm not sure, but probably a special place called a morgue, a place where people are taken when they die. We'll ask about that later."

The sight of Victor Diaz's cruiser on the track forestalled further discussion, for which Harry was grateful. At least Gabriela had asked questions. In her way she was more able to talk of Ernest's death than he was.

No sooner had the car stopped than a second appeared at the far end of the track, lights and siren at full bore. Apparently the sergeant had little opportunity to use them. The silence was all the greater when he came to a halt beside them.

Victor Diaz invited Harry to lead the way, "Please show me, señor Rose."

Harry led them across the sand to the front of the house where he asked Gabriela to wait with the sergeant while he and the captain went inside.

140

"Will you be back soon?" she asked unhappily, the first signs of distress curling her lips.

"Very soon. Then we'll go home."

Inside, Harry hung back while the captain crouched to examine Ernest. The view was the same as Gabriela must have had. He crouched down himself, to see what she had seen. How long had she been there, what brought her into the house?

"This is Ernest Portillo?" said the policeman, "I haven't seen him for some time."

Harry had no doubt, but the question made him hesitate. "Yes, I think so. Who else would it be?"

He looked at the face closely then said, "I'm sure you are right, I think it is señor Portillo."

Satisfied, Victor Diaz stood and surveyed the room.

"Señor Rose, Harry, show me what you did. Touch nothing."

Harry demonstrated, moving to the bedrooms and pushing the doors open with his elbows even though he knew his fingers had already been on the handles. He repeated the pause when he'd first recognised a body in the gloom, then at the window he mimed opening the blind. "Then I did what you've just done."

"Thank you, we will write this down later."

"You think there's something wrong? Something..." Something what? Harry's thoughts raced across a dozen unlikely possibilities.

"Caution, Harry Rose, caution. I have called the doctor, he will be here soon I hope. And also I have called DIC in Puerto Reunión. They will take a little longer to be here. It is as well to be cautious."

"Is there something unusual?"

"It is unusual to be called at my meal in a bar, to be called by a friend who already is known to DIC and is presently accused of many things, even if they appear false, or so I am told. So, yes, I am cautious. Perhaps you should be also."

"And the mark?" Harry stroked his brow to indicate the bloody smudge at Ernest's temple.

"Yes, Harry Rose, there is a small mark which may be anything, but it is a small mark which makes me very happy to be cautious. You say Gabriela was here in this room?"

"Yes."

"We will speak to her together, before anyone arrives, yes?"

They left the house, the captain closing the screen door behind them. Gabriela was sitting on the steps with the sergeant who scrambled to his feet as they came to the verandah. Gabriela came to Harry's outstretched arms immediately.

"Let's go home, at least for a little while. Another policeman is coming and a doctor, as we had guessed. They may want to speak to us, we'll see. Will you join us, capitán Diaz?"

From the steps they turned towards Casa Rosa, only to find the Fairchilds, arm in arm, almost upon them, he short and broad in faded beach clothes, she petite in a blue satin sheath of a dress, immaculate as always, and concealed behind reflective sunglasses.

"Harry!" Bill Fairchild exclaimed in his usual louder-than-necessary voice. "What's going on? Some drama?"

"Ah, Bill, do you know Captain Diaz, from the police in Concepción? Captain, these are my neighbours señora Pérez-Fairchild and señor Fairchild." As he spoke, Gabriela curled herself behind him, attempting to become invisible.

"Señora, señor. Sadly, your neighbour, el señor Portillo, he has died."

"No! Poor guy," the little American said with genuine feeling. Then, looking about him, he added, "And, er, this needs the cops? Sirens, lights, all on a Sunday morning. Something not right, Diaz?"

"Everything is right, señor Fairchild, I was telling señor Rose, we must always be cautious in such matters."

Harry wondered if in all the years he'd known Victor Diaz he'd underestimated him. He'd not seen him in action until his own recent troubles, but he could be as smooth as silk, and perceptive too.

"You were friends with el señor Portillo, you knew him well?" the captain continued.

"No, no, we hardly ever saw him, not socially. He was a neighbour, nothing more." Having been keen to know the inside story, Bill Fairchild drew back, now placing as much distance as he could between himself and his deceased neighbour.

"I wonder when you last saw el señor? Today, yesterday?"

"No, no, weeks, it must be weeks."

"And excuse me, but señora Pérez, did you see him?"

Dolores Pérez maintained her tight, fixed smile and shook her head. Harry noticed the slightest tug on her husband's arm and they turned to leave.

"We'd better leave you guys to it," Bill said casually, then remembering his manners, called over his shoulder, "Good to meet you, Diaz. Come over for a beer later if you like, you too Harry, it's been a while."

"I thought you'd met them before," Harry said when they couple were further away and they'd begun to walk towards Casa Rosa.

"No, you have spoken of them, that is all."

On any other day, Gabriela might have scampered ahead or to the water's edge, but she walked almost on Harry's feet, clinging resolutely to his arm. Even as they mounted the steps to the house she stayed close. She hung in the doorway while Harry cut bread and fruit and cheese, then pulled a cushion on the floor beside his feet while they ate it.

"Not what you were having at the Kasanee, Victor, but something."

"It is perfect, thank you. I must go back in a few minutes, for the doctor. Harry, tell me, why did you go into the house?"

Harry explained again about the screen door, thinking he'd already done so.

"Yes, yes, of course and Gabriela, you heard the door too and went to the house?" he asked, as if he was simply including her in the conversation.

"Papatico was shouting really loud, so I went to find him."

"Yes, yes, that was it. And when you were there, your Papatico was still shouting, eh?"

Gabriela pulled her face that said she was thinking really hard about an answer and Victor let her think. After a few moments she said, "No, Papatico was calling quietly, like Ernest, Ernest," making a low, urgent whisper of the name.

"Ah, so you went in. A bad surprise for you. And dear Ernest, like a man asleep, would you say?"

She nodded. "Papatico was holding his hand." She demonstrated with her own limp wrist. "I don't know why."

"To see if he could help, I'm sure. It is a difficult thing, Gabriela, mi querida, difficult for you, difficult for Papatico, for me too. You and your Papatico will help each other. But now I must return to meet the doctor and maybe soon the DIC. I think it will be the man you have met before, el investigador Scott."

The captain rose and turned to leave the house across the verandah. Harry caught up with him. "Victor, thank you for how you did that," he said, holding out his hand in friendship.

The policeman took the hand in his, saying, "I already knew the answers, Harry Rose, but remember, I am also cautious."

Harry and Gabriela watched as he walked back across the sand. The sky had darkened as the clouds became lower and the wind steadier, yet the usual humidity was absent. It was a peculiar, unsatisfactory day in every way. And now they would fiddle at this and that and do nothing while he waited for the detective to come once again to his house.

On the sofa he reopened the book, determined to speed the passage of time by distraction, but the day's events and Gabriela's need to snuggle yet also fidgety and unsettled, defeated him. He wondered if Ernest was the first dead body she'd seen. Of another human, certainly, but what else had her seven years exposed her to? A dog by the road, an iguana maybe, chickens and fish at the market, but none of these would have prepared her for a dead person. Even less so a person who she was used to seeing and waving and shouting "Hola!", albeit at a distance. The more he thought about it the more he wondered if Gabriela

144

might have had more conversation with Ernest than he did, whether her roaming on the beach, along the track, climbing her tree, had given her closer contact than she'd mentioned. And he wondered if she'd been in his house before, he'd assumed not because she'd never mentioned it, but he might be wrong. He should know such a thing, a father would surely know such a thing.

"It's not bedtime, but would you like me to read one of your new books?"

He felt her nodding against his arm.

"You'd better choose one then."

Which meant she would have to fetch it. He could almost hear her agonising over the dilemma: stay close, or get a book and have her Papatico read to her. She leapt up suddenly, rushed to her room and flung herself back on the sofa clutching *Matilda,* which, of the several she'd chosen in San Felipe, was the one he hoped she'd select.

They settled together again, her fidgeting gone, the familiar resonance of his voice and the comfort of a story smoothing her troubles away. By the time he'd turned a few pages and the brilliant heroine had been introduced, Gabriela's long night under the stars and the troubles of her day had her fast asleep.

★

In the police post Harry once again became señor Rose. He wondered if from that point on it would always be señor Rose in public, Harry for private. Perhaps it should always have been so, although Victor Diaz could not have predicted his friend's troubles. He left Gabriela in the pickup while he wrote out the sequence of the previous day's grim events. When the captain was satisfied, Harry signed it and was given a copy. It appeared to conclude the whole matter, but Harry wasn't keen to let Ernest go so easily.

"Does he have any family?" he asked.

"Maybe, we are not sure, but a brother perhaps and a nephew, in Puerto Reunión. We will hear soon,"

145

"Where did they take him yesterday?"

"The clinic, there is an examination today. We will know more then."

They considered the motion of the ceiling fan for a few moments before the captain shuffled his papers to remind Harry that one of them had work to do.

With her head firmly in *Matilda*, Gabriela hadn't noticed her Papatico had been gone twice as long as he'd intended. Come the evening, when he would read to her again, he'd start where he'd left off, regardless of progress she might have made on her own. It brought them different pleasures and the maximum from the book.

At the school she wanted to stay reading in the truck, but Harry thought otherwise. She could read as easily inside as in the cab. They waited by the administrator's office for half an hour before she could see them and then the interview was extremely short. No, the school had heard nothing from the ministry, but they had received a message from La Agencia de Protección de los Niños. Mention of this caused the woman to give both Harry and Gabriela a very hard look, as if she were surprised to see no malnutrition or bruises. She informed them that Gabriela should come back later in the week for an assessment in preparation for attendance, it would take an hour or so.

Their reception at the Kasanee was more welcoming, Leo and Carla both fussing over Gabriela then putting her eagerly to work collecting a few glasses. On a quiet Monday there was little for anyone to do and it wasn't long before she was back at the table, back with her book. When Leo brought their casado he brought his own plate to eat with them.

"Do you know what happened with Ernest Portillo?" he asked as soon as he was seated.

"News travels quickly, Leo. No, he died, yesterday morning I think, but that's all I know." He could have said a lot more, but would have added nothing to the plain facts.

"It was on the death notices," Leo said, inclining his head towards the TV screen over the bar. "They said family should call."

"Did you know him?"

"No, we knew his name, knew he lived near to you, he was at the market sometimes. They say he's been on the island for many years."

"Before me, that's for sure. he was here when I first came, when I used to come and stay with Brian Carter. I inherited Ernest Portillo as a neighbour."

Leo seemed to lose interest once his most likely source had nothing juicy to reveal and their conversation meandered around a dozen topics before the meal was eaten and there was nothing to keep them at the table. Gabriela was absorbed in her own world, and Harry felt an urgent need to speak to Julio, and if not Julio, then Elena's clever cousin Indira Chavarria.

To Harry's slight surprise Julio was available when he called.

"Before I forget, my laptop. How do I get it back?"

"I'll ask la señorita Chavarria to make enquiries," was Julio's almost predictable response.

"Good. Some sad news, Julio, my neighbour Ernest Portillo has died, yesterday morning." He went on to outline the circumstances and the rôle he and Gabriela had played in events. "There's an investigation of some kind, I thought you should know. But also, I remember he's mentioned in the property papers, about the access across the Casa Rosa property to his place. Could you check it for me, better to be aware than find some surprise when it's sold, or a grandchild suddenly appears claiming it."

"I will look. Is there anything else?"

"Gabriela goes to school for assessment on Thursday, we had a cool reception there today. Otherwise, no nothing else for now."

"I have something for you. La señorita Chavarria has been investigating two possibilities that may be beneficial. The first is quite simple. It is to establish Casa Rosa as Gabriela's normal residence before her mother disappeared. It is for this she will

147

need the documents from the Kasanee. They are not much, but they are something. The second is more difficult. It concerns the wording of the law for children and the word *autorizado,* or authorised. There is a list of such authorised places but nowhere does it say that these are the only places. Also, it suggests that *autorizado* means by the court, but again it is not stated. La señorita thinks perhaps la señorita Estefanía Flores' *autorizado* is the highest authority, as the mother. We need to find her registration and Gabriela's to prove the relationship, but it is a possible way."

"Will she go to court in San Felipe?"

"No, that may be for me to do later, but first she will seek approval from the judge in Puerto Reunión. It is respectful. And it allows the judge to consider the argument without having to respond. La juez Cruz will not simply agree, it will be a matter for a higher judge to decide, but she can agree for us to ask a higher judge."

"Is there any chance it could work?" Harry asked warily. False hope was something he had no need of.

"Yes, certainly a chance. But also if la juez Cruz agrees to the question then it could take some time to be decided and she will not make another order for Gabriela as long as a higher judge is considering the question."

"Ah, I see, a tactic. Indira Chavarria is the legal Wonder Woman once again. You should buy her a cape, Julio."

"Good, yes!" Julio laughed, "Or you should, Harry, ask her. Can you meet her in Puerto Reunión tomorrow at twelve for the papers and your signature?"

★

Gabriela did not want to go to Puerto Reunión and Harry could understand why. She was a little anxious at the prospect of the unknown world of school and had no interest in lunch with a woman she didn't know, but who was somehow connected to her Papatico's troubles. He had his own reservations. He couldn't see Indira Chavarria without also seeing Estefanía. Julio might

148

have brushed it off but if Gabriela saw the same likeness, or worse, mistook la señorita for her mother, that would be a miserable confusion for her to deal with.

He might once have left her with Carla and Leo, but it felt too much like abandoning her in public, which would only risk more gossip. And Pippa was busy teaching two visiting Argentinian ladies how to use light and shade to reveal subtle form and substance in their painting, a world he never entered uninvited. His circle, their circle, had become very small, Gabriela must accompany him and he must be ready for whatever came of the encounter with Indira Chavarria.

From his seat at the restaurant, chosen with the moment in mind, Harry could see the student lawyer as she approached. Smart, confident, purposeful. Anyone else seeing her might think the same but of all the people in the town, he alone knew the assessment to be correct. Apart from perhaps the judge and maybe even señora Mejía. She did look like Estefanía Flores, put her in a cheap dress and scuffed sandals instead of her black and white court clothes and the likeness would surely be irresistible.

"Señorita, good morning," Harry said, standing to greet her.

"Señor Rose," she smiled.

Harry watched as Gabriela lifted her eyes from her book to assess the young woman. Not a flicker of recognition crossed her face. Then she caught Harry's expectant look and remembered her manners. "Good morning señorita," she said quietly.

"Ah, you are Gabriela, yes?" Indira Chavarria said warmly, crouching to be at the child's level. "Your Papá has said many things about you, good things."

"Thank you, señorita."

"Please, Gabriela, will you call me Indira?"

She nodded.

"Good. We will eat and your Papá and I have some papers to look at, then you can tell me everything there is to know about you. We can start with your books, yes?"

She nodded again, this time with her big gappy smile.

"When will you see la juez Cruz?"

149

"Today, if I can. I telephoned and spoke to her assistant. If not today I will come tomorrow or the day after. It is better to be done in person, it remains informal, it commits nobody. I will ask permission which is also a way of asking her opinion. I know you do not agree, señor Rose, but la juez Cruz is really on our side."

"You may be right. It's difficult to believe."

She looked at the papers he'd brought while he read the statement she'd prepared for him.

"I haven't signed so many papers in years," he said a little ruefully. When she looked quizzical he told her of Ernest's death and his and Gabriela's parts in the day's events.

"It is difficult at any time, more difficult when we are young," she said, looking at Gabriela with a softness in her expression Harry hadn't noticed before.

"Do you have brothers and sisters, señorita?"

Again the hint of embarrassment, again the cast down eyes, as if she had been caught being less than cool and detached. Again he saw Estefanía and looked quickly at Gabriela to see if she had noticed too, but there was no reaction.

"Ah, yes, I do," Indira Chavarria said, but didn't expand on the simple fact.

The answer, or lack of it, blunted the conversation. For the first time since Harry and the almost-lawyer had met, the silence between them became uneasy. Gabriela was oblivious to any difficulty and took the lull in conversation as an opportunity to share *Matilda* with her new friend. Indira had charmed the judge, charmed the impressive señora Mejía, charmed Harry and certainly impressed him, so yes, of course she could charm a seven year-old. And yet it did not seem to him that Indira Chavarria's way with Gabriela was anything but genuine. Squinting his eyes he might as well have been watching big sister and little sister.

Did Gabriela have some subliminal recognition that opened her so easily to conversation and giggles? What was her memory of her mother? Harry imagined if Estefanía should suddenly appear, as the waitress or another customer, someone out of context and without any expectation, Gabriela might simply ignore her. Even if confronted with the fact, she would be shocked, wary, reluctant to accept such a thing as true. It might be that she would only recognise her mother again if her reappearance was anticipated on this day or that, if she was dressed as she left, if the slide was in her hair, if she smiled and ran towards her daughter arms outstretched. Maybe the cues and context were more important than a blurry photograph from two years previously or any number of days spent together. Gabriela being scared of forgetting her Mami was more likely a cry of pain that she had already done so.

9

Any expectation Harry had of Gabriela skipping happily out of the assessment with a gold star pinned to her shirt was quickly dispelled. Her face wore the expression of guilty failure, exaggerated by the down-turned corners of her mouth and wide eyes. He'd told her there was no pass or fail, she was to do her best, as always, but there was no right or wrong. And he'd had some confidence that her abilities would be at least the equal of her peers. Her face, and the face of the assessor, la señora Ruiz Acuna, told a different story.

"Hey, Gabriela, what's up my darling? Such a long face."

"I can't write properly," she said mournfully.

That was a shock, but even as she said it he guessed the truth of it, for writing had never featured much in their classroom. His emphasis had always been on learning and using knowledge, hardly ever on regurgitating facts.

"Well, we can fix that, and your reading must more than make up for it," he said hopefully.

She made her non-committal don't-know face with its accompanying shrug.

"Señor Rose, you are right," la señora said, "Gabriela reads well, it's very important and she does well in Spanish and English, but reading is not enough."

There was a hint of condescension in the teacher's tone, a hint that Harry didn't warm to.

"It is the key to everything else."

"Perhaps. But she is a long way behind in other things too, her written mathematics, she has no knowledge of religion, little of music, nothing of our history. Her writing is poor as she has said, but I found she has little skill with a keyboard too. Gabriela says you don't use a computer or a tablet very much, I was surprised to hear that."

"We don't, we have books," too few, he knew as he said it, "and we look at the world around us, we learn from that. Her geography is good, she knows a great deal of the solar system and the stars. And her art is excellent."

"These are valuable achievements," she said, choosing her words carefully, "and they will serve Gabriela very well in the future. She, and you señor Rose, should be proud of such achievements, but for now they put us in a difficult position. Which class, which part of the learning cycle of the school, should Gabriela attend? She is far behind in some things, far ahead in her reading and language. I must talk with the head teacher. We may need to provide a special program for Gabriela."

For a moment Harry had thought la señora Ruiz was going to refuse Gabriela a place in the school. His body had tensed in anticipation of a fresh confrontation with bureaucracy, but instead the teacher was talking of making a special place for her.

"Oh, yes, right," was all he could manage until he remembered that there were others with an interest in her schooling. "Have you any idea when she might be able to start?"

"She should come tomorrow, I think the morning class, it is a smaller group than the afternoon. It will be a day for Gabriela to become familiar with the school. She has her uniform?"

Harry shook his head. For years he'd seen the children of Concepción in their familiar white tops and blue bottoms without ever really considering it a uniform.

"It is simple," señora Ruiz reassured him, "we have some spare for accidents and for charity, I will find some for her. Later you can take her to Puerto Reunión, there is a store there. We have a selection here to buy at the beginning of the year, but not now."

Setting out on her school life in used clothes from the lost-property basket didn't sound like the start he wanted for her, but he thought it better to accept the offer with a good grace, even if she never wore them. He was already counting the minutes until the next departure of *Espíritu de las Islas*.

By the time they left the school with Gabriela reluctantly carrying the little bundle of clothes, a blast on the ferry's horn told them they'd have to wait for its return. She'd said nothing while la señora Ruiz had held up a selection of once-white tops against her body, nor had she spoken as she was required to step into faded blue skirts that hung in heavy pleats below her knees. Her dejected expression during these fittings more than made up for her silence.

"Papatico," she ventured, "will I go to school every day?"

"No, a normal week will be five days, in the mornings, at the weekend there is no school. And then there are other days, holidays, when there's no school."

She didn't answer him, but considered the information carefully while staring straight ahead.

"I'll be a few minutes, no more, I promise," he said as he stopped in the side street by the police post.

Gabriela nodded but still said nothing. She was disappointed by the teacher's reaction to the assessment, uncertain about the clothes she was expected to wear, yet to Harry there was more to it than that. He paused to let her speak if words were ready, but none came.

Victor Diaz was in the outer office when he stepped inside, arriving or leaving, Harry wasn't sure which.

"Victor, er, capitán Diaz," he corrected himself, remembering their new public formality, "good morning. Is there any news of Ernest Portillo?"

"Good morning, señor Rose. Yes, I am told everything is normal, el señor Portillo had a heart condition. There are more tests, but…" he shrugged as if to dismiss further speculation.

"Poor Ernest, you never know do you? The funeral, do you know anything, are there relatives? If not then I'd be happy to…" he trailed off, not sure what he'd be happy to do.

"There is a nephew, Oscar, his brother's son, he will come maybe today, maybe tomorrow, he says he will make arrangements."

★

The clothing store in Puerto Reunión didn't carry the full range of sizes other than at the start of the school year, so Gabriela would have to wear the charity skirt she'd been given at school until her order arrived. At least she had a smart new top, whiter than white and with a crisp red and blue badge. In fresh blue socks and her new shoes she almost looked the part, even if she didn't look like Gabriela. The skirt was the real sticking point, an item of clothing she hardly ever wore, but Harry insisted. Yes, he would ask if girls were allowed to wear shorts, but for her first day she would, unfortunately, just have to put up with it.

"Can I wear my shorts underneath?"

He couldn't think of a single reason to say no. "Try them, we'll see."

She did. They were invisible beneath the blue pleats.

There wasn't much to go in her new bag apart from a notebook and set of pens and pencils, so they added her current favourite, Spanish *Matilda*, and an old one, English *Charlotte's Web*. Her writing may be poor but she could play to her strengths with those two.

With what he calculated were ten minutes to spare, they set off for Concepción. At the point where the drive joined the main track by her tree, he paused slightly to check for any other vehicles. It was habit, there wouldn't be another vehicle, but in looking he caught sight of Gabriela's face and the tears on her cheeks.

He stopped the truck and slid across the seat to be closer, putting an arm around her, encouraging her to lean into him. Little tremors rippled through her, interrupted by shudders of breath. He let her cry without question until her movement subsided and her breathing became calmer. First day nerves or something else? She had a wide selection of things to be tearful about, the only surprise being how little she wept. He put a hand to her head, holding her close and kissing her hair.

155

They could see and hear the ocean no more than thirty metres away, the rhythmic sound a soothing balm for the most unhappy of spirits. To their left the track looped down to the point and Ernest's house, the scene of her most recent trauma. The way to town and school lay to their right, with today's test still to come. And beside them was her tree, the old roble de sabana, the so-called savannah oak. Her tree. It was no more an oak than it was a pine, it was a pink trumpet tree which at unpredictable intervals, as now, would suddenly burst into glorious flower. Perhaps it was no coincidence that the tears came at this point in their journey.

"Did everything just get too much, my darling? These are difficult days, I know. We all expect so much of you, we all think you're so strong, so smart, you'll cope with everything. You are so good I forget how hard it is for you. You know you can ask me anything, tell me anything."

She groaned, half cry, half moan, with more sorrow than any child should have, a sound to break a man's heart. He felt tears pricking his own eyes.

"Is there something, a single something, worrying you right now?"

He felt her nod into his shoulder.

"You can tell me."

She mumbled into his shirt, speaking with the safety of not being heard. Harry eased her away, brushing back the strands of hair sticking to her face. "Tell me," he whispered.

"If Mami comes back while I'm at school she won't know where I am."

It was true, she wouldn't. There were plenty of logical, sensible, grown-up answers he could give her, but none that would address her real fear, that her Mami had gone forever and they would never find each other again.

"You're quite right," he said, cupping her chin in his hands. "And not only school, but all the other times we are away. We should leave her a message whenever we aren't at home. Shall we go back and do that now?"

"Can we?"

"Yes."

He turned the truck and headed back to Casa Rosa, unhurriedly and without thought to their appointment with la señora Ruiz at school. Here was his priority, here was Gabriela's, others could judge as they wished. In the house they each wrote notes, Gabriela's to be in her bedroom, his folded like a tent on Estefanía's bed. Longer letters could follow, but these would serve their purpose for now.

Their reception at the school was frosty, but Harry was unapologetic, explaining only that they'd set out in good time but an urgent personal matter had arisen and they'd needed to turn back. Gabriela's spirits had been lifted to something like her normal self, but he still watched her disappear into the classroom with the same apprehension as every parent on the first day of school. It went further, for when he stepped out ready to head home, he found himself alone, suddenly without his responsibility and the easy closeness of her company. He'd made no plans for his day, unaware until that moment that he needed any.

At the house he mooched around, unable to settle, unable to concentrate for more than a few minutes at a time. The beach held no attraction, particularly with Ernest's house standing mute, glowering down at the sand, the blind at a crooked angle where he'd half raised it to better view the body. It was tempting to go inside and close it.

It could have been a day to visit the Fairchild villa, to accept that latest offer of a beer, but that would always be an afternoon event or, more likely, an evening one. The prospect of small talk and the inevitable references to the Kasanee, to Estefanía and now of course to Ernest, held no attraction for him. Reflecting on their recent brief encounter, it seemed to Harry there was a distance between him and his neighbours which he'd never noticed before. Perhaps it was too long since they'd last shared a beer, perhaps it was the occasion or the presence of Victor Diaz, but something was different. People change, by experience or circumstance, who was to say how much the last two weeks had changed him, perhaps it was he who was different, not the Fairchilds.

A little after ten, when he'd already started checking his watch to see if he should be leaving to collect Gabriela, Julio called.

"I have some news for you, Harry."

"My computer?"

"No, nothing on that. Something else. We seem to have found Estefanía Flores' registration at last. There weren't many places left, it may be that we'll find Gabriela's there too. The copy we've seen is not a good one, but la señorita Chavarria is confident and I think she is right. The details are of Estefanía Gabriela Flores Blanca, the name looks right and also the age, it makes her twenty-four. Registered by her mother, also a Gabriela, Cristin Gabriela Blanca."

His Gabriela's true grandmother. Harry had hardly given that possibility any thought at all. Another way to lose her.

"That's fantastic, a lot of hard work, where was it?"

"In the north, in San Carlos, there was a dispute over the records, there still is, so they have never..."

"San Carlos? The San Carlos I know, the San Carlos near the site at Rio de Los Angeles?" Harry's head was spinning, surely it couldn't be the town he'd once known so well.

"Yes! I hadn't thought of that, I will check, but yes, it must be. A long time since you were there, Harry."

It was. Probably ten years since he'd visited briefly, twenty since he'd lived a few miles down the road in the purpose-built ex-pat enclave close to the dam site. There, he'd had pretty much everything provided for him, but little to relieve the boredom. The company clubhouse wasn't a place to relax or take a drink, whereas San Carlos could at least boast a couple of good bars. Not that the town could boast of much else, it was a dreary place which had been the main beneficiary of the money brought in by the hydro project.

Twenty years ago he might have seen Estefanía's mother, he might have seen the four-year-old Estefanía. Her mother,

Cristin, could have worked in a bar, served him a beer, or brought his chifrijo to his table. But he'd first been to San Carlos many years previously, before Estefanía had been born or even thought of. Other ghosts stirred in other rooms, softly rattling their chains and finding the creak in dusty floorboards.

"Harry? It is good news, do you think? I feel sure we will find Gabriela in San Carlos also."

"Yes, good news and you're probably right." He hesitated over his next suggestion before continuing, "Um, if the records from San Carlos are not being submitted, I wonder, should we look also at the records of marriage, and I don't like to say it, but possibly death too?" He didn't want there to be any such records. A month ago he'd have been happy if they'd fallen between the cracks of a bureaucratic dispute, but now was different. Answers should be found if answers existed, for if not now, when?

"You are right," Julio enthused, "I will ask la señorita Chavarria to extend the search. La señorita is driving to San Carlos as we speak."

Faster than a speeding bullet, no doubt. It was an uncharitable thought, but Harry said, "Good. I will say nothing to Gabriela for now," and wondered why he would feel so cynical about Indira Chavarria after all she had done for him and for Gabriela.

Harry could hardly wait for the conversation to finish, for the goodbyes to be said. Until it was, he felt as if he were holding his breath, every word an effort, unable to think of anything but this new revelation. His thoughts raced over wild possibilities from the wholly innocent to the darkest. Dear God, he might have slept with Estefanía's mother!

There was still an hour before Gabriela would finish school. The pink sand he'd spurned thirty minutes previously became his thinking ground as he paced the waterline, regardless of Ernest's house or any other distractions. He knew well enough it could be purely coincidental, so far as he knew it certainly *was* coincidental, there was simply no connection between himself and Estefanía or her mother. They had probably been in the same town at the same time for a short period in their lives. So

159

what? Wasn't everyone in the same town as thousands of other people for short periods of their lives? The fact has no meaning, no significance. Later in life we sometimes meet someone from that town and it still has no significance. Weren't human brains designed to search for patterns in everything? But the search doesn't mean a pattern exists, even if we wish it were so.

All this he knew. And yet.

Who in San Carlos today would have reason to remember him? Not the taxi drivers who doubled in number as the project progressed, then doubled again as the managers and technicians came to stay. And as the numbers doubled so did the fares, although they could have risen a hundredfold for all the difference it made to the expenses-paid passengers. The fees for the extras also rose steadily, since supply did not increase as quickly or as easily as the taxis: a twist of weed, quality debatable, once the price of a shot of rye, ended nearer to the cost of a bottle; a couple of hours with a little slip of a girl, quality also debatable, leapt from the cost of a bottle to the cost of six. And the fees for everything were collected by the same taxi drivers who delivered and collected the goods. Weed, girls, pizza, whisky: just pay the driver – US dollars, preferably.

Bar keepers and taxi drivers, these had been his only regular contacts among the citizens of that seedy border town, yet who remembered such people without special cause? And who would be remembered by them? Certainly not the sweating bartenders who barely looked at the drinkers who barely looked at them. Nor the barmaids, all curls and flesh, who hardly looked at the drinkers who always looked at the barmaids, even if those looks rarely rose above breast height.

A few might remember an ill-mannered young man from Indianapolis whose head collided with a blunt instrument one night, but even now that he thought of him, Harry could not recall his name, nor what he looked like. Had the perpetrator ever been called to account? Again, memory did not provide an answer. Somebody's son was killed that night, a tragedy for those

160

closest, yet the years had reduced the event to an impersonal footnote.

There was another guy who should remember how lucky he'd been to be abruptly re-assigned to a project on another continent just as an angry husband came looking for the gringo who'd cuckolded him. A gringo who'd added insult to injury by casually bragging about it to the husband's brother. Perhaps the husband and the wife remembered too, but Harry wasn't either, nor was he that gringo. That had been another drama of the moment, now anonymous as it slipped back in time to become no more than an anecdote, perhaps recounted by someone's drunken uncle at a family wedding.

Harry had no reason to remember Cristin Blanca nor the infant Estefanía, of that he was certain, but had they reason to remember him? If they did, then what? It could change everything or change nothing. But what event, trivial to him perhaps, could possibly have made a lasting impression on Cristin?

He might walk by the lapping ocean all day and still have no answer.

The fact was Cristin was Gabriela's grandmother, which might change everything on its own. Should he try and find her in San Carlos? Wouldn't she have first claim on Gabriela? Surely she'd want her granddaughter, want to keep her there, she'd never sanction her staying with him at Casa Rosa. He might keep very quiet about his girl's family, but so long as Julio and his clever assistant knew the facts, this genie would not go back in its bottle. If la señora Mejía didn't take her, la señora Blanca would. And if he wouldn't deny La Agencia, he couldn't deny the grandmother.

A single question pulled him up short. Had Estefanía recognised him on that bus ride from San Felipe? And if not exactly recognised, had some half-memory been stirred in that desperate young woman's head? Yes, the bus was pure chance, it could be nothing else, but everything since then, could events have been helped along by design?

161

Meanwhile, Estefanía's baby would be waiting at the school gate, bursting to talk with her head full of her day while he'd have his head full of San Carlos. The pickup coughed and stuttered until Harry swore loudly, at which it started obediently. He should get it looked at, it was an anxiety he could do without, but he'd been thinking that for a few months.

Outside the school a dozen or so mothers were gathered, chatting as mothers do. Harry parked nearby, then walked towards the gate, ready to nod or smile or share a friendly word or two. The conversations ceased as he approached, only suspicious stares greeted him. Too tall, too pale, too old – what was his business there? Although, when he gave it a little more thought, more likely they all knew his business there, and half his history along with the worst of the rumours. As he waited, muttered exchanges resumed, animated by sideways looks and rolled eyes.

As the children began to emerge he realised that only the youngest were being met by their mothers, the rest, apart from Gabriela, were heading home on their own or in twos and threes according to their routes. He was worried he wouldn't recognise her in the flow of uniforms, but he spotted her at the same instant she caught sight of him. She walked alone, straight faced, looking only for her Papatico, no smiles or goodbyes to new friends.

His instinct was to open his arms and pick her up and twirl her round, but he was uncertain how such a show of affection might be regarded by the watching eyes. Instead he said, "Did that go all right?" and took her hand. She said nothing, but her don't-know-don't-care face told him all he needed to know: it hadn't gone well and she wasn't ready to talk about it.

"I thought we might go to see Pippa after we've had something to eat. What do you think?" he asked, when they'd climbed into the truck.

She nodded, which was better than don't care.

★

Visiting Pippa turned into an overnight stay, which they both knew it might, then Saturday was slow to start until Gabriela began a new painting, her subject of choice being the iguana who'd hung around the patio most of the evening. Harry thought it was a bit ambitious, although he didn't let Gabriela hear him say so. Nothing wrong with ambition, was Pippa's reproach, which she made sure Gabriela did hear.

After the three of them had shared a meal at the Kasanee, Harry and Gabriela wound their way home to Casa Rosa. At the turn close to her tree they could see a car parked down at the point by Ernest's. Harry's interest in visitors had been sharpened by recent events, even to the extent that he felt protective of Ernest's house and belongings. Word gets round quickly when a man dies and leaves his home unattended.

Leaving Gabriela to her own distractions, he walked across the sand and paused at the bottom of the steps. The half raised blind had been straightened and two more had been pulled up. As he reached the verandah, a short, middle-aged man, overweight and balding, appeared from around the side of the house.

"You are señor Rose?" he said before Harry could speak. "I am señor Oscar Portillo, el señor Ernest Portillo was the brother of my father. You live there, yes?" He pointed towards Casa Rosa.

"Yes, we live there." Harry held out a hand which Ernest's nephew shook limply with short fat fingers, cool and damp. "I'm sorry for your loss, señor."

"Ah, yes, yes, thank you señor Rose, he was a good man I think."

The introductions over and condolences given, there seemed little else to say, and they stood in awkward silence for a few moments. Did Oscar Portillo know, or care, that Harry had found his uncle's body? The little man suddenly stepped forward and spread his arms as if to embrace the whole of the bay.

"It is a fine place this, eh?"

"We like it. Have you been here before? To see Ernest?"

"No, no, not for years. As a child, yes, we came. It is as I remember it."

"And now? Will you live in the house?"

"Live here? Live here on Playa de Rosas? Ha, no, no, there is nothing here. It is beautiful but there is nothing. It is also for my sister, we will sell, maybe we have sold already, there are papers, she will have half, I will have half." He made a slicing motion with his stubby hand. "You will sell, señor Rose? I heard you will sell and leave soon."

"No, you heard wrong," Harry snapped back, too quickly, too sharp. More rumours and gossip. Where had his new neighbour picked that up? In Puerto Reunión? Had the story of his troubles spread from the island so quickly? He looked for a reason to end the conversation without appearing rude. Then it struck him that Oscar Portillo had used the same name, Playa de Rosas, as his accuser when she'd called La Agencia. A name he'd never heard spoken before, a name from a dusty property deed, had suddenly appeared twice.

"Perdón, señor Portillo, rumours, only rumours. We have thought of selling, I haven't decided yet, it is difficult at the moment."

The man nodded slowly and looked sideways at Harry. "Difficult, yes, I hear it is difficult," he said, the hint of a smile playing at the corners of his mouth.

Harry pushed back his growing distaste for Oscar Portillo in favour of extracting any useful snippets he might be reveal by flattery or cajoling. He began cautiously.

"You live in Puerto Reunión, señor Portillo?"

"Yes. Well, no, nearby, in Playa Sabina."

"Oh, a very beautiful place. Close to the ocean?"

"Three blocks back."

"Sometimes it is better. Sometimes a bigger house for the same money, eh?"

"Yes, it is a fine house, you should visit, señor Rose, you will be welcome."

"You are generous, thank you, I'd like that. Call me Harry, everybody calls me Harry." He held out his hand again to seal the contract.

"Yes, yes," he said accepting the shake, "Oscar, I am Oscar."

"You've made a good deal for this property?" Harry asked, lowering his head and his voice to emphasise the confidential nature of their discussion.

"Yes, we think so." He looked about him to be sure he would not be overheard. "It will be three times what we expected. My sister is very happy. I have told her it is not complete, there are papers and the lawyers, always the lawyers, eh?"

"Always the lawyers, Oscar. He's from the United States, your buyer, another gringo?" Harry waved towards Casa Rosa and the Fairchild villa, as if such an owner would complete a set.

"No, no, señor Rose, Harry. I think from San Felipe, but I am not certain of this."

Harry turned and looked out across the water, gentle ripples all the way to the reef, nothing to disturb the tranquillity of the whole world. He should keep what he had, and keep the chance of more to come.

"And Ernest, when will the funeral be? Will it be here on the island?"

"Ah, señor Rose, disculpe, the funeral was this morning in Puerto Reunión. I was here yesterday, I came to the house, but you were not here."

★

Halfway home on Monday morning it dawned on Harry that his world was as much altered by school life as Gabriela's. She attended, but he had mornings with holes in the middle, big gaps where once they'd made their classroom wherever they liked. He thought they might find a new rhythm given time, meanwhile he resolved to fill the morning with something more than checking his watch to see if it was time to pick her up. There had been no tears to make them late, neither had there been any smiles to hurry them along. He supposed that would also take time, for friendships to form, for newness to wear off, for her to find her place.

He repeated these thoughts when Indira Chavarria called mid-morning and asked about her.

"It'll take a while for her to settle, she has a lot to deal with," he said, "I think she's strong but I mustn't forget she's seven. My friend Pippa reminds me of that every time I see her. How was San Carlos, señorita?"

"I saw nothing of the town. I don't think there is much to see," she answered, chit-chat not being her strong suit. "I have a copy of la señorita Estefanía Flores' registration. I am sure it is correct. It is a step. Today, perhaps tomorrow, we may see details for Gabriela, but if we do not then it will become very difficult to find her. She may not be registered, or she is registered with another name. If that is so then we must start again, but without some information it will be difficult."

"Did you make any enquiries while you were there? I mean, did you ask about Estefanía or her family?"

"No, señor Rose. But the colleague who found the entry for la señorita will ask questions. She works in a law office in San Carlos, she is a careful. I suggested she should be, er, private."

"Discreet," he corrected, without any idea of why he felt the need to do so.

"Thank you, yes, she will be discreet."

"Do you have any connection, family connection, to San Carlos, señorita?"

"No, señor Rose, no connection," she answered quickly, "El señor Aguilar asks me to give some other news, señor Rose, news which he thinks is good for you and for Gabriela. First, la juez Cruz has sent a message today regarding the question of authority and the word *autorizado*. You remember we spoke of this in Puerto Reunión?"

"Delaying tactics, I think you said."

"Hmm, perhaps more than that. La juez agrees that the question may be put to the higher court, she makes no objection."

"Good, thank you, it was a clever idea you had."

"Perhaps not clever, señor Rose. It is all logic, a way of looking at things."

Harry wondered if Indira Chavarria might shrivel up and die if one day by some awful mistake she were to leave a compliment unchallenged or admit to a life outside of the law.

"You said first, is there more good news?"

"Yes, your computer will be returned. It will be sent to the administrator at El Tribunal Central de Familia in Puerto Reunión, where we saw la juez Cruz. I thought you would prefer that to collection in San Felipe. It may be tomorrow, perhaps later."

"Thanks. Anything else?"

"No, señor Rose. El señor Aguilar may speak with you soon."

"Please tell him I'd like that, I have something to ask him. Is there any news of my passport, can I have it back? I think Captain Diaz may still have it in his office."

"Do you need it?"

"No, señorita, I do not. But I would like it back."

When she'd gone, he wondered at the coolness, the distance, Indira Chavarria maintained. It was admirable in many ways, it spoke of calm, unemotional efficiency. In time, he thought, she would surely excel in her profession. One day she would sit where la juez Cruz sat, or more likely in the higher court where her clever idea for an appeal would be considered. She would be respected, she would speak at conferences, address the students at her old law school, she would be la juez Chavarria. But where would she show her warmth, her human frailty, who would she laugh and love with? For sure it would not be him. Perhaps being first introduced as a potential paedophile was an impenetrable barrier to friendship. Hell, she might detest the sight of him. And there was the extra problem of his friendship with her boss.

To give Gabriela a little space and to avoid running the gauntlet of parental hostility every day, they'd arranged to meet away from the school. He was there, parked and waiting far too early, then watched anxiously in the mirror for her to turn into the street as the time ticked down. She appeared almost to the minute he expected, not walking but running. A little way behind her came a group of children, no more than five or six. It seemed to Harry they were yelling and jeering at Gabriela. She was still thirty metres away when something whistled passed her head and skittered along the road. Harry jumped out of the cab and stood hands-on-hips facing Gabriela and her pursuers. She slowed slightly but the gang stopped abruptly then nonchalantly separated as if nothing had occurred.

He held the truck door open and she piled in without a backward glance.

"Not very nice," he said as they moved off.

She stared ahead, saying nothing. Stealing a glance, Harry saw the tear stains on her cheek. School is so vicious, children can be so vile, especially to the outsider, the newcomer. He felt the anger welling in him, anger fuelled by his impotence and her distress. He was her protector, yet once again he had no idea how best to do so.

He drove slowly, taking the scenic route, as if the longer the journey the further away the school would be. On his own he would have stopped, breathed the air and let the song of the ocean soothe his troubles, but he knew, without asking, Gabriela wanted to be home. And once home his guess was that she'd head straight for her tree and watch for her Mami.

"Will you tell me about it?" he asked as they swung round the last corner. "When you're ready, but soon, OK?"

She nodded. He counted it as a nod in the right direction. In less than a month some part of her innocence, her childhood, had been torn away by accusations and lies, threats and innuendo. Where once everything had shone out of her, now she was driving her miseries deeper inside herself.

It was as he had expected, as soon as they were in the house the school clothes were ripped off and left where they lay, their owner out the back door heading to her familiar eyrie.

"La señorita Chavarria gave me all the good news," he said when Julio called mid-afternoon. "She thinks she'll have

Gabriela's registration soon. I can't help but wonder what it'll tell us. There's something to be said for not knowing."

"Yes, my friend, it is often so, but whatever it contains, Gabriela needs it, it is for her. She will have many difficulties without it. But we don't have it yet, we must be patient, only a little longer I hope. How is our Gabriela today?"

"Not so good. School is proving to be hard for her. It's only her second day but she was chased by a little gang as she left. I may go in tomorrow and talk with the teacher. Although, maybe it's too soon and she's better left to fight her own battles, I don't know. How do you tell?"

"You can't. You can only do what you believe is best. I think poor Gabriela knows nothing of battles. The school should be told, they should be alert. It may pass. Do you know what caused it?"

"Not yet."

"You could try to find out. It may be nothing. I will ask Elena, she may have an idea of what you should do."

"Yes, or Cristela, she's grown now but nearer to those years than we are."

"There is more business, Harry, but first, la señorita Chavarria said you wished to speak to me."

Harry recounted his conversation with Oscar Portillo and the reference to Playa de Rosas. In the telling it seemed like a very thin link to anything of significance.

"No, it is interesting," Julio said. "I have the file for Casa Rosa here on my desk. You asked about access to el señor Ernest Portillo's house. In all the old papers the whole property is called Playa de Rosas, before it was divided."

"So it was a name anyone might've used. Older people might still remember it."

"Yes."

Harry thought for a few moments. "I don't think it gets us anywhere. The woman on the tape might be an older woman who has some local connection or knowledge. That's all. We could have guessed that already."

"It is possible. By the time you bought the property, it had become Casa Rosa. I don't see any names for el señor Portillo's house or for your other neighbours' property, la señora Pérez y el señor Fairchild. You were right to check on the details. Both of them travel across the Casa Rosa property, as you know. But it is for the owner of Casa Rosa to give permission to the owners, it is not automatic."

"Did I give permission when I bought Casa Rosa? I don't remember that."

"No, once it is given it cannot be taken away by a new owner of Casa Rosa. But a new owner of Ernest Portillo's house, such a new owner must have new permission, it is the same for both. It was written that way when the two portions were sold seventy years ago."

"That's weird. Why would anyone do that?"

"Once it was common, less so now, most have been replaced by new agreements. It was to protect the original seller when the land was divided for a new house, they could make sure their neighbours were only people they liked and it could only be sold again to people they liked. But your neighbours also have access from the ocean, there is no permission needed for that."

"I wonder if Oscar Portillo is aware of that, he said there were papers still to be signed and lawyers looking at them."

"And you say he is selling?"

"Yes. Can we find out who to?"

"There is a register of interests. If someone is buying they must register their interest so that objections can be made. Once it was for mortgages and inheritance, now it is for everything."

"And we can look?"

"Yes, there is a small fee, but it is public."

"Should we talk about money, Julio? I think there have already been many expenses."

"Thank you, one day perhaps, but that day is not today. Today we have other things to consider. La doctora, la pediatra, who saw Gabriela, she has sent a report. As we expected it is good, but there are small things to be considered, nothing unusual, she is

170

physically within the average for her age, mentally a little ahead. But she recommends Gabriela should visit la dentista soon, before all her teeth are present. I have a copy for you of course. I would like to send a copy to la juez Cruz and to la señora Mejía at la Agencia, with a message that Gabriela will see la dentista soon."

"Yes, certainly, I can do that."

"Good. You will remember also la doctora made a sample from Gabriela for DNA testing. Harry, soon I think we must consider that la señorita Estefanía Flores does not wish to be found or that sadly she may be dead. We find no record of her death so we wonder if perhaps she has died and yet she remains unknown. It is possible and perhaps we can be certain of whether this is true or not. Every day such deaths occur and people are not claimed by their families. In recent years samples are taken from such people. It is possible now to be sure, even many years later. But a family member is needed. For that we have Gabriela. We can limit the search to young women who have died since you last saw la señorita Flores. We can start in San Felipe, there is a procedure." Julio didn't ask permission, it wasn't Harry's to give, yet clearly he wanted Harry's agreement.

"If it gives us an answer, gives Gabriela an answer, then we should do it, although…" Although what? Harry's reservations were ill-formed: part suspicion, part wariness of piling fresh pain on Gabriela, plus a deep apprehension of where DNA matching might ultimately lead. He could see an irresistible logic which would demand further tests to prove or disprove a new claim or counter claim.

"You are unsure, Harry?"

"No, it should be done, but if it's more bad news we must be careful about what we tell Gabriela. And also *when* we tell her anything. My poor girl has so much to deal with without adding more misery."

A sound from the kitchen made him look up, what might she have overheard? He called out, "Gabriela?" as much to alert Julio as to bring her to him. She appeared in the doorway, her face half

171

hidden by a slice of cantaloupe. For an instant it appeared as a painted smile. The image hurt so much that the barb of pain lasted long after the melon had been eaten.

10

The next day they changed their meeting point, closer to the school gate and within sight of other parents. It removed the threat of pursuit but did little else to improve Gabriela's day. He saw no tear stains but guessed there had been a few shed. Again the wordless stare ahead once she reached the sanctuary of the pickup. Again the single nod when he asked if had been another bad day.

He let it go until they were half-way round the island where he stopped at a spot overlooking the ocean a little along the road from where they could've turned off to La Plantación. He let the engine idle for a few moments before switching off and rolling down the window to catch the breeze and the sound of the water. She still said nothing, but by her silence he knew she understood why they'd stopped.

"Look out there," he said as if surprised to find himself where they were, "off to the right, that's where you walked when you came down from Pippa's the other day. It's somewhere along there you found that fabulous float."

"Float?" Her voice was flat, quiet.

"The blue glass ball, the fishing float."

"It's at Pippa's. Pippa found it, she saw it first."

"Maybe she did, but the finding was both of you together. Neither of you would have found it without the other. Sometimes things are like that, a thing happens but it can't happen without another thing happening too."

He let this idea find a place before he went on, "I know you want to tell me about school, about what's going on there, what the bad things are. But I also know it's hard to tell me without some kind of help. Two good things can start happening when I understand why it's hurting so much. First, and this is the easy part, you'll feel a little better just because you have told me. That may be hard to believe but I promise you it's true.

"Second, the very moment I understand the problem, I can start helping you fix it. Whatever it is, I'm pretty sure it's going to need both of us to do that. What do you think?"

"Papatico!" she cried suddenly, as a girl caught in a quicksand, her face pulled into a miserable shape, her arms reaching out.

He slid across the seat to comfort her, to lend her little body his strength.

"Let's see if it's easier if I make some suggestions and you can guide me to the answers without having to explain the details just yet. Do you think that might help?"

She nodded once. "Yes," she said.

"Good. Well, I wonder if the trouble is about your Mami not being here. That's easy to guess, but is it right?"

"Yes."

"And another part might be about you being new at the school?"

A shrug told him he'd gone cold with that, which he'd thought might be the case and in a way he was pleased to know it and get it out of the reckoning.

"Then the next guess would be that I'm the other part of the trouble."

"Yeess," she wailed and cried into his shirt. He let her do so, but only for a few moments so as not to lose the purpose of their conversation.

"So, other children are saying things about your Mami and about me, saying nasty things to make you feel bad, is it something like that?"

She drew a breath in little shudders before saying, "Yes."

"And the teachers, are the teachers saying bad things too?"

After giving this some thought, she said, "They said I don't have a Mami but I do."

"Yes, you do. I wonder if they meant to say that you don't have your Mami living at home at the moment. Sometimes people say shorter versions of what they really mean. It would have been better to say that your Mami has gone away and for now we don't know where she is, but that gets more complicated and people want to ask more questions when they hear something like that. People, even teachers, like simple facts, simple ideas, simple answers. You and I, we know that it's complicated, even if we wish it were simple.

"So, already there is something that can be done, something I can do. I can go to the school and talk to the teachers and help them understand how you feel, how it is, here in our home. I'll try and make it that you can come with me and hear what I say to them, but that may not be possible. We'll see, but I think they'll speak a little differently about your Mami when they understand."

He gently pulled her away from him, enough that he could see her face and she his. With soft fingers he wiped tears from under her eyes, then kissed her forehead.

"Now my darling girl, there are other things too, things about your Mami and about me, the bad things the children are saying, how they are being mean to you. Are these the same things that la señora Mejía spoke about when she first came to see us, that I am cruel to you and beat your Mami? And worse things too, even that I have killed your Mami?"

With her head in his hands he felt her nod slightly, more like a tremble than a deliberate action.

"And although I love you, and I know you love me, despite that, do you have a tiny doubt, the smallest idea that it could be true if other people say so?"

"Yes," she whispered through crooked lips.

"Then you must hear my words too and know I love you and tell the truth. I did not beat your Mami, I did not treat her badly. And I have not killed your lovely Mami."

"I know," she moaned. After a few moments she said, "Papatico. Que es una puta?"

"Ah, so they say that too. Sometimes it can be just a word to be really unkind to someone. We've spoken a little about sex before and I think you have heard something from Pippa too, but really

175

a whore, una puta, is a rude word for someone who will have sex with anyone for money." Which he knew was true enough, but which told Gabriela nothing of such people, nor of those who paid. He tried a little amplification, a little context, partly as an insurance. "Most people would say it was a bad thing to be una puta, but sometimes it is the only way to get money for food or to pay the rent. Nothing is simple."

Gabriela considered this with tight lips for a few moments.

"No, your Mami is not a whore, ella no es una puta," he said, and hoped with all his heart what he said was true.

"If there's more from school my darling, now is a good time to say it. You can say anything."

"They call you something I don't understand, they say viejo verde. Is it bad?"

"Yes, of course, that would go with everything else. It means nothing really, they are being unkind to you by being rude about me. It is the same bad things that la señora Mejía said when she first came to our home. If they were true la señora would not let me look after you any more, she knows they are not true."

They sat and listened to the ocean for a few minutes before he said, "There'll be other things I expect, nasty little comments, but is there anything else they're saying, anything you want to tell me about?"

"Their Mamás say they shouldn't talk to me."

"Their Mamás don't know the truth, so the children don't know. Let me think about everything for a little while, perhaps we'll talk to Pippa too, then we'll see if the truth will help fix some of this. What do you think?"

"Can we see Pippa today?"

"Yes, let's do that."

He could've turned back and headed straight for La Plantación but instead they drove home so that Gabriela could change out of her hated uniform. Harry made up a bag for an overnight stay, just in case, although there'd be no need to ask. Nothing had changed in the hour since he'd collected Gabriela from school, yet the mood had lifted. Not only hers, but his too. Hearing her put her troubles into words had been as good for him as it had been for her. It was all as bad as he might have expected, but no worse, and that alone was a relief. Not only that but he could do something, even if it was very little, to push back the ignorance and the insults.

When Pippa had hugged them both, and they'd taken refuge from the rain driving in from the south, they sat on her welcoming sofas nursing drinks. Gabriela lounged across Harry's lap, sucking up a fresco while he and Pippa enjoyed the rare indulgence of afternoon gin.

After a while Harry said, "Gabriela, shall we tell Pippa of our troubles, of school and other things, are you happy to do that?"

She agreed without removing the straw from her mouth.

So he told Pippa the stories from school and Pippa listened with a serious face and confined her comments to grunts and shakes of her head until Gabriela said, "And they call Papatico un viejo verde."

"What's that?" Pippa said. "Probably rude."

"Dirty old man is close enough," he said. "I thought I'd go in and see the teachers, let them know what's going on. And put them right on a few things."

He let the suggestion stay unanswered for a few moments.

"What do you think?"

"Yes, why not? It might work, who knows?"

"You're not convinced."

"Small town, small minds. It's the same the world over. But go ahead, like you say, what else should you do?"

These were not the encouraging words Harry had expected. Pippa's usual support and optimism had gone missing just as he needed it to propel him and Gabriela forward. However realistic his friend's doubts and reservations might be, it wasn't what he wanted Gabriela to hear.

"I'll think about it," he said by way of closing the subject.

For the first time he could remember they sat in a less-than-comfortable silence. Pippa had shut some part of herself off from him, from Gabriela too. Opening a fresh topic would only emphasise what was not being said, so he let the silence grow deeper as the rain splattered over the gutters. Gabriela watched and waited, her hands and mouth busy with the smoothie. The remains of Harry's gin lasted no more than a couple of awkward minutes.

"Perhaps it's a bad time, maybe we should go home," he said, more abruptly than he intended.

Pippa stared at him then said to Gabriela, "Close your ears, sweetheart, I'm going to be rude to your Papatico." She paused only slightly before addressing Harry. "Harry Rose, you are an arse. You blunder around from crisis to crisis making no plans beyond tomorrow's breakfast and can't see what's in front of your nose. Your few friends generally go along with you because they love you. How did you ever get a dam built and producing electricity?"

"What now?" he cried, ambushed by his closest ally.

"Even a few moment's thought could have predicted that Gabriela would have a difficult time at school in one way or another. They weren't likely to welcome you with open arms, were they? So who takes the brunt of that? Gabriela of course."

"Plans, you said plans, what plans could I have made for all this?"

"Plans for the future, your future. Gabriela's future. Before all this even started."

"We've been through this."

"But Harry, you're still doing it. Or not doing it."

"Explain, please."

"Only if I can sit beside you and you stop being defensive."

Having puffed himself up with indignation Harry wasn't quite ready to call a truce so easily, yet he could hardly do otherwise. Gabriela lifted her feet obligingly to allow Pippa to slip in close to them both.

"Harry."

"What?"

"Stop being an arse."

He grunted.

"Let's start with school. There's no secondary school on the island, so what will happen when Gabriela is twelve? Twice a day on the ferry? It's possible, I'm sure a few do it. I've no idea what the school is like, but I bet it's a choice of one, just like Concepción. Is that what you want for Gabriela?"

"Well…" he started.

"Or for yourself? Twice a day to take and collect. Think about it." But she wasn't giving him time to do that, not now. "Remember we talked about sport, music, art? What about the wonders of the world-wide-web? All noticeably missing from this corner of paradise."

Again he might have answered, but thought better of it.

"And friends. You and I and the local policeman and Leo Morales are not enough." She turned her attention to Gabriela, but continued speaking to Harry through her. "I know you've started school and even though it's horrible now you may find one or two friends in time, but that's not enough either.

"Let's just assume what we all hope comes true, which is that soon we'll find out something of your Mami, and that you and your Papatico go on living together for many years to come. It may be better for you both to be living in the city, better to come to your Casa Rosa home at weekends, come and stay here with me in the holidays. I think your Papatico should start thinking about that. That's why I'm cross with him, I'm not cross with you. And I still love you both."

"I do think about it, all of it," he protested, "You make it sound easy, but I can't catch my breath between one thing and the next."

"What if something happens to you Harry? What if you are ill, or worse?" He felt the pressure of Gabriela's grip tightening on his arm as Pippa spoke. "Yes, I know we talked about Julio and Elena and I all making sure Gabriela is loved and cared for, but it'll be for us to make it happen, not you. Have you made a will?"

He shook his head. Certainly he'd thought about it, more than once, but…

179

"Are you hoping we'll sort that out too? We'll do it of course. We love you, so we'll do it. But I don't know if that'll help this lovely girl."

Gabriela looked up at him with big eyes. "Papatico?"

"Ah, a will," he began and described what it was and what it meant. When he'd finished his simple explanation Pippa added what it would mean if there was no will and how arguments could arise and how the most-loved people could be left with nothing.

Gabriela briefly considered the idea.

"Will we live in the city?" she asked.

"I don't know. Not now, not tomorrow. But one day we might."

"What about when Mami comes?"

"If we ever leave Casa Rosa we'll have to make sure she knows where we'll be. That will be the most important thing."

The feeble tinkling of Pippa's phone interrupted their thoughts. She slid across so the other end of the sofa and picked up. Julio for Harry. No greetings or small talk, straight to the point.

"Can you come to San Felipe tomorrow?"

"Urgent?"

"Important. Yes, also urgent."

"Not something we can talk about now?"

"Perhaps if you were alone, but better in person. Harry, you should come tomorrow." Julio's manner was all formality, his professional persona squeezing out friendship.

"I really want to go to school with Gabriela in the morning. I'll ask Pippa if she can pick her up." She was already mouthing her agreement. "Yes, that will work, I'll get the bus, I don't trust the truck any more. Your office?"

Julio hesitated slightly. "Home, home will be better."

Two enquiring faces looked for answers when the call finished.

"A legal thing, that's my guess. Something to do with the court or maybe la señora Mejía."

What he feared was something quite different: the possibility of some revelation from the past dug up by the diligent Indira Chavarria.

★

The school was less than helpful. La señora Ruiz Acuna listened sympathetically enough but no, she did not feel that Gabriela should be part of the interview, neither did she believe the staff could have contributed to Gabriela's distress. Hadn't Harry brought Gabriela to the school along with his own reputation? It was something of which she herself had been aware even before he had first entered the school, it was natural that others might be wary. La señora was unaware of any abuse or bullying of Gabriela within the school and such treatment was taken very seriously if detected. She could promise only to be alert to the possibility and to find an opportunity to remind staff and pupils of their duties of tolerance and good manners. And yes, begrudgingly, she would make a record of his visit and his comments, but in what capacity was he complaining?

It left him angry and bitter, the two natural offspring of impotence.

The clanking ferry did nothing to improve his humour. Late arriving, even later setting off for Puerto Reunión, it meant an extra hour's wait for the *directo* to San Felipe. Pippa's comment about this being Gabriela's route to school in a few year's time stuck with him. Of course it was not what he wanted for her or for himself. But there was a trade-off: Casa Rosa was their home and had benefits far beyond the conveniences of city life. Could they have both? He'd all but forsaken the city since Estefanía had brought Gabriela to Isla Concepción, now it held even less attraction than it had then.

Julio and Elena's suggestion of becoming Gabriela's adoptive family came suddenly back to him. Was that what was so urgent he had to go to see them, had they progressed that idea quickly and now it had come to a critical moment? How long ago had they mentioned it, last week or two, even three weeks ago? He

181

hadn't given it another thought since the evening they'd made that loving suggestion. It swirled round his head again as the bus carried him to the capital. Gabriela's attachment to Casa Rosa was intimately bound up with her Mami and her Mami's return. Without that she had little to hold her there beyond familiarity and Harry himself. In years to come she might remember it fondly as an idyllic playground, but would it be more than that? Or would the taint of her missing Mami, of the visit from La Agencia, and of Ernest's death, forever blight her memory of Casa Rosa? Too late to change any of that now. Too late to change where the bus was taking him.

"Harry!" Elena's welcome was as warm and genuine as ever. Either Julio hadn't shared the development he'd come to discuss, or it was less poisonous than Harry feared.

Julio, too, embraced him as fondly as always and Harry's worries began to dissolve. They ate and shared drinks and the small talk of close friends until Elena made an excuse to be elsewhere. In his little office off the courtyard, Julio quietly closed the door and took a folder from his desk drawer before settling awkwardly into an armchair. He handed the file to Harry without speaking.

"This is the development? It's very slim."

"I didn't tell you the whole truth, there are two developments. This is the first. It is the most important."

Harry opened the flap and saw the edges of two sheets.

The first was a certified copy of the registration of the birth of Estefanía Gabriela Flores Blanca, just as it had been described to him. Harry lingered over it, reading every word so as to avoid seeing the second sheet, which surely could only be Gabriela's birth or Estefanía's death. When he could delay no longer he slipped the second paper to the top. *Nacimiento*, a birth. Gabriela's. At San Carlos, weight at birth 3.2kg, 47cm, full term, ten o'clock at night on a Saturday. Father: Stuart Henry Rose, Ingeniero, 52, Resident of Casa Rosa, Isla Concepción. ID: British passport 51603660A. Mother: Estefanía Flores Blanca, 16, Resident San Carlos. ID: 103694705. The witnesses were Marco

Umaña, the registrar, and a Mariela Fonseca. There was no entry in the space for the father's signature.

It was a piece of paper with marks on it. The more he looked at it the less the marks meant anything. He kept looking at it until he could no longer avoid looking up at Julio.

"Did you tell Elena?"

"No, not yet. This is difficult because you are our friend. Harry, you are our family. Also my client. So you are first. But I will tell Elena, I must, or perhaps you will."

Harry's gaze returned to the paper. "It's dated a few days before her fifth birthday," he said.

"It is the limit for doing so. Five years. After five years it is difficult. There is a process, it is difficult. But we know this."

"You haven't asked me."

"There are many questions," he said, looking slowly at Harry. Eventually he said, "Are you Gabriela's father?"

"I don't think so."

"But you could be?"

Harry drew a deep breath. "It's possible."

"Did you know about her registration?"

"No."

"But you are not surprised."

"Not completely. I thought Estefanía might have named her Gabriela Rosa or Rose. I mentioned that to you before."

Julio nodded. "Yes, you did, and I thought it was a good idea, just as we called our son Stuart. Now we can see she does have your name after all. She is Gabriela Rose Flores."

"Yes."

"Did you give Estefanía your passport?"

"No. But she could have seen them any time. They're in the desk drawer."

"Pure chance which one she chose. Is the number correct?"

"I think so." Harry paused before asking, "What does this mean, Julio?"

"It changes everything."

"Doesn't it matter whether it's true or not?"

"If you accept it as true then it is true, who will say it is not? You may challenge it if you wish. A test is simple. Do you want to challenge it?"

"I don't know. It's a shock."

Julio leant towards him, his voice low, "Do you want to be her father or do you want to be her Papatico?"

"Just today I'd started to think it would be better for Gabriela if she lived here in San Felipe. Isla Concepción is nothing, there is nothing there for her."

"Your Casa Rosa is there, your home, her home is there."

"What do you think is better for her?"

"San Felipe or Casa Rosa?"

"No. Papá or Papatico."

"If you are Papá you can be both. If you choose to not be her father, then you can only be Papatico. Choose Papá and she need never know, never find a difference. Choose Papatico and one day she will ask why you didn't choose to be her Papá."

"Can we ask Elena?"

"Of course! And perhaps you would like a drink, a little whisky, if it is not too early. I would like one, I will not go to my office today."

Elena joined them eagerly, although when she saw their serious faces her own smile evaporated. Harry caught the glance toward Julio for approval before she sat by him on the little two-seat sofa.

"Elena, you should know these things," Harry said. "This, I think you are already aware of, but here is the paper. It is Estefanía's birth in San Carlos."

"Yes, Julio told me. Is it important?."

"It is a step," Julio said. "One piece leads to another."

Elena looked at the paper for a few moments, then looked up expectantly. He passed her Gabriela's registration and waited. Recognition of the vital fact took only a few seconds. A sharp little intake of breath told Harry when she had reached the critical entry.

"Oh Harry!" she cried, a hand at her mouth, "Did you know?"

"No." He shook his head slowly, "And it may not be true. Most likely it's not true."

"What will happen?"

"I don't know, I thought you might help me," he said softly. "Listen, let me tell you."

He explained how it seemed he must decide, and quickly, whether to accept what had been recorded or contest it. Accept, and an inevitable train of events would be set in motion, a choice which would indeed change everything. To contest it would mean the grim process started by the call to La Agencia de Protección de los Niños would continue and might become even muddier. As he laid these things out for Elena, Harry had a vision of that process and how absurd it would look to be fighting to keep Gabriela in his care while denying she was his child.

"Julio," he said as a thought occurred to him, "did la señorita Chavarria find the registration and have this copy made?"

Julio nodded.

"Did she say anything?"

"Nothing. She brought the certificate directly to me, she said I should see it. That was all. Why do you ask?"

"Something she said to me once. I said I might not want to know about the past and she said that I might have to know."

"How should I help, Harry?" Elena asked.

"You have already, thank you. Just telling you about it, talking about my choice, has helped. I must accept the certificate as it is, I should be Gabriela's father, her Papá. I hope you agree."

"Yes, I do," she said easily, then looked at Julio for his confirmation. "Yes, we do, certainly, for Gabriela and for you, Harry."

"Even if it's not true?"

"Yes, even so. I will tell you why I think this way. Have we all been saying that Estefanía intended you should look after Gabriela, even if she was only thinking of days rather than years? Wasn't Gabriela left in your care? Of course she was, and here is proof of Estefanía's intention. If you are her father then it is easy, and if you are not then she trusted you with her child, not just for days but for all of her life. A mother does not do that lightly."

"But she kept it a secret, she was scared I wouldn't take it on."

"Perhaps she was trying to tell you when she spoke of naming her Rosa or Rose, perhaps she was seeing what you thought of the small idea without telling you the big idea," Julio said. "Maybe she hadn't had the big idea at that moment, only later."

"She did this when Gabriela was nearly five, yes? After five years she knew how much you loved Gabriela, how much Gabriela loved you," Elena said, with a certainty that would tolerate no argument.

They fell silent, each turning the new knowledge around to look at it from different angles, each seeing which way it settled into their friendship, each imagining a new future shaped by a piece of paper. Harry could not escape from the unasked question of how he might be not only Gabriela's recorded father but her real father. Would they one day remember that they hadn't asked him, one day in a year or ten when they were sharing a pleasant meal in this same welcoming home, then would they casually say *We never did ask, Harry, how was it you could have been Gabriela's father at fifty-two when Estefanía was barely sixteen and you'd never met?*

He was briefly tempted to tell them, get it all said, all confessed, now, while there were a dozen other more important aspects to distract them from his history with prostitutes. Perhaps it was their love for him which stopped them asking. Perhaps they'd guessed already.

Harry broke the silence, nervous of more questions, "It answers something, gives us a way forward, but I feel as if now it's all the more important to find Estefanía. That isn't your second development is it?" He knew how anxious he sounded.

"No, it is different," Julio soothed. "We will come to that, but you'll think about this before I act tomorrow? The court will wish to be informed immediately. I will also contact la señora Mejía at APN."

"I won't change my mind, not now. I see no reason to tell Gabriela of the new, er, situation. Better for her if nothing changes. For now, at least."

"You see? Already you are Papá and Papatico. It is good. I'm sure we will come back to this many times but for now there is something else." Julio pulled another file from his desk, took some papers and handed them to Harry. "We have searched the register of interests for Casa Rosa and your neighbours. Together they once made Playa de Rosas, as we discussed.

"There are several entries to note. Look first at your own Casa Rosa, there is an interest registered, by el señor Giancarlo Duarte. You will see the interest is in purchasing or inheritance. You may be surprised at this, as you probably don't know el señor Duarte, but this is not unusual. Property brokers and agents always want to know when property comes available, especially desirable property. And it helps the property owner because they know immediately that there is an interest. For somewhere more remote like Isla Concepción it is less usual, but still normal.

"His name is also attached to the property of Ernest Portillo, again el señor Duarte is interested in purchasing. It is probably how the nephew, Oscar, was able to move to sell so quickly. The buyer is waiting to hear from him as soon as the property is available. But Harry, I should say we do not know if el señor Duarte is the purchaser. You will see that Oscar himself had also recorded an interest, in the event of his uncle's death. Again this is normal, many families would do this, to prevent one brother or sister taking what should be shared or had been promised elsewhere. It means that a lawyer will look at the recorded interests to be sure all claims are satisfied before disposing of a property.

"Now we see the other property, your neighbours la señora Pérez and el señor Fairchild. On the third entry there is once again the name of Giancarlo Duarte. He has covered all three properties of the old Playa de Rosas. Why not? It makes sense if he is interested in one then he might as well put his name against all three. But there is more than one interest here. On the first entry you see there is a mortgage from the Banco Nacional which was taken out three years ago. Is it large or small for their house? You may have an idea but I cannot guess. It is not huge, so let us say that it is normal."

Harry was ahead of Julio's careful commentary. "The next line doesn't look normal. It looks like a great deal of money for a second mortgage. Even in a crazy world, two million is huge. On Isla Concepción it is unbelievable. Perhaps the lender doesn't know where the property is. You could probably buy most of the town for that. And a few favours to go along with it. Do you know this lender, Sindicato de Avatar?"

"No, not yet. I have begun a search for them and for el señor Duarte."

"Julio," said Elena, "Why is it important to know about the mortgages?"

"It may not be important, it may be nothing. When we know a little more about the interests we may see it is important."

"Money is always a motive," Harry added. "I've been wondering about el señor Oscar Portillo and his sister who both once knew the place as Playa de Rosas. They need me on their side to give them the access they need, or give it to their buyer."

"Their buyer would, certainly, but they would inherit the property with access. The law says that if Ernest had access then so too could his family who inherited. There is a sense in that. A new owner is different."

"So they still need me. Or they need me out the way."

"Julio, Harry, could that be true?" Elena looked from one to another. "That would be a terrible thing."

"True or not, it reminds me there's something else. Would you help me draw up a will."

★

Harry spoke low and calm to his pickup. "C'mon, not now, not tonight, please." After a few seconds to rest he gently urged it again, "This time, and I promise I'll get you looked at." The engine coughed twice then threatened to falter before one cylinder fired, encouraging the others into action. A few minutes later he trundled onto *Espíritu de las Islas,* the setting sun almost blinding him as he stopped.

Before he'd switched off there was a pounding on the window.

"Papatico! Papatico!" A split second later she was in the cab and across the seat to hug him.

With his face buried in her hair he breathed in her scent. She was as sweet a cocktail as girl children are meant to be, full of sugar and spice, with a splash of beaches and laughter. He held her tight and kissed her head and wondered how he could ever have had the tiniest doubt about the choice he'd made.

"Hello my darling, what are you doing on this rusty old barge? Have you stowed away, looking for adventure?"

"No! We've been to Maxi and bought loads and loads and loads," she said, spreading her arms wider with every word.

"Anything nice?"

"Everything!"

"Where's Pippa?"

"We're right next to you!"

They were. In the glare he hadn't recognised Pippa's 405 when he'd driven in beside it. As the ferry slipped away from the jetty she was there at the open door, then climbed in to sit beside them. Gabriela ducked as they exchanged their own embraces.

"You're a happy man tonight, Harry. Good trip?"

"The more I've thought about it the better it seems."

"Light at the end of the tunnel?" It was a careful question, leaving room for evasion if the light was not for Gabriela's eyes.

"One tunnel maybe. Lawyers and legal stuff mainly, something for the judges to consider," he added as explanation for his daughter. His daughter. Sitting right there beside him. The sudden reality of it made him jolt as if in pain. He tried the idea again and found it pleasing. His daughter, through convenience or genetics made no difference. With her snug beside him, with the gentle motion of the ferry carrying them towards their island home in the purple haze, the warmth of a new contentment flooded through him.

189

At Pippa's they ate well and drank well, which was not to excess but to satisfaction. For almost an hour afterwards Harry read to Gabriela with her head on a cushion on his lap. Each time he stopped, thinking she was asleep, she murmured drowsily for more until he was too tired to continue and he carried her to bed. At the door he waited a few seconds longer than he might, just for the pleasure of seeing her.

"Harry, what's happened?" Pippa asked as soon as he sat back with her.

"You first. Did Gabriela talk to you, how was school?"

"She didn't say much, OK was all I got out of her. I didn't push it. I didn't see any tears."

"And picking her up, that went OK?"

"Just as arranged."

"That's good, thank you. She's been great this evening. Just wonderful."

"So, what was the urgent call to San Felipe?"

He put a finger to his lips then reached into his bag for the vital document. He watched as her eyes flickered across it, widening at the point of the crucial information. Just as he had done, she read it again carefully before looking at him, incredulous.

"How is this possible? It can't be true, can it? Did you know?"

"I didn't know, of course not. Estefanía chose to name me as Gabriela's father, perhaps for her own benefit, but more likely for Gabriela's. And now for mine too. I'm accepting it without question. As Julio said, who will contest it? And see when she did it, she and Gabriela had been at Casa Rosa for almost five years."

Pippa looked again at the paper, then slowly she said, "You knew Estefanía before she came here, didn't you?"

The slightest pause betrayed him. A whole lie became impossible.

"There is a slight possibility we could have met, that is all. So far as I remember I never saw her before that day on the bus."

"So there's a possibility that it's true. Was it guilt made you take them in?" There was an unfamiliar edge to Pippa's voice. It wasn't a loving edge.

"No, I don't think so. Maybe I wanted to give something back."

"Will you have a test done?"

"No."

"The court might want one, don't you think?"

"Julio thinks not. They'll be happy to accept the official version and happy to drop the whole awkward affair. I thought you'd be happy, but I don't think you are."

"It's certainly a surprise. It'll take a bit of getting used to. I don't know what I think. Ask me tomorrow. Will you tell Gabriela?"

"One day. Everything has changed but nothing has changed. We'll treat each other the same and one day she'll see this paper and understand what it is and won't be surprised by it, it'll be what she always thought."

★

For a few days their troubles were kept at arm's length. Details of Gabriela's birth were acknowledged without comment by either la juez Cruz or la señora Mejía, no further revelations were forthcoming from la señorita Indira Chavarria's enquiries and the DIC investigation by Daniel Scott made no fresh contact. When Julio called, it was to confirm he'd drafted a will for Harry to check, but there was nothing extra about property or mortgages. Armed with his new status, Harry would have been happy enough to meet any new challenge, but none presented itself. Even Gabriela's misery at school appeared to have abated: outright abuse replaced by sullen hostility.

Of Estefanía there remained no word.

Saturday passed in what might be their new normal with a trip to the market, a quiet afternoon followed by a meal at the Kasanee, where Gabriela was predictably fussed over by Carla and Leo. Something of the old warmth seeped back into Harry's welcome too, as a few regulars managed muted greetings. He told no one of his new parenthood, contenting himself with suggesting to Leo that one or two things had changed and he was feeling confident. A new beginning, he called it.

It should have meant a smooth transition from food and wine into deep and rejuvenating sleep, but it didn't. Instead the very things which had apparently lessened in the daylight hours grew to their worst proportions in the darkness. A comment Carla had made about a problem with *Espíritu de las Islas,* and the service being reduced or worse, suspended, troubled him greatly. To be marooned on Isla Concepción might once not have mattered greatly to him, but now the prospect was threatening, even dangerous. It played in to every difficulty they faced. What if the ferry could not be repaired? The idea of a replacement being found quickly was laughable. It was the island's lifeline, without it Concepción would become untenable.

A little after midnight, having wrestled with all his present ills and several phantoms from the past he abandoned his sweaty pillow. As he crept about in the darkness he caught a movement beyond the jicaros, a movement at odds with the breeze and the water. Stealing closer to the window he saw a figure walking by the water's edge. Even in the thin light of the moon he recognised Bill Fairchild, as much by the floral shirt as any distinguishing feature. He was headed homewards. Perhaps the prospect of losing the ferry had ruffled his sleep too.

Harry poured a scotch and stepped softly to the verandah, intending to sit in his chair until the demons had grown tired of their sport and left him in peace. But his steps took him further, down the stairs where he paused by the struggling roses. Two fresh blooms were defiantly wafting their delicate scent into the slow night air. He went on, across the deserted sand until the water lapped at his feet. To his right poor Ernest's house sat in silent darkness. To the left a light at the Fairchild villa flickered behind the foliage. Whether it was from inside or out Harry couldn't tell.

Should they stay in this perfect place? It seemed absurd to question it, for how could they not? This was paradise, unspoilt, unhurried and beautiful beyond words. It lay on the shores of the vast Pacific yet was sheltered from the worst the ocean could throw at it. It was close enough to all conveniences without being cursed by them. More than all that, it was home, not only his but Gabriela's, a better home than her mother could ever have dreamed of when she begged at his table at the Kasanee.

And yet. Her school was a problem, one that would only become worse in time. He wasn't the man to make a proper job of home schooling, even if he had brought her this far and would happily take her further. He would never be patient enough to study and comply with rules and required curriculum to be approved for such a thing. She needed, no, deserved, a good education. He caught himself being ambitious for her, his flight of fancy taking her to university and from there travelling the world before settling to some highly respected career. Electrical engineering perhaps, although he smiled at the thought.

It wasn't only education, there was the catalogue of other deficiencies so clearly spelled out by Pippa, deficiencies for which there were few remedies. In a perfect world he and Gabriela would remain healthy; she would be a natural athlete with no need of sport; with Leo's help she would master the guitar and play at the Kasanee to enthralled audiences; Pippa would lead her to artistic heights and international acclaim; Gabriela would gain a distance-learning degree from Oxford or McGill; she would have pen-friends who would come to stay and become lifelong confidantes.

Were pen-friends even a thing any more?

Unrealistic, romantic for sure, but whether he'd ever bring himself to abandon the dream, that was another question. He'd chosen this life, not lightly but deliberately and the years with Gabriela had proved its value.

With his glass empty and the wind beginning to stir, Harry wondered if he might be ready for sleep. He retraced his steps, through the jicaros and the roses, their scent lost on the breeze. On the verandah he looked back to the shore. It would be beyond difficult to leave this magical place.

He settled back into his bed and almost immediately felt sleep taking him, like fog rolling in from the ocean. The first dream images had just appeared when a noise jerked him awake again. Inside or outside? A crash of glass or splintering wood? He pulled himself upright, the better to hear any recurrence. A noise certainly, but what? Low and muffled. He stepped across to Gabriela's room and drew close to her sleeping form. She breathed softly in untroubled sleep. A light across the window, moving. Car headlights or a flashlight? The low-level sound a little louder. The light brighter.

Outside the sound growing, a low roar. The light orange, yellow.

Fire.

Ernest's house was burning.

Harry jumped down the steps onto the sand and ran towards his neighbour's. A little way from it he stopped, amazed at the speed and intensity of the flames after so short a time. The side of the house was well alight, thick dark smoke curled from under the roof. A small explosion from within shattered windows and fed oxygen to the flames. Was it a movement or smoke in the window? Could Ernest's nephew or his sister be inside? Had they come for the weekend unannounced, left a pan on the stove?

He raced over irrelevant possibilities, struggling to find meaning or reason in the crackling, roaring destruction. A million sparks hurled themselves skywards in the flames and smoke. Already burning fragments were drifting down towards Casa Rosa.

"Gabriela!" He cried her name in despair and ran to the house.

At the top of the steps he met her screaming his name.

He scooped her in his arms and held her tight for a few moments.

"Be calm now," he told her, advice for himself too. "Go to your room, get your bag, collect your things to stay at Pippa's. Then put other things in too, some books, all your precious things. Be quick but don't panic, our house is not on fire. I'll do the same. I'll collect your Mami's things from her room."

She seemed stunned, orange light flickering across her face, bright in her wide eyes.

"Gabriela. Now, we'll do it now." The urgency in his voice mixed unhappily with the need for calm.

She turned stiffly and they went in, but she still clung to him. He threw his wallet, passport, phone, and a few clothes into a bag. In Gabriela's room he grabbed a blanket from her bed, yesterday's clothes from the floor, her precious Héctor and her Mami's photo along with the nearest books. Already smoke was seeping into the house but Gabriela was stuck to him. In Estefanía's room he took her Bible, her tray of cheap jewellery and the photo of the baby Gabriela. The splintering roar of the fire grew louder as he hesitated over what else was essential.

Nothing. Everything could be replaced.

Outside they felt the heat on their faces immediately. The pickup was only a few steps away but wreathed in smoke. Carrying her to the cab he pushed her in.

"Scoot over!" he urged.

She reluctantly let go of him and he jumped up beside her.

For a moment the engine coughed. He tried again too quickly, too anxious to be moving and it failed. The smoke had enveloped them, lit horribly by the flames behind it. One more time. Not too quickly. Nothing. Deep breath. Abandon ship.

He staggered down the sand, half-carrying, half-dragging her with him. In a few metres they were in clear air, but he took them further, close to the water. Only then did they look back at the blazing remains of Ernest's house. As they did so part of the roof collapsed inward, sending up a huge column of flame and burning debris and pushing out a billowing bank of black smoke that reached halfway down the beach.

With the collapse of the roof the blaze intensified, decreasing the noxious smoke. Casa Rosa drifted in and out of sight through the haze, backlit by fire in the scrub behind it. Between the house and the Fairchild villa a lone bush burned fiercely. Harry prayed that the tiles and stucco walls would resist longer than Ernest's wooden roof had done. But there were low hibiscus and pampas grass close to the walls, it only needed one to ignite by a window and the fire would be under the eaves and into the house in moments.

"Will you stay here while I go and check the house?" he asked her.

"No! Papatico, no!" she cried, tightening her grip on him.

He pulled out his phone. The island's volunteer firefighters would all be sound asleep in their beds and twenty minutes away if they responded at all. It was academic. No signal. *Los bomberos* could sleep on.

"We must go to the Fairchild's, wake them. We'll go by the water, then up to the house."

Together they walked and ran, Harry carrying both bags while Gabriela ran so close to him she threatened to trip him up. As they turned toward the villa, Harry saw Bill Fairchild standing hands-on-hips looking at the fire. He was surprised by their sudden approach from the water's edge.

"Jesus, Harry, you gave me a fright! This looks bad, can anything be done?"

"No, it's gone."

"Yours too?"

"No, not yet. Will you look after Gabriela while I go back?"

"Sure."

But Gabriela clung tighter and wailed so miserably he thought better of it. Ridiculously, he recalled that his will had only been drafted, not signed and sealed. He would have to stand with her and watch to see if their house burned.

11

The early morning rain doused the last of the flames but the ugly footprint of the house continued to smoulder and steam. Wisps of smoke still rose from the ashes and the occasional collapse of a charred timber sent up plumes to hang in the still air. At least they could breathe, but the rain had released a foul stink that pervaded the whole property.

As the fire had slowly subsided they'd ventured closer until around five in the morning Gabriela had finally released her hold on him. By sitting on the sand just below the jicaros with Bill Fairchild in attendance she could keep him in sight while he inspected the side of Casa Rosa closest to the flames. Some grasses had ignited but burned too quickly to spread the fire to the house itself. The smoke-stained wall and eaves revealed just how close they'd been to disaster. At the back, blackened patches across the ground showed they'd been doubly lucky. Then the rain had come.

Gabriela finally fell asleep on the verandah at Casa Rosa, resisting all persuasion that she should go to her bed. She would not stay in the house without him. He covered her with the blanket he'd grabbed from her bed and tucked Héctor in beside her. There'd be no lasting harm from a night with little sleep, but the terror of the fire would surely leave an indelible mark.

Around eight he found two bars of phone signal. Pippa's line was out of service, but he roused Leo and told him of their night. Would he go to Victor Diaz's house and inform him of events, not as an emergency, but for information? Of course he would, and Carla would offer a prayer for them both.

With Gabriela asleep, Harry slipped down the steps. The pickup sat as they'd abandoned it, blistered paintwork and a dozen scars of burning where embers had landed. In the back a loop of nylon rope had caught and melted into a blackened imprint of itself. Otherwise the vehicle appeared to have survived intact. He climbed in and tried the key. The motor turned but with no suggestion of starting. A job for later.

He couldn't resist the temptation to take a closer look at the smoking ruins of Ernest's home. As he approached the stench intensified, making him gag on an empty stomach. The smell was of burning, of course, but he wondered what else might be mixed in with it. The gruesome notion of a person or animal being trapped in the house and roasted alive pressed on the edge of his thoughts although reason told him otherwise. The figure he fancied he'd seen was no more than smoke and flame. Even so, that movement would have been exactly where he'd found Ernest lying dead two weeks previously. His ghost in the flames, perhaps. The fire and the fear mixed badly with his exhaustion.

There was nothing left. The sparse metal skeletons of the cooker, a bed frame and two chairs were identifiable, of the rest only ash and rubble and smoking timber remained. No charred hump that might be a body, no suggestion of a corpse impaled on the bedsprings. But still the vile smell.

He didn't venture further than the perimeter of the debris. If there was an unnatural source for the fire he wouldn't know what to look for, certainly there was no paraffin odour, or anything like it. Such a thing can linger at a fire for days after the event. His other thought was that if there were anything gruesome to find then he would rather not be the one to make the discovery.

Bill Fairchild joined him after a half hour. Harry saw him from a distance walking casually towards the point, for all the world as if he were out for a Sunday stroll. He'd changed his clothes since they'd stood together as helpless spectators. Harry hadn't. He was grimy and sweaty from the night, no doubt as foul smelling as the remains of Ernest's house.

"How is it, Harry?" Fairchild said when he was still a little distance away. "Smells real bad."

"I don't know what it is," he called back.

His neighbour came closer and surveyed the scene.

"You OK? And the girl, she's OK too?"

The words jarred. It was a time for strange things, it had been such a time for several weeks, from the moment la señora Mejía had stepped out of her car at Casa Rosa and reprimanded Victor Diaz. Now here was something else. The girl, he'd said. It wasn't new, Bill Fairchild never used her name. But today, after all that had happened, surely today was a day to have concern, to have feeling for a child traumatised by the night, a child you'd sat beside on the sand while she'd whimpered in fear at being separated from her Papatico.

"We're OK. Shaken up, you know," Harry said in as measured and non-committal a way as he could manage.

"It makes you wonder about this place."

"It does." He maintained the casual tone as he added, "Did you see anything last night, Bill?"

"No, same as you, saw the fire and came out. You gave me a shock, Jesus Christ you did, coming up from the ocean like that."

"Nobody else on the sand, or up here?"

"No, not that I saw."

There were a hundred things Harry could have said but none seemed appropriate. Bill Fairchild may have had his own good reasons for prowling the sands at the dead of night, a short while before fire had engulfed an empty house, but he was unlikely to share them with Harry. They stood together, unspeaking, as men do who know each other but who have no bond of friendship to underpin the silence.

Harry recognised Victor Diaz's white pickup, his own, not the police Toyota, as it came into sight along the track. The destruction had provided a better view in that direction, with no house nor trees and bushes around it to hide an approaching visitor. The pickup stopped twenty or thirty metres from the end of the track. Victor got out slowly and stood, taking in the whole scene. Only when he had satisfied himself of the complete picture did he raise a hand to acknowledge their presence. As he

199

walked towards them he stopped and bent down to inspect something at the edge of the burned grass beside the track.

"Did you call Diaz?" the American asked Harry behind his hand.

"No," Harry answered perversely.

"Good morning, señor Rose, señor Fairchild. Have you..." he motioned with his hand toward the still smoking remains.

"No," Harry said, "I thought it best not to. And still too hot, still glowing, see." He pointed as another small collapse sent up ash and sparks.

"What can you tell me of this?"

"I'll get back, not much I can do here," Fairchild said, moving away.

"You can tell me nothing, señor Fairchild?"

"No, Harry's your man. Good to see you again, Diaz."

They watched as he left them, his step a little quicker than when he'd approached.

"So, Harry Rose, we are here again. Where is Gabriela?"

"She's asleep. It was a long night. For both of us."

"Tell me about the long night and Ernest Portillo's house."

It didn't take long. Without the fear and the heat, without the chocking smoke and Gabriela's tears the story was a short one. Only when he'd finished did Harry mention seeing Bill Fairchild on the beach a short time before the fire and how when asked, he'd suggested he hadn't been there.

"You think it is important?"

"No, Victor, probably not. But it's a bit odd, him being around like that, and then this."

"And yet you were also out in the night, later than el señor Fairchild. When someone saw you would they also think it was, er, interesting, so soon before the fire began?"

"Did someone see me?"

"Perhaps, I do not know."

They stayed for a few more minutes, Harry unsure what else he should be doing, the captain apparently happy to patrol the edge of the burning, occasionally poking in the ashes with a metal stake he'd picked up.

"Some coffee? Something to eat? I need something," Harry said.

As they walked to Casa Rosa, an overwhelming tiredness enveloped Harry, so much so that he was barely able to put one foot in front of another. Gabriela was stretched out on the couch and he sank into the chair beside her. Alone, he would have slept immediately.

"I must sit a minute."

"Stay there Harry Rose," Victor said, "I will get some coffee, some breakfast."

After he'd poked around in the kitchen for a few minutes he returned with coffee and cheese and fruit. When Harry had recovered a little, Victor said quietly, "What of your other troubles, Harry?"

"Slowly, it is better," he said, before studying the policeman's face for a moment or two. The man seemed older than Harry had noticed before, with hints of lines where he hadn't remember any. "Are you my friend, Victor? I hope so. I will tell you. We have some news which makes us optimistic. Important news which I will tell you one day soon. This week, I think, la señora Mejía will be happy and la juez Cruz too. We will see, but I think it'll be good."

"I too will be pleased for you, and for this child, esta querida niña." He spoke the words with such tenderness Harry wondered how he could ever have doubted his goodwill.

As they finished their coffee and Diaz made to leave, Harry asked, "What will you do now?"

"For the fire? I spoke to Oscar Portillo before I came here. He will come later, or tomorrow. I will speak to an investigator, ask him for the next action. Is there something else?"

"No. It was very frightening, that's all. I worry. Too much, or too little, I don't know which."

★

Harry woke, disoriented, in the chair where Victor Diaz had left him. In his dream Gabriela was calling his name from the water's edge but he couldn't understand what she was saying. Half awake, dream and reality merged.

"Papatico, there's no water."

"Where? No water where?"

"Here. In the sink."

He shook himself awake and went to look. She was right. No pressure, no water. The pump was old and had failed before. Repairing it, or worse, replacing it, was a messy job that needed care and patience. He tried the light over the sink. Fine. A look at the main panel showed the pump had tripped out. Another job, but sooner rather than later. They had bottled water to drink, but the well provided everything else.

As he stood at the back of the house wondering how long it would take to fix, his worries were interrupted by the familiar sight of a battered Peugeot lurching across the potholes.

"My God," Pippa said as she climbed out. "Come here you two, I want to hug you both. This is terrible."

They were both very happy to oblige.

Harry told the tale again, skipping lightly over his own fears and the escape from the pickup. No point in a graphic repeat of that episode, not with Gabriela still raw from the experience. He omitted the part about Bill Fairchild too, and his own moonlit wandering. To compound it all they were now without transport and without water.

"I can probably fix both," Harry concluded, with more confidence than he felt. "Could you take Gabriela to town, get something to eat, then come back and see how things are? Maybe we could stay with you tonight if it's not fixed."

With a pang he feared he'd assumed too much. Gabriela might still be too fragile to be separated from him. He stooped to hold her and say, "Darling Gabriela, I should've asked you. Will you go with Pippa while I fix the truck and see about the pump?"

"Yes," she said with a seriousness to match his.

"You should stay with me at La Plantación even if you get it fixed," Pippa said. "I was coming over today anyway, then I saw Leo and he told me what had happened." She paused before adding, "You look grey, Harry. This is horrible."

One reason Harry hung on to the old pickup was that it was repairable without needing to be hooked up to a computer for diagnosis. Running through the age-old check-list of fuel supply and mixture and sparking in the places it was meant to spark, he identified the main problem quickly enough. From his work box he found enough cable to make a replacement that would last a while.

The water pump was another matter. If he was lucky it would be the motor, if he was not it would be the impeller. In an hour he'd disconnected it, dismayed at the filth and gunk he found accumulated in it. It had certainly been working harder than it should have. Possibly, just possibly, a thorough clean might extend its life for a few days until he could get a replacement. He lugged it out to the truck ready to take to Pippa's.

Along the sand Harry saw Ernest's nephew poking at the ashes. He should at least go and commiserate with him over the loss of his inheritance.

"Ah, señor Rose," Oscar Portillo said cheerfully enough.

"It's Harry, remember? Oscar, I'm so sorry about the house, there was nothing we could do to save it. Did you have Ernest's things?"

"No, they are gone. There was nothing to take, nothing valuable."

"But the house, that was valuable."

"As I told you, we are not using it. We are selling it."

"What about your buyer, wasn't he going to use it?"

"I think no, the bulldozer maybe, we will see. He may be saved the expense. And there is some useful insurance."

Harry was shocked at the man's attitude, how could he lose such a thing and not care. More than not care, more as if he'd been relieved of a burden by something being settled.

"We almost lost Casa Rosa," Harry said, more as a rebuke than to gain sympathy.

"Fire is a terrible thing, eh señor Rose?," he nodded, "In these old houses, out here where nobody can help, one spark and, boof, there is fire. And then it burns until there is nothing. It does not ask questions and debate answers, no, it burns until there is nothing. Nada. This is still hot, do you know?"

"Yes, I know."

"You and I, señor Rose, we are thinking of Ernest, what if he had been here, eh? Who knows what may have happened? We know, eh? In the night, we are asleep and the fire is round us before we are awake."

"You speak as if you've known a fire like this."

"No, no. But I look here and I can see. You can see. And if there are children, huh? Boof."

The same images had been in Harry's head more than once in the hours since he'd woken to the sound of burning. The smoke and the dancing light of flame in Gabriela's window would stay with him for a long time. And with Gabriela too. The night had made frightening memories for them both, yet this man with his ghoulish commentary frightened him as much as the fire itself. There was no suggestion of sympathy or understanding for Harry's experience, nor Gabriela's trauma. If anything, he was taking a bizarre satisfaction from events. So vividly did he recreate the nightmare, Harry wondered if he had been present in the darkness beyond the flames. The idea triggered different fear, a fear that he'd set the blaze himself. He needed to get away from Oscar Portillo.

"I'm doing some work, I, er, must get on," he said, turning away before the man might extend a hand or wish him well, or safe or luck.

Oscar Portillo did none of those things. Harry doubted that he even watched him walking back to Casa Rosa.

They would be away from the house until he could replace the water pump, a night at best, more likely two or three if a new one had to be brought in from San Felipe. He should repack their bags, not just the frantic selection of last night, but a few more things to last them. He sat on the edge of his bed, checking through what he'd chosen in that smoky minute before they ran to the truck. He'd done such a thing once before, years ago in another life when an alarm had driven him from an apartment. Then he'd snatched the nearest but not necessarily the dearest of his possessions. His passport was the single common item between the two evacuations.

He laid out the meagre treasures on his bed. Gabriela had very little of her own and next to nothing from her mother. Héctor would always be a treasure, yet how many children of her age would have only one bedtime companion? It had made emergency packing a little simpler but sitting alone with the creature in his hands he could have wept for her.

She had no toys. How had he never bought her a toy beyond the toddler's push-along truck with wooden wheels and a cargo of wooden bricks that had sat unwanted under her mother's bed for years? She'd be a teenager before she'd had a chance to be a child. All that Pippa had said, and more, clarified as he sat there. When had he last played with her, as a child should play, not in his grown-up way, not in his grown-up teasing and play-acting way, but as a child might?

And now that he had time what should he pack for her? As he looked round he saw he'd missed nothing, there was nothing to miss. A single photo of her mother in its cheap little frame was a sad record of family, something he'd try to improve on in the coming weeks and months. In the thrill of fatherhood it was easy to forget there was now the possibility of finding her grandmother. With his own position more secure he could see himself following that link sooner rather than later.

If Gabriela had little for a child, Estefanía had even less for a grown woman. She would, of course, have taken her everyday treasures with her when they'd waved her goodbye at the ferry, but she had less than Gabriela in her room. A few clothes, her Bible, Gabriela's photo and her tray of cheap jewellery and hair slides. Even the tray was no more than a box lid. The glass in the photo frame had cracked sometime in their bumping running flight from the house and the truck. It had at least been broken in a good cause, not through some avoidable clumsiness.

Harry picked up her Bible and weighed it in his hand. The red faux-leather binding appeared to be no older than Estefanía, perhaps it had been a childhood gift. Its pages had been closed since the day she left. Harry had an idea that Estefanía looked at it from time to time, but it seemed more of a sentimental possession than something more. So far as he was aware, she'd never been to a church since coming to Isla Concepción.

He let it fall open, on the off-chance that Estefanía might've tucked a photograph or keepsake between its gilt-edged pages. There was nothing, but the flyleaf was more revealing. The inscription was to Gabriela. It was Gabriela's Bible, not her Mami's. It had always been placed by Estefanía's bed and there it had stayed, apparently hers and waiting for her return. The writing was in Estefanía's blocky print. *My Darling Gabriela you may find truths for all your life between these covers keep it with you always hugs and kisses Mami*. Below it Estefanía had drawn a smiley. There was no date.

To find such a precious thing, a personal note from her Mami to Gabriela, was wonderful to Harry. His poor girl had nothing else, but now she'd have at least one permanent reminder of how much her Mami had loved her. Perhaps Gabriela had once seen the words, for surely Estefanía would have shown them to her when she'd given her the Bible. The moment probably held little significance for a young child and so it had slipped from her consciousness. Perhaps it would be reawakened when he showed it to her later.

The house still smelled strongly of smoke. It had pervaded everything. All the bedding and their clothing would need to be cleaned or replaced. Harry wondered idly if Oscar Portillo's useful insurance would cover the expense, not that he wanted anything more to do with the man. He stuffed a garbage bag with a selection of Gabriela's newer clothes and a few of his shirts and put it along with their overnight bags in the pickup. He couldn't resist another trial of his makeshift repair and was rewarded when the engine responded immediately.

He sat at the wheel enjoying this small success, half expecting Pippa and Gabriela to return at any moment. Oscar Portillo had disappeared, presumably back to Puerto Reunión, and the place was deserted apart from himself. He saw it as a stranger might see it, with black strands of ash and fire across the sand, a charred timber still defiantly pointing skywards from the place that had been Ernest's home, the last power pole in the line with its wires looping down to the scorched ground. The precious message from Estefanía came back to him as he sat there. Had he missed some nuance concealed in her words, some colloquialism in her Spanish that eluded him? The more he thought about it the more the words seemed deliberate, more formal than a mother's note to her young child. Perhaps she had thought too carefully about her message in the context of a Bible, rather than dashing off a simple inscription as she might in any other book she'd give to her daughter.

Harry took the book carefully from the bottom of the holdall and read Estefanía's words again. Nothing new revealed itself. He leafed through it more carefully than before, but still found nothing slipped into the pages. As he let it fall open in his hand the soft leatherette of the covers hung down on either side of his palm as the book divided itself in equal parts. But they hung down unequally because the back covering was stiffer than the front. Pieces of thin card had been pushed through slits close to the binding to help the covers keep their shape. He removed both, but as the front cover was now no more than fabric it behaved as such, whereas the rear cover still kept its shape. Closer inspection revealed a second stiffener which he withdrew carefully. It was an unaddressed envelope, a little smaller than the original card.

His hands shook a little as he flipped it open. What had Estefanía chosen to hide in here? Before he'd unfolded the first document he saw it would be a birth registration. It was Gabriela's. A little different from the one he'd so recently acquired, but to his relief it contained the same information. This was the original, his was a copy from the register. Estefanía had kept it safely out of sight, available should she need it but not for anyone's eyes until then. And not for Harry's eyes at all. It confirmed what he knew already: she'd chosen not to gamble on his reaction to being named as Gabriela's father.

He guessed the second paper would be Estefanía's own registration and so it was. Two fifty-dollar US bills completed the collection.

These four things made up Estefanía's secret stash, safer in a Bible than anywhere else. Which had come first, he wondered, the inscription or the hiding place? Maybe it was an awful prescience on Estefanía's part, maybe it was a family tradition to use a Bible as a safe place for such things. None of it made any difference now. It wasn't the book itself or the inscription which had made him snatch it up in the smoke for Gabriela, it was the lack of anything else she might hold precious.

He put everything back in the envelope and slid it back into its hiding place. He couldn't think of anywhere safer for it to be.

★

At Pippa's they walked by the sea, close to where they'd found the glass fishing float. Gabriela was outwardly much recovered, but Harry thought a walk would be better for them both than hanging around La Plantación, dwelling on the previous night. Gabriela stayed close, keeping Harry and Pippa within range of a quick dash, but something of her usual self had begun to return.

It seemed to Harry that something of Pippa's usual self had also returned. The edge of irritation he'd felt before his last trip to San Felipe, the distance he'd sensed when he'd told her of his new parental status, both these unfamiliar scowls had disappeared as completely as the sand is smoothed by a wave.

As they climbed the hill back towards the house, Gabriela alternately complaining of tired legs then scampering ahead of them, Pippa said, "Harry, dear Harry, I owe you an apology for last week."

"No," he said, "no, you don't. You're right and you've been right all along, about friends especially, but all the other stuff too. She needs more, she should have more than she has."

He told her about the Bible and snatching up her precious things as the house filled with smoke and how few there had been, how easy it was to collect everything of importance in only a few seconds, how even with careful thought and time to think, he couldn't add anything to that hasty grab. And since the Bible was in the conversation he told Pippa of the inscription and the hidden papers and the hundred dollars.

"It's not much of a legacy is it?" she said.

"No, it isn't. And here's another thing you were right about: my will. Julio has drafted one, I'll get it signed this week."

"Now I feel worse than ever. I shouldn't have spoken how I did. I suppose I'll have to do mine now."

He stopped and pulled her round to see if she was being serious: she was.

"Damn right you will."

"Actually Harry, it was something else I had in mind. It was Gabriela. It was when you showed me her birth certificate and you were so happy. You bounced off the ferry like you'd won the lottery. When you showed me I wasn't very nice to you. I was jealous. I'm sorry."

"Jealous? I didn't know. I didn't think. Of me being named as her father?"

"It's never simple is it? It was all mixed up with the idea that you might really be her father, her biological father. I was jealous of that. Once, we might have, but we didn't. And then there's you having a baby with a girl young enough to be your granddaughter. That hurt. I know it shouldn't have, but it did, even after all these years."

"A slight possibility of."

"However bloody slight it was, it was possible. Which means you were fucking her and if not her then someone like her. Too drunk to remember, but possible. Yes?" she said, with great emphasis on the final syllable.

"Yes."

"Thank you. Hence my feelings. And if you make me cross by being an arse we'll have to do this another time."

At the sound of Pippa's raised voice Gabriela had come back down the slope to join them, then she begged a carry. Harry wasn't inclined to refuse her, not immediately.

"Come on then, I'll give you…" but he stopped himself in the instant he was about to say fireman's lift. "I'll put you across my shoulders, you're too big to sit on them."

She made a face but was curious enough to find out what it was like.

"First, you have to pretend to be a sack of potatoes, can you do that?"

"Potatoes? Can I be something else?"

"Yes, how about coffee beans?"

"Um…"

Before she could decide he was down beside her and lifting her across his shoulders, her head and an arm one side of his neck, her legs the other. He very much hoped that she'd want to get down quickly. They walked on, up toward the house, ten paces, twenty paces, thirty, before she complained.

"Papatico! Put me down."

He stopped but kept her hoisted. "Quiet!" he said, "Coffee doesn't talk."

"Pleeeease!"

"Since you ask so nicely," he said lowering her gently onto her feet. "See if Tatiana is still hanging round the house. Go quietly and look carefully."

Gabriela danced off ahead of them. The house was not far and they watched as she tiptoed across the terrace.

"Tatiana?"

"Your resident iguana. Gabriela gave her a name."

After a few more steps they stopped to watch as Gabriela crept about, peering in all the nooks and crannies and up under the eaves.

"There was something else," Pippa said quietly, "a different jealousy."

"Whatever it was, I forgive you, it's gone now. You don't have anything to apologise for."

"Actually, it hasn't completely gone. And I want you to know. Whatever the truth has been over the years, I know Gabriela lives with you, not me, but I always felt we shared her. You thought that too. The first thing you did that day La Agencia came calling was to call me. Then later we talked about how we could take care of her, and what happened if you weren't around, what I would do for her."

"Yes," he said, a little uncertainly.

"We both love her, and care for her, and we're on the same footing, she's not ours, but we carry on as if she is. And in her different ways she loves us both. Then suddenly you get promoted, suddenly she really is yours, just with a piece of paper and a wave of a wand. So, I was jealous of that. And if you want to know, I still am."

"I didn't know, I should have thought. I'm so sorry, Pippa."

He put his arms round her and hugged her tight to his body. It was a hug she returned in full.

After a while he said, "You'll always be special for Gabriela, and you'll be special in ways that I will never be. It doesn't make up for what you're saying, but it's something. It's a very important something."

"Thank you, Harry. I'm still jealous. You and she will get closer now, I see it in you already. No matter what you say or what you do I'll be left behind. You'll both still love me in your way, but it'll be different. It can't help but be different."

"I think if Estefanía had been writing in a name for Gabriela's mother she'd have chosen you. No consolation, I know, but it's what I think."

She freed herself from his embrace so as to be able to pull his face to hers. "That's a lovely thing to say, thank you," she said before kissing him. "While we're being honest and kind to each other, there's something else I want to talk about later. Come on,

211

let's get something to eat and drink. But first, you and Gabriela both need showers. You certainly."

★

Once he'd cleaned the pump the fault had been easy enough to diagnose. No amount of time and energy would repair the unrepairable. That meant a visit to Puerto Reunión which he could squeeze in while Gabriela was in school but chose not to. A night at Pippa's could easily become two or as many as were needed.

After he'd collected Gabriela and they'd lazed away an hour over lunch at the Kasanee, he dropped her off at La Plantación and returned to Casa Rosa for another bag of laundry and to take measurements for the pump. From the turn by Gabriela's tree, the house looked forlorn without its nearest neighbour. When he reached the verandah and found his book and empty glass where he'd left them and the door wide open, the place felt deserted and alien, abandoned long ago by people he'd never met. Inside, the smell of smoke persisted. He guessed it would always be there until they became inured to it. Outside by the back door the stink from the fire had lessened but he could still taste it in the air. The two ends of the water pipes stared mutely at each other across the space where the pump had been. It was as if the local scavengers had already started stripping the place of anything worth taking.

Casa Rosa no longer looked like their home, nor did it smell like their home. He turned and looked towards her tree. The house may have already forgotten them, but the tree would always be her tree. In years to come she could return and look down the track and smile to herself to see it still standing and know it was hers, know its knots and footholds, know the hours she'd spent in its branches waiting for her Mami.

His jingling phone took him from his reverie.

"Señor Rose?"

"Señorita Chavarria, we haven't spoken lately. I should say thank you for all your work, all you've discovered."

"It is good that you are pleased but there is still work to be done. I must tell you that la juez Cruz will decide on her actions with regard to the new information in Gabriela's registration, tomorrow. It is courtesy that someone should attend. El señor Aguilar has suggested I be there. Perhaps you would wish to be present? It is not necessary."

"In Puerto Reunión?"

"Yes. We expect only that she will dismiss the case."

"She might not? What did you hear?"

"There were no details."

He'd spent weeks waiting to hear the word *dismiss*, yet with his newly bestowed parenthood he'd almost forgotten there was still a process to be followed. More than a piece of paper, a dismissal would be public recognition of a new status, a rejection of false charges. It would be the official start of their new life. A rebirth.

"Tomorrow morning? At ten? Yes, I'd like to be there. Do you know if la señora Mejía will also be in court?"

"Perhaps."

He had an urge to ask her to have lunch with him, to celebrate the outcome, but he didn't want to tempt fate. And she might easily sidestep a simple invitation. He chose his words carefully.

"Will we have lunch?"

"Perhaps. Will you bring Gabriela?"

"No. There is school, although…"

"It is better she is at school."

Easy to make arrangements when Pippa could be relied upon to fill any gaps in care or collection. It would be different if she weren't there, even for the few weeks she'd suggested she might be gone. He couldn't be anything but pleased for her, although his first thought had been more selfish. She'd resisted previous invitations to attend small exhibitions of her work in the United States, but now it seemed that someone wanted to make it worth her while. Three good galleries, San Francisco, Chicago and Toronto, the chance for comfortable travel with minimum effort and buyers supposedly queuing up for her work. He'd tentatively questioned why she'd agreed to the trip, but her *why let someone else get rich when I'm dead?* was unanswerable.

It brought his own situation into even sharper focus, not that it needed much sharpening. Everything since Victor Diaz had raced along the track with la señora Mejía close behind him pointed in one direction: he, they, should leave Casa Rosa. He weighed the idea, let it run its full course of never seeing the place again, becoming the visitor from the city when he came for the weekend, bringing supplies for Pippa, an exotic bottle for Leo and Carla, another for Victor Diaz. He'd bring Gabriela, of course, but not always, she'd be growing into her own life of music or sport or whatever she chose, just as Cristela and Stuart had done.

Right on cue Julio called.

"Hello Julio, I've just spoken to Indira Chavarria, she's already told me about the court tomorrow, good news she thinks."

"Yes, we hope so. But now there are new developments, some for later, perhaps when you come to San Felipe, but one thing is urgent."

"Should I come now, Julio? Something serious?"

"Yes, my friend, it is serious. It is Gabriela's mother, we believe it is Estefanía Flores."

Harry's throat tightened at the mention of her name. He daren't ask what new pain was about to be inflicted on his suffering child, although Julio's voice gave little room for optimism.

"There is a match with Gabriela's DNA." He paused long enough to leave Harry in no doubt where the match was made before confirming the worst. "Sadly it was found among those who have died without a name. There is a process, it is not complete, I have asked for a second check, a precaution, but we are told that the result can be trusted."

"Ooh no," he groaned, sinking into his chair, every ounce of energy knocked out of him. Hadn't they suffered enough? "What happened? When? Too many questions, I don't know where to start."

"One answer and now many more questions, yes. I know nothing more, the results say nothing of Estefanía Flores, only that Gabriela's mother is among the unknown. But there is one thing, an important thing and we must act quickly. The body is still held, but not for very long. Less than a week, I have already requested an extension."

"How is that? Where is she?"

"She is in San Felipe, in the facility for those waiting to be claimed by their family, waiting for a name to be found. It seems she has been there for more than a year, nearly two, but there is a limit and that limit is almost reached. It may be extended or we may ask to move la señorita elsewhere.

"Harry, the testing tells us that Gabriela's mother is deceased. It does not tell us that Gabriela's mother is la señorita Estefanía Flores. I'm sure it is so, but an identification will be needed. Most likely it will be you who will do this, especially in view of the information on Gabriela's registration."

Difficult as it would be, he knew he could deal with such a thing, but there was Gabriela to be considered. She too would have a claim to see her mother.

"Is she, er, injured? I mean, recognisable?"

"There is a match with a deceased woman in the facility in San Felipe. For today that is all I know, Harry."

"What should I do?"

"Arrange to come to San Felipe at the end of the week, you will stay with us of course. Also you should advise la juez Cruz of the match. I will tell la señorita Chavarria before she comes to Puerto Reunión."

"And Gabriela?"

"She should come also. There will be arrangements to be made. A funeral. You should prepare her."

Just like that. Prepare her for news of her mother's death, prepare her for her mother having been dead for a long time, prepare her for the news that all those hours in her lookout tree had been wasted, the tender notes in case she returned while they were away were all useless, the careful preservation of her

215

room and her pitiful belongings were a pathetic waste, the note in a Bible was the only thing left, that and the dollars slipped into the cover.

"Yes. I should. I will. Have you told anyone else yet?"

"No, you first, Harry. Elena, tonight."

"I'll talk to Pippa and see what she thinks."

"I think there is also someone else to be told," Julio suggested.

"Oh God, yes, Estefanía's mother. If she can be found. Will you…?"

"Ah, no, I had not thought of la señora Blanca. I was thinking of DIC, el investigador Daniel Scott, who should be told. He too has been searching for la señorita."

"Easy to forget, yes, he must be told. As soon as possible."

An accusation of murder should have been indelibly printed in his mind, yet in the midst of all his other trials it had been the forgotten trouble. It had been preposterous from the moment he'd heard it said, and he could never take it seriously, even if the implications were unspeakable. At least now the manner of her death would become known and that last cloud could be blown away. How much better if it was the manner of her living that brought the relief.

"El investigador Scott will be my next call. We will hear soon enough of the circumstances. Harry, I am sorry to bring you this news."

"You said there was something else, something when I'm in San Felipe."

"It is not urgent, it concerns the property, it will wait, I will show you."

216

12

The road to La Plantación was never so long, nor so short, as his drive after receiving the news from Julio. He wanted to be near Gabriela instantly, to hold her close and stroke her hair and wipe away her tears. He wanted the drive to never end, for him to never see her run from the house and meet him with her beautiful gappy smile. Above all he wanted the moment of telling to be in the past and not in their immediate future.

Even as he considered how he should share the awful knowledge, fresh doubts circled. Fresh doubts or, he conceded to himself, new excuses to delay the moment of telling. What if Estefanía had snatched Gabriela from her real mother and it was not Estefanía lying stiff in a refrigerator drawer, what then? Surely he should wait for absolute confirmation before leading Gabriela down the miserable path? And shouldn't Estefanía's mother be the one to identify the body? But who knew if Cristin Blanca was traceable or even alive? And how long since she'd seen her daughter, how long since she'd cared one way or another? Even as the uncharitable thoughts entered his head, he reproached himself for such meanness. A mother never stops caring.

As he swung the pickup round the last turn he caught a glimpse of Gabriela and Pippa standing together at the top of the trail down to the ocean. They were a good pair. Despite her fears to the contrary, Pippa would surely become even more important to the child in the coming days and weeks. And Pippa would give him good counsel before he launched into the latest tragedy in Gabriela's young life.

When the evening was almost done and he'd carried the sleeping Gabriela to her bed with the fate of her mother still unspoken, Harry poured nightcaps for himself and Pippa. From

217

the terrace the slope of darkness fell away below him to the sparkling silver of the ocean. Standing there with the dome of stars above and the black earth beneath his feet, was supremely peaceful, as close, he guessed, to walking in space as he was likely to come.

"Julio called after I'd spoken to Indira Chavarria. There is news of Estefanía." He spoke to the universe, not turning to Pippa.

She said nothing.

"It looks bad."

"I thought there was something else, but sometimes it's hard to tell with you, Harry. What did he say?"

He relayed the conversation as best as he could recall it, no embellishments, no tears or commentary.

"I suppose we knew really. Even so. What do you feel?" Pippa said when he'd finished.

"Sick for Gabriela, sick at the prospect of telling her. There's still the slightest of chances it's not Estefanía, but that's not worth hoping for, it'd probably be worse for everyone. It would mean… I don't know what it'd mean. Even if I thought she wasn't Estefanía I think I'd probably say she was. Then it'll be done with."

Pippa considered this for a moment before saying, "It is Estefanía. Estefanía is Gabriela's mother, no question."

"I hope so. I hope it's her. Never thought I'd say that."

"Poor girl, never had much did she? What about you, what do you feel for yourself?"

"Tired. Very, very, tired. It was like being hit hard." He clenched his fist and held it against his stomach as he spoke.

"When will you tell her?"

"I don't know, I thought you might offer some of your good advice. I thought it would be as soon as I got here or tonight, but I wasn't ready. Not in the morning, not when I'll be off to Puerto Reunión for la juez Cruz. And I hoped you might be around when I do tell her, so maybe in San Felipe with Elena and Julio, will you come? Can you come?"

"Yes, I'll come if you think it would be better."

218

"I think she should have everyone who loves her and who she loves right there for her. Then there's seeing her mother, what do you think about her seeing Estefanía?"

"Probably a good thing, but maybe you should know how Estefanía looks before you suggest it. Go before her, see her, see how she is. When you see her I think you'll know. And ask Elena what she thinks. You and I, we come from a different place, they do things differently here."

"Yes, and probably better."

"I think you might ask Cristela too. She's the nearest thing she has to a friend of her own age."

They talked late into the night about life and death, theirs and others, about unfilled dreams and unexpected pleasures, about how best they should shape Gabriela's future. They talked until they fell silent and asleep in the warmth of the night under a billion stars while the child slept quietly, holding Héctor close to her heart.

★

At El Tribunal Central de Familia there was a delay, urgent business for both la señora Mejía and la juez Cruz. It was something, Harry supposed, that he and Gabriela were no longer urgent business, that they could be shuffled to the end of the day without a second thought. But as they had slipped down the list of priorities, he couldn't help but wonder who had replaced them? Which child was now in danger, who would receive the unwelcome visit? Who among them would be fortunate enough to have friends like his, an ally as diligent as Indira Chavarria?

He knew almost nothing of her other than confidence beyond her years and abilities beyond her training, while she knew a great deal about him. It made an unequal relationship and such inequality is always unsatisfactory. An ally certainly, but not from sentiment or feeling, a paid ally. A mercenary.

Killing time in a café until their appointment with the judge, sitting as friends would but as allies must, Harry couldn't resist another probe.

"Your time with Julio will soon be over. Will you stay in touch, señorita?"

"Yes, of course, el señor Aguilar has been most generous."

"And different work than you might have expected."

"Perhaps, yes," she smiled.

"A good outcome."

"It seems so, although la señorita Estefanía Flores is still to be, er, confirmed, is she not?"

"Yes. I meant good regarding..." Good regarding what? She'd wrong-footed him again with her unwavering precision. She wore her professional aura as easily as her black court suit. The impossibility of seeing beneath it only made him wish for it all the more.

Her likeness to Estefanía remained, although now he had to remind himself of it, seek it out in her features. With the prospect of seeing that true face once again, cold and grey in the worst of places, he wondered if he remembered Gabriela's mother at all.

"It will not be easy for you to see la señorita Flores again," she said with a hint of compassion. Not for the first time, Indira Chavarria's insight unsettled him. She could guess his thoughts while he could see nothing of hers.

"No, not easy. But it will be an end to the uncertainty and that's the only good thing about it."

"We must hope so. I wonder if you will know her. And Gabriela, I wonder if she will know her mother."

"Do you think I might not? Do you know something? Is she injured?"

"Ah no, no señor Rose, I have no knowledge of la señorita. But knowing a face is sometimes difficult. There are examples of witnesses who can swear honestly that they saw a person do something and yet another will swear that it was a different person."

"Stress or panic, a threat, these can make the mind play tricks."

"We are taught to question certainty. Everyone has doubts. The man who is certain may be lying, to himself if no one else."

"Yes, I can see that," Harry said warily. She was dancing rings around him again. "Is there something you are thinking of, something you wish to say, señorita Chavarria?"

"Will you be certain when you see la señorita Estefanía?"

"You think I may not be?" he said, more sharply than he intended.

"You once said that you may not want to know the past about la señorita. A little lie to yourself. You once said I looked like la señorita, yet nobody else has said this. Gabriela saw nothing, there was nothing in her eyes when she looked at me. I wondered if perhaps you wished it so. A brown-skinned young woman to take the place of another. A little lie to yourself. The mind plays tricks, as you say."

Harry was ambushed by her candour, in all his years in the country he had never quite got used to the customary plain speaking; his polite upbringing of euphemism and tight-lipped denial remained too deeply ingrained.

When he'd recovered he said, "Perhaps," and looked away to close the conversation. It was better to keep la señorita as an ally.

The judge's room was exactly as he remembered it, devoid of anything but bare essentials, the three chairs lined up waiting for them. On the desk the solitary file, as before. As he sat, flanked as previously by his almost-lawyer and Arsenia Mejía, the emotions of that first visit rushed back, he was once again ready for a fight, even though he was anticipating an altogether happier experience today. He'd been too angry. Or not angry enough. The talented Indira Chavarria had steered him through that, deftly excusing his ill-temper and frustration, quietly impressing her legal superiors. Here she was again, with surely her farewell appearance in this provincial backwater.

La juez Cruz smiled at him before opening the folder marked with Gabriela's name. He watched as long fingers slid between the covers before carefully separating them, as if a precious painting or ancient manuscript might be kept between them. Harry hadn't noticed how pale and slender her hands were. They were elegant, manicured, even beautiful. How could he have missed such hands? Then he looked away quickly before the lawyer or the agent from APN might follow his gaze or his thoughts.

"Señor Rose?" the judge was saying.

"Yes. Sorry, yes."

"It was not necessary to attend today, but I am happy you have done so, señor Rose. La señora Mejía has given me your new information. This case is not usual, from the start it was not usual, and now it continues to be so. To find that you are the father, it is a surprise for everyone."

There was no malice or prejudice in the judge's voice, a hint of scepticism maybe, but nothing to suggest that she might challenge his new status. Harry had considered this moment, weighed what he should say not only to judge Cruz, but to anyone else who might be tempted to comment on his fatherhood.

"La señorita Estefanía made me a beautiful gift," he said, knowing that both the judge and the social worker would fully understand his meaning. He knew too that it was true and easier to say because of it.

"A beautiful gift, yes," agreed the judge. "La señora Mejía has requested the process of finding a new home for Gabriela should be ended. She has spoken to el Departamento de Investigaciones Criminales and they raise no objections. I accept la señora's request. Gabriela will stay with you, señor Rose. It makes me happy to say this."

"Thank you. There is something else." Harry turned to Indira Chavarria for confirmation that he should share the news of Estefanía. She nodded her agreement. "Yesterday we received bad news, information that la señorita Estefanía Flores is dead. Muerto. We have been told she's been dead for a long time." The words grew thick in his mouth as he spoke them, the finality of them rising up like floodwater to drown him. After a moment for breath he continued. "She is among the unidentified in San Felipe. DIC may not have known this when you spoke to them, el investigador Scott was informed yesterday."

222

"Ah, señor Rose, that will be a great sadness for Gabriela and for you."

To his surprise, Harry felt the touch of Arsenia Mejía's hand lightly on his arm.

★

"Julio?"

"More information, Harry. Some details of Estefanía Flores. She has been moved from the facility to, er, una funeraria, er, La Funeraria de las Tres Marías. It's not far from here."

"Thank you. Will we…?"

"Will you come on Friday? I've made arrangements for you to visit. There is still the question of identity, although it seems certain. And a detective, un investigador, will also be present. A formality, but there is a process."

"Yes, I'll be there. Pippa and Gabriela too. We'll come tomorrow."

"Good, it is better."

"There are arrangements, the funeral, but I thought you might do this."

"I will."

A dozen other questions silently came and went in a blur before Harry could focus on the topic that worried him the most. He would never let Gabriela see her mother if she'd been disfigured, if she was anything less than beautiful. He would manage, but Gabriela's final image of her Mami must be beautiful, a lovely thing to cherish always.

"Have you seen her, Julio?"

"No. I will come with you on Friday."

"Have you heard anything of what happened?"

"Ah, yes, there is a police report. A traffic accident. A truck. Very quick. There are few details, but there is nothing good to be said, only that it was quick."

For all the possibilities, accusations of murder, allegations of abuse and hints of slavery, for all the million things that could have happened to Gabriela's Mami, it came down to the mundane: hit by a truck. Harry could hardly believe he'd heard the answer, an answer so unworthy of all the drama and suspicion surrounding her disappearance. He'd been braced for some unspecified horror, some incomprehensible event that even now could sweep him into its consequences. Death was death but the manner of it did make a difference to the living. A truck was understandable, a fractured skull was understandable, a child would understand.

"In San Felipe?"

"Yes."

"Soon after we...?"

"Yes, soon after." Harry heard the turning of pages. "It was, er, two days I think, yes."

Only a few hours after *Espíritu de las Islas* had carried her away, smiling and waving as she went. Two nights. Long before she was missed. What were they doing when her soft flesh met the metal? Where were they at the moment of impact? Was Gabriela in her bed or her tree? It didn't matter then, it didn't matter now, they couldn't go back and save her, they couldn't plead with her not to go, claw at her arm and pull her back from the ticket office. It didn't make any difference, but he had an urgent need to know.

"What time of day, does it say, Julio?"

"Yes. Early morning."

"Ready to come home."

She may have been, but Julio said nothing.

"And her purse, her ID, her cédula, didn't she have it?"

"It was never found. It may have been stolen."

Before or after the fatal encounter? Which event precipitated the other? *Oh, Estefanía,* he silently wailed, *there'll be tears for you yet, your daughter's will mingle with mine for sure,* he felt them brimming even as he sat dumbly holding the phone.

"Tomorrow Harry, we want to see you and Gabriela, come tomorrow."

"We will, in the afternoon."

He'd been working, almost finished with fitting the new pump when Julio had called. Another ten minutes at most and it should be ready to test, but he was unable to move from his chair. She'd been a theoretical match with a swab in some laboratory until this moment. Now she was certainly Estefanía, certainly Gabriela's Mami, certainly dead. There was a chance she might still be whole, with a little cosmetic attention she might still be beautiful for Gabriela to see.

She swirled around him, images of her stood before him with a coffee, a sandwich she'd made for his lunch, beers, one for him and one for Victor Diaz. She'd slipped so easily into his life after the first awkward weeks when neither of them quite knew why she was there. What if she'd never come to Casa Rosa, what if he'd never spoken to her on the bus, what if he'd never held her baby, what then? Then she might still be alive. But the past was unforgiving, remorselessly grinding its way through the twists and turns of Estefanía Flores' life to the moment she stepped in front of a truck in San Felipe.

At length a feeble energy entered him. Mechanically he attended to the pump, giving it a cursory trial before collecting another bag of smoky clothes and chucking it into the pickup. As the engine ticked over, he sat, hands on the wheel, staring at his home, wondering if they would ever sleep at Casa Rosa again. Abruptly he stamped his right foot down and the pickup lurched forward, sand and stones spraying from under the tyres.

★

For an hour or so, Gabriela was quiet, content to switch seats across the aisle, first by Pippa, then with Harry, then Pippa's turn again. She'd rejoiced at the prospect of a day in the city away from school, then jumped round in gleeful circles when she heard they'd be staying at Cristela's house and there'd be no school until after the weekend. But an hour into the drive, boredom, mixed with excited anticipation of the days ahead, made her fractious. The rain restricted their view of the passing landscape and she'd exhausted reading and I-spy and her new colouring book. When she began jumping from one seat to the other, Pippa eyed her disapprovingly, and made that disapproval plain to Harry, too. Not long ago she would have said something to Gabriela herself.

"Gabriela, please sit and put your belt on," Harry said.

For an instant she looked at him as if she might disobey, a look that said *who are you to tell me what to do,* but it passed as quickly as it had appeared. She did as she was asked, albeit with pursed lips and folded arms. No wonder she was erratic, Harry knew he and Pippa were both scratchy, pre-occupied with the real purpose of their journey, one that carried them towards the reckoning in La Funeraria de las Tres Marías. He was sure Gabriela had no inkling, although he was just as sure some sense of their anxieties had transferred itself to her. The burden of telling her grew heavier with each mile, even if he did excuse himself by the need for absolute confirmation. There would come a moment when he had no choice but to speak.

On the outskirts of a little town the bus slowed to a crawl. A little distance ahead they could see the flashing blue and red of police lights where a knot of jostling vehicles were being forced into a single lane. Their bus was halted close to the accident and Gabriela strained to see what was happening, slipping out of her belt and leaning across Harry to the window. On another day he might have tried to distract her for fear of some gruesome event causing distress. It was a mystery to him why he should be cursed with such sensibilities when the sight of blood so quickly drew a crowd. Too late to change himself, he could at least allow Gabriela's natural curiosity to be satisfied.

The bus inched forward, giving them a perfect view of the incident. Police and paramedics milled around, pointing and gesticulating. One was taking photographs with an archaic camera and flashgun. The crushed remains of a motorcycle were visible beneath the wheels of an oversize green SUV more suited to combat than the school run. A few metres in front of the vehicle were two orange plastic sheets, apparently randomly discarded in the roadway. The ribbed sole of a running shoe protruded from beneath a corner of the sheet nearest to them. As they watched a policeman lifted the other end and briefly inspected the victim before letting the plastic fall back.

Then they were gone. The curtain dropped on the tableau and the grubby houses thrummed by until they were once more in open country. Gabriela slumped back into her seat, still and staring. Pippa caught Harry's eye with an expression suggesting he should seize the opening which the tragedy had so conveniently given him. She might be right, but he was lost for words. He'd been groping his way towards an opening to suit a completely different scene after a visit to the funeral home, now two bodies in the road demanded a script re-write.

"Papatico, what were those orange things?" Gabriela asked in a way that suggested she already had a good idea of the answer.

"Ugh," he said, caught in the middle of composing his own opening on the same topic, "plastic sheets I think. Someone had put them over the, er, people, the motorbike riders most likely."

"Why?"

"To be respectful, maybe. So that people wouldn't stare at them. And to keep them dry too."

"Were they dead?"

"Yes."

"Why do they have to keep dry when they're dead?"

"They don't really, it doesn't matter. But people often like to treat dead people as if they are still alive, in some small ways. So they cover them to keep them dry, as you would if the person was alive. And if the person was all twisted then you might straighten them out, to make them more comfortable, as it were. It makes no difference really, but it makes us feel better."

"What will happen to them?"

"They will be taken to a special place, to be examined."

"A morgue," she interrupted.

"Yes, you remembered, good. The police, their families, everyone, will want to know why they died, even if it seems obvious. There are rules to be followed. Then their friends and families will come and there'll be a funeral."

"And they'll be buried."

"Yes, they'll be buried in a cemetery, somewhere like the one in Concepción near your school."

Gabriela considered this for a few moments, while Harry collected his own thoughts, pleased she could talk so openly with him, wondering why he'd been so worried when she had no fears at all.

"Will I be dead one day?" she said.

"Yes, we will all be dead one day. We are born and live and die, it's the same for everyone. For me, for Pippa, even for you one day, many, many years from now."

"When will you be dead?"

"We don't know, we never know. One day we are alive and the next we are not."

"What happens when you're dead?"

"Nobody knows, but the best answer we have is, nothing. It's hard to imagine nothing so people make up stories, but really there's nothing."

She was quiet again, although he could see she had more questions, even if she didn't know what they were or how to ask them.

"Are you thinking about your Mami?"

"A little bit," Gabriela nodded.

"Is there anything you'd like to ask me, anything at all?"

She shook her head.

"We may find out what has happened to her quite soon. It's one of the reasons we are going to San Felipe. We may find out tomorrow."

"Will Cristela be there tonight?"

"I think so, I didn't ask."

"Can we make another song when we get there?"

"You'll have to ask her."

A great tension flowed out of him, Gabriela was as prepared for the difficult day as he could hope for. From across the aisle Pippa gave him an approving smile.

Elena and Julio met them with the same warmth and love as always, but the welcome was subdued, a low-key version of previous visits. The adults set the tone, but Cristela and Stuart picked up on the quieter note, no doubt coached by their parents beforehand. The family fussed over Gabriela as much, if not more than usual and the evening passed as amiably as ever, despite conversation being stunted by the unspoken topic of Estefanía Flores. Every part of their lives, past, present and future, seemed influenced by Gabriela's Mami, both in her life and, more oppressively, her presumed death. Each of them was waiting for Harry's appointment the following morning to release them from Estefanía's spell. Even Gabriela was spellbound, although she didn't know it. One way or another, although there was little doubt which, it would be the following evening before they would able to speak without first carefully considering each word.

Everyone apart from Gabriela sought early nights through tiredness or simply to hasten the passage of time. As they said their goodnights, Julio motioned Harry aside. "There is no place for talking tonight," he said, passing him two buff envelopes, "Here are two things for you to see if you wish. There is a copy of the reports of la señorita's death, the one we believe is la señorita Estefanía, the person we will see tomorrow. These are the papers I spoke of yesterday, the circumstances of her death, the time and place and so on."

Harry nodded, taking the envelopes. "And the other?"

"The property, Playa de Rosas, the people with interests in your neighbour's villa. You remember? I said we would find something about them. It's not much. We can talk about everything tomorrow."

Harry took the papers, along with a Tomintoul nightcap, to his room and stretched out on the bed. In the house around him he guessed others lay the same, unsleeping, apprehensive of the day ahead. Gabriela, thankfully, had fallen fast asleep the moment she lay her head on the pillow. Her tomorrow was perhaps the longest of all.

Did he want to know about Estefanía's death, any more than he already did? If there was nothing to add why had Julio handed him the papers so discreetly? As the whisky spread its gentle spiciness round his mouth, a myriad thoughts spun through his head without reaching any conclusions. Estefanía whirled around him, now at the Kasanee, now on the bus, now walking with Gabriela by the ocean. Surely he must remember her, surely he'd know her, even pale and stiff at the funeraria? Then la señora Mejía took her turn, just one of his new cast of characters. He'd found a grudging regard for her, something he wouldn't have expected at their first meeting. And then there was the unspoken sympathy at their parting. What was her life when she wasn't protecting children? He could hardly think of her without thinking of Gabriela, how she'd clung to him that first day, terrified of being taken away. And at the root of every thought was the lost Estefanía, who lay elsewhere in the city, still waiting to be named.

He slit the fatter of the two envelopes and drew out the papers.

The post-mortem report was long and detailed, some of it beyond his understanding of language and content, but as he skimmed through it the vital elements were clear enough: ...*well nourished female of about 25 years...fractured skull...bleeding in the brain...broken collar bone...no evidence of drug abuse...at least one pregnancy...no evidence of recent sexual activity.* That brought him up with a start. He read the section again. No mistake, *no evidence of recent sexual activity.* Not a fact he was expecting to discover, but one which he found curiously reassuring, even if having the knowledge also made him feel like a perverted snooper. But either way, it seemed a poor reason for Julio's discretion.

The police reports covered several pages, the last of which was the latest update regarding identification and the DNA match made to *la niña Gabriela Rose Flores.* Harry turned back to the first summary of the accident.

As Julio had said, Estefanía had died two days after leaving Casa Rosa. The details were spelled out in the curious stilted language reserved for police reports. It told how an unknown female, estimated to be between twenty and twenty-five years of age, had been struck by a garbage truck after stepping into the road without warning and without looking. She was apparently struck only once and was later found to be dead by paramedics. Two small personal items, a crucifix on a broken chain and a hair clip were assumed to belong to the victim but no ID, purse or wallet had been found.

A garbage truck. The type of truck made no difference to anything, but he wished it had been otherwise. Julio had missed telling him that detail and he imagined he'd do the same when it came to telling Gabriela. He scanned down the page to see the time of day: five-thirty in the morning. Early. And there was the location too, Avenida 7 / Calle Umberto. He let his eyes rest on the words. Marks on the paper, no more than that. It could have been anywhere, like the truck, the particular street changed nothing, a truck moved, a woman stepped out, bones broke, life ended. The exact location didn't matter. But he knew Calle Umberto, even if he hadn't been there for years. There was a place on the corner where they used to keep a good Scotch and had clean rooms above.

The statements of the truck's crew were short. The driver did not see her until the last second, she ran, she was not looking. He stopped but too late. They were not going quickly, thirty, thirty-five at most. They were working, not speeding. The other saw it differently, but only slightly. The woman had come from the building, Bar Pension Pacífico, looking backwards, not at the street. She was looking behind her when she stepped into the road. He had no chance to speak before she was in front of the truck and they hit her. They were not going quickly, he didn't know what speed but not quickly.

The Pacífico, on the corner, that was the place. No purse, no wallet, looking back over her shoulder to what? Who was standing behind grubby net curtains blearily watching her scuttle from the building, watching her walk in front of a truck? *No recent sexual activity* might have a very narrow definition.

231

Julio must have recognised exactly where Estefanía had been killed and drawn his own conclusions, the same conclusions that now tempted Harry. A stranger to San Felipe, a stranger to Estefanía, such a stranger could easily dream up a dozen reasons for her to be leaving a cheap hotel in the early hours, a dozen more for a purse or wallet to go missing, and none of them would require discretion. He should become that stranger and create a better ending for his Gabriela's Mami. Visiting an old friend, leaving early to get the first bus home, a wallet spilt into the gutter by the impact and taken by an opportunist thief; there, he'd done it, that was easy. In the hours to come he might even improve on it. He might even believe it.

Harry put the papers back and let the envelopes slip to the floor before he savoured the last few drops of Tomintoul. He'd have no trouble identifying her, a hair clip and Bar Pension Pacífico had done that already.

★

"Papatico, when will you be back?"

"An hour, perhaps two." Harry looked at Julio for confirmation but received only a shrug. "If it's longer I will call Pippa. OK?"

"Can I come? Pleeeease."

"No, darling girl, not this morning. Maybe later."

It seemed to Harry that Gabriela really wanted to ask where he was going, and why, and was it about her Mami, but she didn't want to know the answers, so she'd settled for the fringe questions, the ones that could safely be asked and answered. She didn't need to be a genius to appreciate the day was different to any other. The adults around her were all pretending everything was normal when even being there all together on a school day, a work day, was anything but. Even Cristela had been given a day off. Little wonder Gabriela was clingy and nervous of him leaving without her.

"Gabriela, we talked about the judge and la señora Mejía and how it has been decided you will always stay with me, no one will take you away. You know that."

She nodded, but with little enthusiasm, it was old news.

"Good. I thought for a minute you were worrying about that. There's no need, it's settled."

"Will you find out about Mami today?" she blurted out, courage getting the better of her fears.

He pulled her back up into his arms, tenderly stroking her face. He said gently, "Yes, I think so, but for the moment nothing is certain. When I come back I'll tell you if I know anything. I promise."

"Will we stay here tonight?"

"Yes, I'm sure we will."

A ten-minute drive brought them to La Funeraria de las Tres Marías, a low white building at the end of a leafy drive. They were ushered into a small anteroom where Daniel Scott Ramirez, the investigator from DIC, was waiting for them. They shook hands stiffly.

"A sad day, señor Rose."

"Yes."

The three men stood awkwardly, unsure of what lay ahead of them in the next room. Harry was about to ask the detective if he had already seen Estefanía's body, to ask him if her face was damaged, when a woman in black opened the door and motioned them in to the viewing room. White blouse, black suit, she would, he thought, fit perfectly in judge Cruz's court.

Twenty ornate chairs were arranged in two arcs around a plinth dressed in white silk. On top was a plain dark coffin, open to view the occupant. Harry looked away quickly. He wanted a page to turn and her face to be there right in front of him, not to have her features gradually revealed as he slowly approached. Julio and the detective hung back, deferring to him as the prospective chief mourner. Eyes on the floor Harry went to her. Only when he was standing close by the coffin did he lift his eyes to her face.

Grey. She was grey. The months in a freezer had chilled the colour out of her.

He reached out a hand as if to touch her, to see if she was as cold as she looked. There were no marks on her face, no graze or blemish to disfigure her looks. She was whole. He'd been holding his breath since the call from Julio, the news of the DNA match. Now he could breathe again.

Harry let his eyes linger on her, reminding himself of her mouth, her nose, her sleeping eyes. Her hair was tied back, not at all how she'd have worn it, but it was neat and clean as if someone had cared about how she looked today. She was wearing no make-up, he would ask about that, see if something could be done, a little rouge, a hint of lipstick, just a touch, no more. It was what she'd have done for herself.

"Harry," Julio said.

He looked up, surprised to find his friend close beside him.

"Harry, there is the question of identity."

That question, he'd forgotten all about it.

"Señor Rose," said the detective, "Can you say who was this person?" He had a file open in his hands and a pen poised for Harry's reply.

Harry looked again. He wanted it to be Estefanía Flores, it must be her, it could be no other. But would he have picked her out in a roomful of corpses, a roomful of twenty-something women who'd all been dead and frozen for nearly two years?

Harry nodded.

"Señor Rose?"

"This is Estefanía Flores, Gabriela's Mami."

"You are sure?"

"Sure enough."

"And you señor Aguilar, do you agree?"

"I hardly knew her, but yes, I agree."

Investigador Scott made notes in his file then asked Harry and Julio to both sign the form. When they had done so he slipped the file into his briefcase. From the case he took a ziplock bag, which he handed to Harry.

"Señor Rose, we believe these belong to la señorita Estefanía Flores. Do you recognize them? You should have them."

He could see what they were without opening the bag. A crucifix on a broken gold chain and a pink hair-slide with a blue butterfly. He could find both on a hundred stalls in a hundred markets but these cheap trinkets banished any shadow of doubt as to who lay in the coffin.

Harry took the slide from the bag and held it close to Estefanía's hair. The colour transformed her. If Harry had believed in such things he could have imagined the ghost of a smile pass across her face. What was it he'd said to Gabriela about doing things for the dead that we're really doing for ourselves?

Abruptly their allotted time was up. Estefanía must be wheeled back to the wings while another mother, another daughter took centre stage; people were waiting.

Before they left there were arrangements to be made, although for Harry it was more a case of arrangements to be agreed to. There were only seven people to mourn Estefanía, there'd be no procession, no band, no party, just the essentials to be attended to. And a touch of make-up, the crucifix and the slide, he wanted those things attended to before he came back with Gabriela.

As they returned to their cars, the detective said, "Señor Rose, this will be the end of the investigation. An unhappy time for you, but perhaps a new beginning too."

"Thank you," Harry said and was about to ask about Daniel Scott's father, but he had little appetite for a new conversation and none for a renewed acquaintanceship. He'd let investigator Scott fade into the past, just as his father had done.

Harry and Julio were almost home when Julio said, "No doubts, Harry?"

"None at all, thankfully."

Julio parked in the shade of the bougainvillea in the little cobbled drive at the front of his house. They sat in silence for a few moments, preparing for all that would follow, not only in the coming minutes and hours, but both aware of an altered future, the shape of which was as yet unformed.

The house was quiet apart from Gabriela's tinkling laugh leaking down the stairs from Cristela's room. In the courtyard they found Pippa and Elena, who looked up expectantly. Harry nodded.

235

"It's a little thing, it means nothing really, but I'd like to talk to Gabriela before we talk about it ourselves," he said. "Pippa, will you be with me?"

"Of course I will." She put her arms around him and kissed him.

"I will ask Cristela to come down, Gabriela will be sure to follow," Elena said, sweeping Julio along with her into the house.

Harry and Pippa settled together on the swing seat, holding hands softly as friends and lovers do.

"Papatico! Papatico!" Gabriela yelled as she leapt down the stairs and out to find them. She jumped on the swing and squeezed between them.

"What have you been up to?" he asked her.

"Cristela has a new guitar and she let me play it. She showed me how to play Estrellita!" The morning's pleasures tumbled out of her, sharing her excitement in a quickfire account of how much she'd packed into little more than an hour.

He let her talk until the torrent abated. After a pause he shifted on the seat to be able to look at her more easily. Her face was still full of life and excited anticipation. There would never be an easy time.

"Gabriela, I promised to tell you about my morning. I have sad news of your Mami. There was an accident, your Mami died. There was a truck and your Mami didn't see it when she stepped into the road. It was a long time ago, but nobody knew who she was, so nobody could tell us."

Gabriela looked at him steadily, her expression blank.

"Was Mami under an orange thing?"

"I don't know, but probably, yes."

"Did she go to the morgue?"

"Yes."

"Was she buried?"

"Not yet, but very soon, tomorrow I think. It hasn't been decided."

"Where is she?"

"In a special place, a special morgue. I saw her this morning. We'll go together later on, this afternoon. It will be our way of saying goodbye to her."

"Is she still dead?"

"Yes."

"Can we talk to her?"

"If you want to. You can tell her anything you like."

"Can she talk?"

"No, but we can imagine what she might say to us. She would certainly say that she loved you."

Gabriela considered this for a few moments, dwarfed by the enormity of it, unsure of what she felt or what was expected of her.

"Can I go back and play with Cristela now?"

13

Harry had thought carefully as to whether there was any respectful way to carry Estefanía Flores' ashes back to Concepción. Their bags and the rack space on the bus gave him few options. In the end, he'd gently guided Gabriela into having the plastic container in its velvet draw-string bag placed in his holdall. With due care, it meant that the flask could be maintained in an upright position, a little detail important to her. "Making Mami comfortable," she'd said, and there'd been no good reason to disagree with her.

There had been tears, how could there not be, but it seemed to Harry that Gabriela had taken the events of the weekend in her stride. Perhaps he'd watched her too closely, analysing each word for signs of hidden turmoil, scrutinising every expression for suppressed emotions, but he found no cause for alarm. Even so, something had changed, either in her or how he saw her. The death of a parent is often a defining moment in life, whatever the age of the child or parent. It marks both an ending and a progression of sorts, to a future of independence, however unwelcome that may be. It should be no surprise if his daughter's spark was less bright, her smile less broad.

At the funeraria she'd been silent, wide-eyed and transfixed by the sight of Estefanía. The staff had done well with her hair slide and the hint of colour in her cheeks, even if the grey could not be completely disguised. After sitting quietly for a few minutes, Harry had spoken softly to Estefanía, telling her what a fine daughter she had and how proud she would be of her, how well Gabriela could read, how she knew her stars and had started school and loved painting with Pippa. Gabriela had said nothing but as they came to leave Harry said, "Goodbye Estefanía, and thank you." Gabriela, hotly clutching his hand, echoed him with a heartfelt "Goodbye Mami, I love you."

The funeral and cremation had been a brief affair. Seven mourners, two attendants, a few words from Harry, Cristela playing Estrellita on her new guitar at Gabriela's urgent pleading, and a prayer from Elena. "There must be a prayer," she'd said.

Afterwards they'd walked in a park then lunched in a restaurant where they laughed and said good things about Estefanía and remarked how pleased she would be to know what a good time they were having. Harry, when he caught himself watching, feared it was a performance for Gabriela's benefit, it was not, after all, his way, the Anglo-Saxon way. But for Elena and Julio it was spontaneous and showed their children, as well as Gabriela, how death should be regarded, even sudden, premature death: as a part of life. Gabriela's Mami could be spoken of, she could still love her, miss her, and she could say so.

Now they were heading home to their new lives, lives devoid of the constant reference point Estefanía had provided. Removing that centre of gravity gave everything else different weight, threw everything into a different orbit. Harry could feel the change already. He looked across at Pippa and Gabriela, each engrossed in their books and with an hour of the journey to Puerto Réunion still ahead of them. Somehow, he must keep Pippa in their lives, not just as the ever-ready friend who'd help and advise him, not merely as the stand-in grandmother for Gabriela, but as a permanent fixture with regular contact to keep her as close as possible. For an instant he found himself thinking of cohabitation, even marriage. He dismissed the idea immediately but it left an after-image on the retina of his mind's eye.

A billboard flashing by reminded him of property. He pulled out the notes he had about Playa de Rosas. As Julio had said, they didn't amount to much. He'd discovered that Giancarlo Duarte was an agent for a handful of foreign companies, nearly all involved in property or other investments. Some of these businesses had spawned local subsidiaries which had acquired and developed land. Julio had pointed out one of these, Tierras Pacífico, as being the same one as had previously made overtures to Harry, Ernest and the Fairchilds. It seemed that although the attempted acquisition was dormant, their agent Duarte retained a watching brief. No harm in that and little he could do about it even if he wanted to. The other party who'd registered an interest, Sindicato de Avatar, was no more than a shell, with an accommodation box number for an address. Julio had discovered that any mail was forwarded to another box in Panama City. Yet this shadow company claimed an interest in Bill Fairchild's villa far greater than it could possibly be worth.

"A mistake perhaps," Julio had said with little conviction.

"And Oscar Portillo's buyer, is that Duarte, acting for one of his employers?"

"Perhaps, there is no information so far."

What were they returning to at Casa Rosa? Their home, certainly, but would it feel like home, wouldn't they forever be reminded of what it did not have, while its virtues became marginalised. There was always Pippa of course, and surely she would never be prised away from La Plantación, even if she could be tempted to visit them if they lived in San Felipe.

A void of uncertainty and inaction threatened to open before him.

On a whim he called Julio's office. His friend was unavailable, *unless it is very urgent, señor Rose.* Julio was well served by his staff.

Harry contented himself with a voicemail. "Julio, can you contact Duarte and see if he's interested in buying Casa Rosa, see if you can find out if he's buying Ernest's place. Time we took the direct route, let's see what a good price looks like. Maybe see what someone else would give for it too. I'm not committed either way, not yet, but let's find out where we stand. And how about putting your name on the register of interests for all three properties, see what that stirs up."

He looked across at Pippa and Gabriela. The child was still engrossed in her story, but Pippa was regarding him with raised eyebrows.

"It's worth finding out," he shrugged.

As they neared the outskirts of Puerto Reunión, Harry thought he would look again for the boards trumpeting the airport renewal and the up-scale marina. They were still standing, although the marina was tilting sideways. The bus took him past too quickly to be able to read the small print.

Once in the pickup he swung away from the ferry, heading back on the main road the way they'd just come.

"A small detour," he announced. "It won't take long, a little journey of discovery, if we're lucky."

He drove out of town to the first placard, the marina, then past the second and on further until he was sure he'd have passed the third if it had been upright. It could have been scavenged for firewood, but with luck it would still be in the ditch. They drove slowly, half on the road, half on the verge while Pippa and Gabriela scanned the scrubby banks of the brown stream.

Two spindly poles sticking out of the ground marked the spot. He pulled up a few metres beyond them and jumped out. The board was still there, half submerged and ready to be buried by the loose earth and stones of the bank. Harry fished under the seats for a length of twine that had escaped the fire, tied it to the back of the truck then scrambled down the bank to the board. He found a bracket still screwed solidly to the wood and hitched the twine round it.

"Pippa, can you gently ease forward? I'll keep an eye on it. You remember how to do gentle?"

She gave him her most withering look before expertly inching forward. The twine tautened to the point of breaking before the board slurched free. Harry scrambled down the bank and flipped it over. He recognised the picture of the idyllic cabins on stilts over the water, but the name of this paradise had meaning where previously it had none: Playa de Rosas. The developer's logo tucked in the bottom corner was a laurel wreath surrounding the letters VV.

"See this," he called out.

They came and saw. Harry used his phone for a couple of pictures of the board before flipping it back on its face and down into the stream. In the cab he pulled out the information on Giancarlo Duarte and glanced down the list of names. Vida Verde seemed to fit well. He also snapped the marina and airport signs on the way into town and sent them all to Julio with the message *Vida Verde – a Duarte company*.

The excursion had given them a long wait for the ferry, but at least they were first in line. Pippa bought ice-creams while they strolled around the quayside. Harry even remembered to take a few photos, for Gabriela's sake if not his own. If it weren't for Harry's scorched pickup, they might have been mistaken for tourists.

"Pippa," he said as the ferry backed away from the ramp, "How long till you're off on your gallery tour?"

"About six weeks, why?"

"I'd like to get all this settled before you go. Decide about Casa Rosa, find out what's going on. I suddenly realise how isolated I'm going to be. We're going to be."

"Where will we live?" Gabriela said, hints of suspicion and anticipation mixed in her question.

"I don't know, my darling. We can talk about that, we can talk about a lot of things."

"I want to live in the city, I want to live in San Felipe."

★

The Kasanee was quiet, late afternoon was never a busy time. Leo and Carla had taken a few hours off, as was their normal routine, although Harry had forgotten until he walked in. Without Carla in residence the kitchen was closed and the bar was in the care of Alex, who was more often seen drinking than serving. Harry knew him slightly, enough to nod a greeting if they passed in the street, enough to exchange a few words in the Kasanee.

"Leo? Carla? Soon, maybe ten minutes, four-thirty for sure. You want a beer, señor Rose? A fresco too?" He gestured vaguely towards Gabriela.

"Thanks Alex, sure."

With no company to engage them, no buzz of chatter to distract them, Gabriela sat bored while Harry took stock of the bar. It was tired. Hard to see when it was full of life and Leo, when Carla sent out inviting aromas from the kitchen, but in the quiet of a grey afternoon with the muted TV screen flickering its banality to empty chairs, he could see the Kasanee for what it was: tired. He couldn't remember Leo buying a single new item for years. The last big spend had been on the coffee machine, but that, like so much that was new to Concepción, came second-hand from a failed business in Puerto Reunión. The Kasanee was still comfortable, the more so by its familiarity, but Harry saw as if through a fresh lens that it would soon reach a tipping point. It would either continue to sink slowly to the point where it would not be worth reviving, or the renewal must start soon.

"Gabriela! Mi cosita!" Carla yelled as she and Leo came in with bags of supplies. Gabriela leapt up immediately to be kissed and hugged before Harry also received his share of both.

"Will you come and help me with all this, Gabriela?"

She jumped at the chance of time in Carla's kitchen while Leo settled beside Harry with a beer.

"How was San Felipe?"

Harry told him the headlines but left most of the details to his imagination.

"Leo, I don't know what will happen to us, me and Gabriela, but the way I'm feeling now we might leave the island." He said it as much to see how it sounded as to alert his friend to the possibility. He let the idea sink in for a moment before continuing, "If we do, would you like to have my share in the Kasanee back? I like being a part of it, I always have, but if we left I can see you might want me out of it."

Leo took a slow swallow of his beer before answering. "You should be more careful with your investments, Harry. You make a bad bargain, you'd give it away before any talk of money. Sure, I'll take your share back for half what you gave me. How's that?"

Harry was surprised at the speed of the agreement, unsure of Leo's sincerity.

Leo leaned forward and shook a disapproving finger at Harry, as if correcting a naughty child. "No, I do not want your share back, wherever you live, but thank you for the offer. Because I am honest I will also say, keep your share a little longer and you might double your money, perhaps more if we make a better bargain than you would make."

"Something new?"

"Yes. We have interest in the Kasanee, a suggestion of a good price, more than we might expect. You remember the marina business? It could be more than just talk. So keep your share Harry, it might be worth something."

"Ah, the marina. Let me guess, Vida Verde? Did you hear from a man called Duarte, Giancarlo Duarte?"

"Vida Verde? I don't know the name. But Duarte, yes, the agent for a development."

"Vida Verde is the company he's acting for. Look." Harry flipped through the photos on his phone.

"In Puerto Reunión?" Leo said, "I never stopped to look."

"Remember we had offers, Ernest Portillo had one, so did Bill Fairchild, a couple of years ago? Duarte was involved there too. Now this Vida Verde has their name on the marina, the airport and Casa Rosa."

"Casa Rosa? The same? They must have money to do all that, but you don't know, maybe it's all big talk."

"Will you sell, Leo?"

"For a good price, I think so, yes."

"What will you do, you and Carla?"

"Who knows, eh? Twenty-two years we've been at the Kasanee. Good years, yes. But maybe it's enough. Carla tells me often how big is the world."

"Have you mentioned this to anyone else?"

"No, but everyone knows. Everyone along here to the end of the road, by the old boat ramp, they've all had letters. Big smiles everywhere. But we'll see, the Kasanee is not just a property, but a good business. We'll see what happens."

Harry saw Gabriela advancing towards them, concentrating on the drinks on her tray. A step behind her, Carla watched like a mother hen.

To his surprise Carla joined them and sat beside him.

"Harry," she said tenderly, "Gabriela told me of Estefanía. A great sadness." She reached out and laid a hand on his, gently squeezing it. "But what of your other troubles? Is everything settled, is it good?"

"Yes, it's settled, it's good. But now what? I don't know what we'll do."

"Has Leo told you?"

"Yes. Big changes for you two. Maybe, eh? When all the talk is done."

"Talk, talk, big talk. We will wait. For now I'll wait in the kitchen. You want patacones, Gabriela?"

"Patacones!" she cried. Those fried delights were irresistible and Carla knew it. Gabriela nodded vigorously until she caught Harry's critical look. "Pleeeease!"

She was gone in an instant, dancing along behind Carla.

"Gabriela, mi cosita, she is well I think, yes?"

"So far, yes. Julio and Elena were a great help. Cristela and Stuart too. I'm a lucky man, Leo."

"Señor Rose, the lucky man." Victor Diaz's voice was right behind him, his hand on his shoulder.

Harry spun round and stood to shake the captain's hand. "Victor! Very good to see you."

"Ah, señor Rose, likewise." He was in uniform, in a public place, there'd be no Harry here. "Look, I have something for you."

He passed a brown envelope to Harry. One feel and he knew it was his passport, his Canadian passport. "Good. Thanks," he said.

"Information from San Felipe, el investigador Scott, DIC. He said it was finished. And la señorita Flores, that is not, um, so good. But it is decided, er, complete." The policeman stumbled over his words, more in his heart than he could express to Harry standing in the Kasanee.

They sat and talked and Leo brought three more beers before Carla and Gabriela brought the patacones. Uppermost in their minds were the changes bubbling up like a storm on their horizons. Changes for them all except the captain, yet it was he who mentioned it.

"Leo and Carla, they've told you about this place? Yes, of course they have told you. No Kasanee, that will be something to think about. You still have your part in this?"

"Yes, I do. It may be talk, just talk. But Victor, I must tell you before it is also talk, I am also thinking of selling, Gabriela and I, we may leave Concepción," he looked at his daughter to see if the idea was still to her liking, "We may move to the San Felipe, a new school, a new start."

"You will leave? Yes, you have a new life, you and nuestra querida niña." He made a big fist under Gabriela's chin to which she made as if to bite his knuckles. "The young must leave Concepción, if they can."

"And you Victor, will you look elsewhere some day, something new on the mainland?"

"Ah, señor Rose, you must understand. I am Diaz, capitán de policía rural, yes?" he said, tapping his epaulette as he spoke. "Before this I was intendente. Once I was nothing, then by work and clean hands I was inspector, then to sargento, then to intendente, now capitán. Progress, yes? More pay, more pension. Very good. Ask where I started and I will tell you I was first in San Vicente. You know it? Nearly in San Felipe. You drive through it now and you don't see it, a suburb, nothing more.

"It is not so simple, this progress. There are two ways of this, er, promoción. In the first you move towards the centre. You start in Puerto Reunión or Santa Ana, somewhere on the edge, and the progress is towards San Felipe, where you may one day

246

be commandante or comisionado. In the second you move away from the centre, a little further with each promoción until you reach the limit.

"You can see which way it has been with Victor Diaz, yes? The second way. So, you ask me something new on the mainland? I ask you what is this capitán de policía rural good for now? Answer that question and I will tell you how long I will be in Concepción."

The captain's summary seemed depressing, fatalistic, yet Harry knew it might well be accurate. At the same time he wondered if perhaps Victor was content to have his pay and pension secured and a life not too taxing.

"You'll have a quiet life if the Kasanee closes and we all go to San Felipe."

"Quiet, yes. Better, no."

They drank more beer and ate more snacks from Carla's kitchen, until the Kasanee began to fill with the voices of regulars. Leo returned to his duties and Victor shifted uncomfortably in his chair, ready to go home to his wife and supper.

"Have you seen anything of Oscar Portillo?" Harry asked as Victor stood to leave.

"Yes, he was here. With his sister. They were over by the house, by Casa Rosa."

"Any reason?"

The captain shrugged. "I had a report from the fire, el señor Portillo may also have been told, for insurance."

"Anything interesting?"

"The old freezer maybe. Some extra burning under the base." He made a motion with his hands, one under the other. "Nothing certain."

★

"Can I stay here, Papatico?"

"No, we'll go together, we're invited."

Gabriela pulled her most imploring face and groaned her most agonised "Pleeeease."

"Nice try, but no, we're going. If you're…"

"Yes? If I'm good? I am. I will be."

"If you are, then you can come home after we've eaten. Which doesn't mean you have one chicken leg and scoot, OK?"

They could have walked directly to the Fairchild's villa, but the late afternoon, just as the sun begins its precipitous descent into darkness, was one of their favourite times to dawdle at the water's edge. Then, and also occasionally a little before sunrise, when the shape of the land is just recognisable, but painted with colours from a different palette. These times were the perfection Harry had fallen in love with, still loved, despite the souring of the affair.

"Papatico, if we live in the city how will we see the stars? Will there be a place to lie down and have star stories? Cristela says she's never done that. She doesn't have a place."

"That's a very good question, I hadn't thought of that. Once, when I was very young, I stayed in a house that had stairs up to a kind of terrace on a flat roof. That was the first time I ever watched the stars. We should find a house with a roof like that."

"Can Cristela come and lie on the roof with us and have star stories?"

"Of course she can. If it's clear, would you like to lie with the stars tonight, on the sand?"

"Can we?"

"Yes."

To celebrate, Gabriela skipped ahead of him, squealing, then did handstands in the lapping wavelets. They passed the Fairchild place and walked until the rock and forest crowded down to the water, stopping them from going further.

"Come on, we're late," he said, turning back and up the beach toward the villa.

They were a hundred metres away when they heard raised voices, or more accurately, they heard Dolores Perez-Fairchild abusing her husband. The detail was lost on the breeze, but the

248

anger was palpable. It stopped Gabriela in her tracks. Her expression of loathing said more than any words she could have spoken.

"We don't have to stay for long," Harry said.

"Must we?" she pleaded.

"Yes, we must. But we'll go quietly, along by the bushes."

"To listen."

"No! Well, maybe a little."

They slipped silently along the top of the sand by the bougainvillea in front of the wall, hidden from sight should anyone be looking out from the villa. They were rewarded only by a few distinct words, "you must choose," before a door slammed and the shouting ceased. At the end of the wall Harry jangled the old bell-pull before pushing open the gate to the garden.

At the side of the house on the terrace between the pool and the oversize dining table, Bill Fairchild was waving away smoke from the barbecue.

"Harry, glad you could make it," he called, beckoning them towards him. "And you brought the girl too."

The girl clung to Harry, almost hidden behind him.

"Gabriela, it's Gabriela, that's her name, Bill."

"Yeah, sure, we know each other, eh?" He squatted down briefly to smile in her face, and for a moment Harry feared he would pat her head. No wonder she had begged to be let off this torment.

"A few beers," Harry said, passing over the clanking bag he'd carried round the beach from home.

"Put 'em in the cooler. Lola'll be out any time."

Harry opened two bottles but there was nothing in the cooler for Gabriela.

"There's Coke in the house."

"Gabriela, you can go inside and ask la señora if you could have a Coke. Please."

She shook her head fiercely.

"Then run home and get some juice. And don't be long."

She was gone in an instant.

"Harry, I gotta tell you something." Bill Fairchild came close and lowered his voice. "That Oscar, the one that's got the Portillo place now, what's left of it. He was up here a few days back. You and the kid were away. Him and his sister, Noelle, they came in for a few drinks."

"I didn't know you knew them."

"No, no, we don't. The thing is, Harry, they're selling the property, know that?"

"I heard something," Harry said as vaguely as he could.

"Not just selling, but selling well. Listen to this. Four times what he'd thought. Four times! Jesus Christ!"

"You can't buy paradise. Isn't that what you said last time the developers came sniffing round?" Harry knew a little more than Bill Fairchild gave him credit for, and wasn't about to toss the advantage away. A little provocation, a slight deception, these were both repayment for forgetting Gabriela's name.

"I know, I know. But four times for Christ's sake! Gotta think about that."

Especially if you're already mortgaged to three times, thought Harry. But there was more to be had from this before he showed his hand.

"Well, that's all very good," he said, as if it were all just a theory of purely academic interest, "but I was talking yesterday to someone who said the whole deal had fallen through, the people had plenty of talk but no money."

"No, not this one, Harry. Believe me, these guys are serious, I know it." The humour had drained from his face.

"So, will you sell?" Harry said, still innocent.

"Maybe. But will you?"

"Me?"

"Yeah, you, Harry boy. You hold the keys."

"Ah, señor Rose, you are here," Dolores Perez said, emerging from the house wearing her biggest smile.

"Harry. It's Harry."

"Yes, of course. You are alone? You don't have the girl?"

"Gabriela. She'll be back soon," he said, although wishing she would not be.

"Lola, we're just talking about Playa de Rosas, seeing Oscar and Noelle the other day, the great offer they've had. Harry's not so sure."

"Will you stay here now, señor Rose? After all that has happened?"

"Happened, señora?"

"Yes, yes, the fire, the police, the girl, her mother. What is here for you?"

If anything were going to persuade Harry to stay at Casa Rosa it would be the Fairchilds telling him he should go. He tried out another idea on them, one that he'd been playing with on and off since Pippa had suggested it.

"We might keep the house, even if we lived somewhere else. Paradise, remember? Hard to find anywhere better."

"You are staying? Is the mother also back? When was this?" Dismayed, she turned to her husband as if for an explanation, why had she not been told of this development?

"Estefanía Flores, the mother as you put it, she is dead," Harry said steadily.

"You know this, Harry?" Bill Fairchild found his voice again.

"I know this."

"And you are keeping the child?" Dolores Perez was angry and incredulous that he would do such a thing. "What do you want with a girl of eight, a girl like that, the housekeeper's brat?"

Before he could answer Bill Fairchild cut in with his own ill-temper, emphasising his words with a stabbing finger. "Let's cut to the chase, Harry, stop this fucking around. Are you staying or selling?"

"I just don't know. I guess you want to go, but to get what you want from it, Casa Rosa has to be part of the deal. No Casa Rosa then no Playa de Rosas luxury resort with cabins on stilts and swimming pools and suites at a thousand a night. How did it get to be like this?"

"Business, Harry, just business. Nothing personal."

With sudden realisation Harry swung round on Dolores Perez. "Eight. You said Gabriela was eight."

"So?"

"She's seven."

"Seven, eight, nine, what does it matter?"

"It matters like this. Eight is what somebody said when they made a phone call, somebody who never mentioned her name. Eight is what the judge was told. Eight is what somebody who didn't know and didn't care might say. Did you make that call?"

"I don't make any calls," she said, dismissing the idea with a wave of her hand.

"No? You want Casa Rosa, you can have it, special price. Eight times what they offered two years ago because eight is my favourite number right now. Plus the phone call. Who was that?"

The Fairchild's prize was in sight but the price was higher than they'd bargained for. They said nothing.

"It wasn't you, I know that," Harry said to the American.

Still they didn't speak.

"That's too big a silence, it says you know. Who called? Whose idea?"

"You are crazy man," Dolores Perez said, turning to flounce back to the house. Harry grabbed her hair and yanked her back into a chair.

"Son of a bitch! Enough Harry!" Fairchild yelled.

"You think I wouldn't? I'll break both your necks right here, right now. Who called?"

In his fury, Harry yanked hard on the woman's hair, twisting her head round so much she cried out in pain. Fairchild stepped forward to rescue his wife, arms outstretched to pull Harry away from her, but height and reach were to Harry's advantage. The heel of his right hand met Fairchild's nose in a single jabbing, anger-fueled blow. The man fell back, blood spurting across his face and down his shirt.

"Who called La Agencia?"

"Fuck you Rose! Let her go!" Fairchild shouted through a stream of blood and snot. "It was the fucking maid, it was Natalia."

Harry was dumbstruck. Why would the maid do such a thing, what harm had he ever done her? Perhaps she believed what she'd said about him? In his amazement he could think of no other reason.

"Your maid? Natalia? Where is she?" he said stupidly, his grip on Dolores' hair loosened.

"Who the fuck knows where she is, who cares? Fairchild said, "She's gone, weeks ago."

"Why?"

"Because we kicked her out, that's why. Jesus! You fucking broke my nose."

"I'll break more than that. Tell me."

"You are crazy man!" Dolores Perez screamed at him.

"Shut the fuck up," Fairchild told his wife. "You got us into this."

"Hah! I got us? No! I don't lose money then borrow more and lose that too. I don't do deals so we have nothing. I don't do promises I don't keep."

"Kill each other later."

"It's business, just business. A few things went wrong, then a few more, it was nothing. But some guys got upset, wanted money and didn't want to wait. Heavy duty guys, not your regular little credit union folk. They sold me to another company, the same people who want Playa de Rosas. All or nothing. I told them I'd make sure it happened."

"Did you kill Ernest, set fire to his house?"

"Jesus Christ! What do think I am? You think I kill people? No, no, no. Ernest was just a lucky break. The fire, I don't know, but not me. Fuck! You saw me that night. We watched it burn."

"Oscar then, he burnt it?"

"I don't know, OK?"

"So, these people bought you."

253

"Yeah, but you wouldn't budge. I couldn't see how to shift you. Then the idea of a little misinformation came up, something to shake things up."

"You made Natalia call La Agencia. Then you kicked her out, told her she'd be in trouble if she ever told anyone."

"It's not personal, I said that. We were in a jam. And look, for Christ's sake, it's all going to work out, there's no harm done, we all walk away with something. You'll get everything you want and lose nothing. You can find another fucking beach. Nobody got hurt. Jesus Christ, have another beer and calm down."

"No harm done!" Harry roared. "You sit there and say that. No harm done. Have another beer! I should let you bleed to death just for that. No harm? Just something to destroy lives. Mine, Gabriela's – that's her name by the way, Gabriela, she's my daughter, she's seven, not eight like you had Natalia say. You'd destroy friendships worth more than money, destroy this beautiful place. Not personal? What's personal then? I should break more than your nose. Still might."

He turned his attention to Dolores Perez, curled in the chair beside him, still ready to snarl and spit defiance. He wound her hair tight back round his hand then shook her head.

"And was this your idea, Lola Perez? Yes, I think it was." He pulled her head up and down to make her nod her agreement. "I should make you crawl on your belly and beg forgiveness from that child, my daughter, that brat you so despise."

"So perfect, eh señor Rose? How you get a child with a housekeeper, eh?"

Harry drew back his free arm ready to lash a backhand across her face: a blow to carry all his anger, a blow to repay the agony they'd so carelessly inflicted.

★

They watched until the last possible moment, until Pippa's waving hand disappeared beyond the frosted glass of airport security. She was off on her trip, full of the excitement and anxieties appropriate for such a tour. She'd be away six weeks, which was longer than Gabriela had ever been without seeing her.

Pippa had stayed three nights with them in their new home in San Felipe, their first guest, and they'd loved her company, Gabriela said it made it feel like their real home. Pippa was also the first to share their rooftop, not quite so beautiful as the terrace at La Plantación, not quite that sense of walking in the infinity of space, but still they'd floated up among the stars and forgotten the sleeping city around them.

When Pippa would return she'd stay again before they delivered her back to Concepción, back to her home in the gentle fold of the hill above the ocean. That was all for the future, before then they had journeys of their own to make.

From the airport they swung north, away from the city, into the lush green of the hills. Grudgingly, Harry had conceded that his truck was past its best and splashed out on a newer SUV, something altogether more suitable for their new urban lives. As they drove towards San Carlos he allowed himself a small satisfaction with the comfort of the ride.

When they'd been on the road an hour or so Gabriela asked, not for the first time, "Who are we going to see, Papatico?"

"We'll be meeting Cristin Blanca, she is your Mami's Mamá. You've never seen her and she's never seen you. She is your grandmother, your abuelita."

"Is she very old?"

"No, not very, not as old as Pippa, not as old as me."

Gabriela digested this information for a few minutes. Slowly her new world was falling into place: the school, the house, the walk home, the park, more clothes and books than she'd ever had and now, most recently, the prospect of a wider family.

And there were still her Mami's ashes in a black flask in the velvet draw-string bag: part of her was going home too. Harry had explained the idea of scattering those ashes and made a few suggestions, nudging Gabriela gently in the direction of Estefanía's childhood home in San Carlos, encouraging her away from Isla Concepción. They'd reached a happy compromise, one which had needed a covenant to be included in the Casa Rosa sale along with a stiff penalty for failure to comply. Gabriela's tree, the ever-embracing savannah oak, her lookout, her climbing frame, her friend and refuge, must remain untouched while a ten-metre square around it would be maintained as a garden. Together they'd scattered half of Estefanía's ashes in those ten metres. The remainder was heading to San Carlos, where, with a little help, they'd find the right place for them.

Author's note

The story of Arcturus and Spica, which Harry tells Gabriela, is a loose retelling of a folk tale of the Catlolq people of Vancouver Island, British Columbia. The story was described by Franz Boas in *Indianische Sagen von der Nord-Pacifischen Kuste Amerikas* (1895). The website starmythworld.com proved to be a valuable resource in researching such stories.

Particular thanks are due to my son Thomas for his detailed and robust critique of the almost-finished Casa Rosa. In addition, Thomas, together with my daughter-in-law Mariana Granados, provided invaluable advice in finding the right level and usage of Spanish throughout the story.

Although she has had less input to Casa Rosa than previous stories, my daughter Caroline is long overdue public appreciation for all her advice and support over the years. The journey continues, her creative energy is an inspiration.

Thanks also to all those friends and strangers, readers of my previous work, whose encouragement has been invaluable. Often it has arrived unexpectedly at precisely the right moment – when the creative flame was at its lowest and writing seemed worthless.

No note of gratitude can be complete without including Grace Keating, ever-supportive, my muse and editor supreme, without whom this story and many others might never have been told.

DJW

Surrey, British Columbia 2019

Also available from Askance

A Habit Of Dying
DJ Wiseman

Amongst the old photo albums Lydia Silverstream discovers a disturbing journal, the key to one puzzle but an enigma in itself. In her attempts to re-unite the family albums with their rightful owner, Lydia travels the country from Oxford to Essex, Cumbria to Sussex. As the story of the blighted family is pieced together from the fragments of history, the tantalizing journal with its deeper, darker secrets comes to dominate both past and present.

A well crafted, intriguing and enjoyable tale. – *Oxford Journal*

A well written, well paced piece of puzzle-solving that will please family history buffs and fans of old-fashioned detective stories alike. – *Daily Info Oxford*

There's a great deal to enjoy here, believable characters with a great plot twist near the end. - *FH Book of the Month*

Order direct from the publisher at askance-publishing.com

Also available from Askance

The Subtle Thief Of Youth
DJ Wiseman

The aftermath of a summer storm reveals the grotesque secret hidden for years. As mud and water cascade through Whyncombe St Giles and Germans, they unearth the remains of Melanie Staples, a schoolgirl lost for over a decade. As a second girl goes missing on the same day resources are stretched and we glimpse the darker side of Cotswold life as the great and the good close ranks.

An intriguing and original mystery – DJ Wiseman has a real gift for creating and telling a strong and carefully crafted story. – *Helen Ward, Oxford Info*

As surely as the deluge strips away the landscape of the parish, the secrets of the villagers are peeled back to reveal the raw truth of the past. A beautifully layered tale.
– *Simon Humphreys, author*

Order direct from the publisher at askance-publishing.com

Also available from Askance

The Death Of Tommy Quick And Other Lies
DJ Wiseman

Old certainties prove to be anything but as genealogy sleuth Lydia Silverstream responds to a dying man's plea. Her work, her home, her stuttering relationship, even her skills as a researcher, all the familiar patterns are disrupted, leaving her with more challenges than ever. And why won't a mother tell her son who his father is? It all goes to show, as always, there's so much more to a family's history than certificates would have you believe.

This is a wonderful book. I greatly enjoyed A Habit of Dying, the first book to feature Lydia Silverstream, but the follow-up, The Death of Tommy Quick and Other Lies, is astonishingly good! - *Peter Calver, Lost Cousins*

Order direct from the publisher at askance-publishing.com